WHEN HEROES FLEW

H.W. "BUZZ" BERNARD

Severn River
PUBLISHING

Severn River Publishing
www.SevernRiverPublishing.com

This is a work of fiction. Names, characters, businesses, places, events and incidents are either the products of the author's imagination or used in a fictitious manner. Any resemblance to actual persons, living or dead, or actual events is purely coincidental.

ISBN: 978-1-951249-97-7 (Paperback)
ISBN: 978-1-951249-98-4 (Hardback)

ALSO BY H.W. "BUZZ" BERNARD

Eyewall

Plague

Supercell

Blizzard

Cascadia

When Heroes Flew

Never miss a new release! Sign up to receive exclusive updates from author Buzz Bernard.

SevernRiverPublishing.com/Buzz

To the memory of the men who truly "wrote" this story, the aircrews who flew Operation Tidal Wave on August 1, 1943.

And to the memory of my wife, Christina, who grew up in pre-war and wartime Nazi Germany.

"The longer you can look back, the farther you can look forward."

—Sir Winston Churchill

PROLOGUE

On a bitter December day in 1928, Egon Richter, seventeen, and his father, Gerhard, crunched across a snowy field in the *Hunsrück,* the high rolling plateau south of the Mosel River in west-central Germany. Underneath a bleak, colorless dawn, their breaths trailed behind them in thin, silvery streams.

They had come to hunt wild boar, hoping to down a fine, fat hog for Christmas dinner. As they approached the edge of a woods, Gerhard held up his arm, hand extended. They halted. Well back in the forest, half hidden among the firs and spruce, a shadowy form, low to the ground, shuffled haltingly through the semi-darkness.

Egon and his father waited in silence for almost ten minutes until the form reached the tree line, the delineation between forest and field. There, the shape came into sharp definition: a huge hog, an old boar, battle-scarred and limping. With one tusk broken off and an open wound across his flank—testimony to a recent duel, no doubt—he appeared in no condition for another fight. Yet when he spotted the two men, he squared up to face them, the coarse hair between his massive shoulders rising in a bristling warning.

He snorted a cannonade of steam into the brittle cold, then launched a mock charge, kicking up a spray of dirty snow and dead grass. But he proved incapable of even a short dash. One of his front legs gave way and he pitched snout-down onto the frozen ground, furrowing through the icy cover like a snowplow.

Egon raised his rifle, a Mauser bolt-action—a relic of the Great War in which his father had fought and been wounded a decade earlier—and positioned the front sight over the hog's heart. He pictured the pig on the holiday dinner table, his family seated around it in anticipation of a sumptuous feast.

The boar lurched to his feet, but refused to flee. Instead, he stood his ground, grunting and snorting, his tiny red eyes locked on the hunters in what seemed to Egon pure hatred. The animal stalked forward, this time cautiously, favoring his gimpy leg. Still, he displayed the determination of a beast spoiling for a fight. Egon steadied his aim.

"Don't," his father said, his voice soft and raspy in the cold. "He's an old warrior. Let him live. Honor his service and bravery."

Without looking at his father and holding his aim, Egon responded, "*Nein, Papa.* He challenged us. I will answer that. I, too, am a warrior."

He squeezed the trigger. The gunshot reverberated over the frigid *Hunsrück*. The boar staggered, spun, then collapsed into the snow. He attempted to rise, but was able to lift only his head. Egon worked the bolt on the Mauser. An empty shell casing arced into the frosty air. He fired again. The hog ceased moving.

Egon, overflowing with celebratory enthusiasm, dashed forward. He knelt by his kill, expecting to feel his father's approving hand on his shoulder. No such touch came. He looked behind him. His father, unsmiling, arms folded across his chest, remained in place, ankle-deep in the crusty snow.

Egon shrugged, laid the rifle against the boar's bristly hide, and withdrew his skinning knife.

1

En route from Hardwick, England, to Benghazi, Libya
March 26, 1943

At ten thousand feet, a lone United States Army Air Force B-24 bomber roared southward over the Bay of Biscay off the coast of France. The plane, piloted by Captain Al Lycoming and his copilot, Second Lieutenant Lenny Sorenson, "Sorey," was not on a bombing mission. Rather, it had been dispatched to Benghazi, Libya, from its home base in Hardwick, England, to join up with a small bomber force already in place in North Africa. The reason for their deployment had been rather obscure, only that they were to participate in an operation involving "experimental bombing tactics."

They edged around Spain, keeping a watchful eye out for German fighters based in the so-called "neutral" nation. Al had been warned that the Nazis apparently held their own definition of what constituted neutrality, so he kept the crew on high alert.

They cruised without incident for over an hour, but off the coast of Portugal the peacefulness ended. Tail gunner shouted a warning over the interphone. "Aircraft coming up on our six. Fast."

"How many?" Al called back.

"One."

"German?"

"Can't tell."

"Get ready to shoot."

"Roger that."

"All positions, prepare to fire."

Al turned to Sorey. "Let's take 'er down, gain some speed."

"Ready."

The tail position again: "Hold on. Looks like a friendly. He's peeled off to our port."

Al glanced to his left, out the cockpit glass. A fighter tore into view, then slowed as it came abeam of the bomber. The fighter bore an RAF roundel on its side.

"Hold your fire, everyone," Al called. "It's a Brit. Spitfire."

Sorey leaned forward to see around Al and get a good look at the fighter. "Probably out of Gibraltar."

Al nodded.

The Spitfire waggled its wings and accelerated away.

Once the B-24 reached the Straits of Gibraltar, Al relaxed. He pressed his throat mike to make an announcement. "We've reached Gibraltar, so it should be clear sailing from here on out. We'll grab some gas in Casablanca, then press on running parallel to the North African coast to Benghazi. The stop in Casablanca will be brief, about forty-five minutes, so get out and stretch your legs. But don't go wandering off looking for Bogart and Bergman or you'll end up AWOL and sitting out the war in Leavenworth."

In response came a chuckle or two, a series of "Yes, sirs," and a few double clicks—an informal radio signal of acknowledgement.

Sorey turned toward Al and raised his voice to be heard over the bellow of the bomber's four big engines. "Of all the gin joints, in all the towns . . ."

"Jesus. You memorized lines from the movie?"

"Seen it four times."

Al rolled his eyes. "War is hell."

"Nothin' else to do but sleep, eat, and fight."

The stop in Casablanca ate up an hour, but once airborne again, Al got them back on schedule. They flew eastward along the north coast of Morocco and, after that, Algeria, the deep blue Mediterranean Sea below them, a gray-smeared cloud deck of altostratus above. The air proved smooth, unlike the thermal-ridden summers that could send them bouncing up and down as if riding an invisible roller coaster.

"Sorey," Al said, "take it for a while, would you? I just wanna close my eyes for a few minutes."

"Yes, sir. I got the controls. Have a good snooze."

Al shut his eyes and allowed his thoughts to drift off to Sarah, his wife, and their last night together in the States before he'd shipped out for England.

They had married just after he'd joined the Army in mid-1941, guessing it would not be long before the US entered the war. He also thought if he volunteered early he'd have a better chance of doing what he wanted, being an aviator. His thoughts turned out to be correct.

He and Sarah had been separated during much of his flight training—he spent time in locations such as Santa Ana, California, and Tucson, Arizona—but after he'd received his overseas orders in the late summer of '42, she had taken the train— several, in fact—from Oregon to New York. First the SP&S—

Spokane, Portland, and Seattle—from Portland to Seattle. Then the Empire Builder to Chicago, followed by the 20th Century Limited to Grand Central in New York City.

The five-day slog proved exhausting in railcars crammed with GIs, but well worth it for the chance to spend a day or two with Al before he deployed to Europe.

The night before his scheduled departure, they journeyed to the Glen Island Casino in New Rochelle for dinner and dancing. The venture had set him back a small fortune, over fifteen bucks, but for a chance to sway to the Glenn Miller Orchestra, it seemed a tiny expenditure. Besides, he figured, he wasn't going to be spending much money once he entered combat. And as always, there lurked just beyond the horizon of their happiness the unspoken fear, the unacknowledged reality, they might never see one another again.

They sat at a table near the dance floor, sipping Manhattans after dinner and listening to the orchestra run through the new favorites of a nation at war: "V for Victory Hop," "American Patrol," and "Don't Sit Under the Apple Tree."

During a break in the music, he slid a crumpled photograph, something clipped from the *Arizona Daily Star* in Tucson where he'd completed his B-24 training, across the table to her.

"My baby," he said.

She looked askance at him.

"Second-best baby," he corrected.

She nodded her approval. "That's what you fly?"

"It's a B-24 bomber. It's called a Liberator."

"A Liberator? Like what we're doing for Europe, trying to liberate it?"

"Yes. I guess that's a good way to think of it."

She studied the picture. A hint of a frown crept over her face.

"I know," he said. "It's not quite so sleek and glamorous as the B-17."

"That's the one they call the Flying Fortress?"

"Yeah. It's the bomber that gets most of the press."

"I can see why."

He hung his head in mock shame. "Even the guys who fly the Lib say it looks like a pregnant cow."

She laughed. "It's not that bad. It just looks . . ."

"Different?"

He knew it did. With its slab-sided fuselage, twin vertical stabilizers, and a high-mounted straight wing that spanned one hundred ten feet, it bore a much more businesslike and boxy appearance than the popularized Flying Fortress.

"Yes, different," she said. "Tell me about it. You know, the stuff you can, the stuff that isn't secret."

He took a swallow of his Manhattan. "Well, without giving away any numbers, it's actually a bit faster, has a longer range, and typically carries a bigger bomb load than the B-17." He paused for a moment, then added, "But it's a handful to fly."

She locked her gaze on him, and he read the trepidation in her eyes.

"I'm a good pilot," he said. "I love flying it. I know what I'm doing. It's just that it's not like driving a Packard. More like driving a garbage truck."

She reached across the table for his hand. "I know you're a good pilot. But I'll never stop worrying about you. You're the most important thing in my life."

"And you in mine," he responded, and meant it.

"Promise me you'll come home," she whispered.

He couldn't, but knew he had to. A part of him, the intellectual part, understood he might not return, that people in Axis fighters and behind flak guns would be trying to kill him. But another part of him—the youthful, not-yet-battle-tested part, the part that bore a sense of invincibility—brimmed with excitement and anticipation over embarking on a "great adventure." A ripple of guilt surged through him. He realized how hard it must be for Sarah, and all the others left behind—wives, girlfriends, parents, children—to see their loved ones off to war.

"I don't know," he responded. "I don't know how I can make that guarantee. There are just too many—"

"Promise me, damn you, promise," she hissed, and gripped his hand so fiercely he thought she might bruise it. "I know you'll be lying. But I want to hear the words. Please say them." Her eyes brimmed with tears as her gaze bore into his soul.

"I'll come home, Sarah, I will. I love you so much. That's all the incentive I need. Somehow, someway, I'll make it." He attempted to force genuine conviction into his words, but it proved futile.

"How many missions?" she asked, her voice husky with emotion.

"Before I can come home? Right now, twenty-five." Twenty-five opportunities for the enemy to make sure he wouldn't.

The orchestra returned from its intermission and launched into "String of Pearls," and the audience applauded.

"Let's dance," he said.

"I don't know," she answered. "You look so handsome in your uniform, I'm not sure I want other women noticing you."

He stood. "I understand. I guess I could easily be mistaken for Clark Gable."

She frowned and gave him an icy stare. "Sure, if you grew a mustache and a couple of inches, maybe."

Holding hands, they wove their way onto the dance floor.

A stratus of cigarette smoke, like an early morning overcast along the Pacific coast, hung over the floor. The aroma of sirloin steaks and spilled whiskey floated through the casino. He pulled Sarah close and buried his face in her honeysuckle-scented hair as the Miller band began one of his favorites, "Tuxedo Junction."

They glided across the hardwood floor to the soft oop-pah oop-pah of the trombone section as the musicians fanned hat mutes in front of their instruments. They seemed to become one, floating through an ephemeral world of beauty and peace where no one else existed, as if he and Sarah had the casino to themselves.

The orchestra moved from "Tuxedo Junction" to "At Last," and the magic of the evening seemed endless.

———

"Sir, Benghazi's coming up." Sorey's voice over the interphone snapped Al awake. He didn't realize he'd fallen asleep.

"Sorry, Sorey. Didn't think I'd go lights out like that."

"Been a long day, Pops, I know. But I'd like you at the controls with me when we set 'er down."

Al hated his nickname, "Pops," but realized he'd earned it because his advanced age, thirty, made him the oldest member of his ten-man crew. Not that it really mattered. Everyone on the crew sported a nickname. It had become an esprit de corps sort of thing. Even the bomber had a name. In fact, all American bombers did. Not only did they have names but also elaborate artwork on their noses to accompany them.

The artwork, in truth, often bordered on the prurient by featuring long-legged, big-breasted women in the nude or only scantily clad. The bomber names themselves could be suggestive. *Strawberry Bitch, Male Call, Bangin' Lulu, Wicked Woman.* Al supposed a lot of the nose art would not necessarily be welcomed back in the States, but in combat theaters, men called the shots, and sexy ladies depicted on B-24s and B-17s were SOP —Standard Operating Procedure.

Al's Liberator had been christened something a little different . . . nothing lascivious. It went by *Oregon Grinder* and bore a cartoon logo of an organ grinder, wearing a top hat with "OREGON" stenciled on it, stuffing an evil-looking dancing monkey, a caricature of Adolf Hitler, into what was, in effect, a meat grinder.

Why Oregon? Not only did Al hail from Oregon—Forest Grove outside of Portland—but so did Sorey, who came from Astoria at the mouth of the Columbia River. Sorey, though a junior officer, had proved an excellent aviator. Al guessed that Sorey's experience as a salmon fisherman who frequently transited the Columbia River Bar, a highly dangerous stretch of water where the river emptied into the Pacific Ocean, had taught him how to handle rough weather, strong currents, and powerful winds. Nobody could land a B-24 in gusty crosswinds better than Sorey. Al loved the short, stocky, ruddy-complected lieutenant.

Together they'd chosen the name for the bomber and come up with the concept of the cartoon. A third member of the crew, Tech Sergeant Bryce McGregor, the radio operator, had painted it.

Now *Oregon Grinder* approached Benghazi late in the day. The slanting rays of the sun cast long shadows over a dusty, barren landscape. Patches of green speckled a narrow strip of land adjacent to the Mediterranean Sea, but south of there sat nothing but an ocean of sand, the Sahara Desert, that stretched for over a thousand miles into French Equatorial Africa.

Khaki and army-green tents of all sizes, and a few wooden buildings that appeared to lack structural integrity, dotted the sprawling Benghazi complex that boasted five separate runways.

"Holy crap, look at that," Sorey said. He pointed out the front of the cockpit windshield, down and to the right.

A string of camels, herded by men in long brown robes and

headgear that looked like piles of white rags, plodded along a fence outside the air base.

"We're not in Kansas anymore," Al said.

"Shit, Kansas is a rain forest compared to this place," Sorey responded, then added, "Oh, to be back in green, green England."

"I was told this would be only a brief TDY."

"Hope you didn't believe that temporary duty shit," Sorey grumbled.

"Has the Army ever led us astray?"

Sorey laughed.

They landed *Oregon Grinder* and taxied it to a hardstand of sorts—really just firm, smoothed sand—where they shut down the engines and deplaned.

Al and Sorey dropped onto the ground through the Liberator's open bomb bay doors, where they joined up with the rest of the crew.

An Army major with bushy eyebrows and wearing lightweight khakis that had seen better days greeted them.

"Gentlemen, welcome to Benghazi. I'm Major Norman Appold of the 376th Bomb Group. We're better known as the Liberandos."

Al saluted, then stepped forward and shook the major's hand. "Captain Al Lycoming, 93rd Bomb Group, the Circus."

The 93rd's nickname had been shortened from Ted's Traveling Circus, the tag it had earned when Lieutenant Colonel Edward "Ted" Timberlake commanded it and it was frequently called upon to "take its show on the road" and deploy outside of England. Timberlake had since been promoted to a staff position. Now Lieutenant Colonel Addison Baker led the Circus.

"Look, I know you guys are tired," Appold said. "Let's get you over to the mess tent where you can grab some grub, then get you bedded down. Not much in the way of quarters here, but the cots are firm and the blankets warm."

"I thought it was supposed to be hot here in the desert," Sorey chimed in.

"Not at this time of year. The nights are chilly. But that's a good thing. Makes the scorpions lethargic and kills the flies."

"Scorpions?" Sorey said, a tinge of alarm in his voice.

"The national animal of Libya. The cool weather slows 'em down, but best you still check your boots in the morning before you slip them on."

Sorey shook his head in disbelief and glared at Al. *What have you got us into?*

"Okay, gentlemen, follow me to the 'dining room.'"

Major Appold sidled up to Al as they walked. "I'll brief you and your men in the morning about a special mission we've got planned. It'll be just four birds, three Liberando ships and yours. I understand you're relatively new to the Circus, but Lieutenant Colonel Baker said you're one of the best pilots he's got. That's great, because we're gonna need a lot of skill on the trip we've got planned."

They reached the entrance of the mess tent.

"Well, eat hearty, sleep well, and I'll tell you in the morning about the adventure we've got coming up." Appold slapped Al on the shoulder and disappeared into the growing darkness.

Al watched him go and wondered, as Sorey had suggested earlier, *What have I got us into?*

2

Benghazi, Libya
March 27, 1943

Major Appold convened the promised briefing at ten o'clock in the morning in a small wooden structure that reeked of stale cigarette smoke, dried sweat, and whiffs of aviation gas that weaseled into the room through ill-fitting doors and windows. From outside, the cough and throaty roar of B-24 engines being run up from time to time competed with Appold's resonant voice.

"Good morning," he said. "I'll get right to it. I'm sure you're wondering why you were dispatched from Jolly Old to the desert—and in a way I am, too—so I'll begin by filling you in with some background info."

He walked to a map of Sicily that rested on a rickety wooden easel.

"Near Messina, on the island of Sicily, there's a set of ferro-concrete train sheds that protect supply trains carrying weapons and food bound for what's left of Rommel's army in Tunisia. The trains are ferried across the Strait of Messina from the mainland of Italy, then moved into the sheds. We've gone after the sheds several times with high-level raids, but our bombs haven't been able to penetrate their roofs. So I thought a different approach might be called for."

Appold paused and took a swig of coffee from a cracked, steaming mug.

"I went to our group commander, Colonel K.K. Compton, and suggested mounting a low-level attack on the sheds using just a handful of bombers. I was kinda surprised, but he jumped at the idea, and even suggested bringing in a B-24 or two from England. I don't know why—I wanted to use just our Liberando crews—but decided not to stir the pot once I got Compton's okay. Maybe he thought it would be good experience or something."

"You do realize," interjected Al, "we're high-altitude bombers, not hedgehoppers. We don't have any low-level credentials."

"Neither do we, Captain, but I think we can pull this off. I'd love nothing better than to poke a stick in Rommel's eye, and the Italians'."

"Yes, sir. We're on board with that. What's the plan?"

Appold pointed at the map again.

"I'll lead our three Liberando ships and your bird to a fighter strip on Malta—that's about fifty miles south of the southern-most point of Sicily—on March 29, and we'll launch from there, after dark."

Appold continued his briefing for half an hour, filling in logistical, navigational, and tactical details. "Any questions?" he asked when finished.

"Can I assume," Al said, "since we'll be hugging the ground when we attack, the bombs will be on a delayed fuse?"

"Absolutely. I know at two hundred miles per hour and rooftop level our bomb-trail will be dangerously short. I don't want us blowing up the guys behind us."

After the conclusion of the briefing and the question-and-answer period, Al and Sorey, along with Captain George Coleman, *Oregon Grinder's* navigator, walked together back to their tent quarters. George, a skinny Jewish kid from Brooklyn, had joined the military two years before Al. Despite being from opposite sides of the country, Al from Oregon and George, or "Rabbi" as the rest of the gang called him, from New York, they got along well. In fact, they became fast friends, perhaps because they were the "old men" of the crew. George wore a look of perpetual bemusement on his face, a face that appeared to have been snatched from a cubist painting, but he proved a serious and capable officer. Still, from time to time, he couldn't resist taking a shot at his aircraft commander.

With a smirk on his face, he turned to Al. "Well, here's another fine mess you've gotten us into."

"You watch too damn many Laurel and Hardy movies," Al snapped. "Good grief, that must be all you and Sorey do, go to movies."

"We get our asses shot at once in a while, too."

Luqa, Malta
March 29, 1943

A cool evening breeze wafted over the small island of Malta as ground crews at a fighter strip in the town of Luqa refueled four B-24s from Benghazi. A dull overcast hid the moon.

Major Appold gathered the pilots, copilots, and navigators from the Liberators in a ramshackle shed perched on the edge of the runway and reviewed the plan for the attack.

"Okay, men, just to refresh your memories, we're going around the top of Sicily, keeping under radar all the way." He unfolded a crumpled map of Sicily and placed it on a table. "Like this." He indicated a west-northwest course out of Malta, then around the western tip of Sicily. "Once we reach Trapani, we'll turn east, passing north of Palermo."

"Altitude?" asked one of the pilots.

"We'll be skimming the wave tops."

Al winced. When he'd first heard "low level," he'd assumed a thousand feet or so. He looked at Sorey and George and could see they didn't like the notion of barreling through sea spray any more than he did, especially on a cloudy night with no moon. But maybe if they had a difficult time seeing, the Italians might have a tough time spotting them, too.

Appold continued his briefing. "The IP may be hard to find. It's an unmarked spot of water between the Lipari Islands and Messina, where the rail sheds are."

"Lipari Islands?" George said.

"An east-west string of tiny islands about fifty miles northwest of Messina. Don't worry, Captain. Just stick together and we'll be fine. I'll get us there."

Al hoped so. If they got separated, the mission would fall apart. They had no landmarks, other than the unmarked Initial Point, they could use to navigate on their own.

"One final thing," Appold said. "If we can't get to the sheds in Messina, our alternate target is Crotone on the mainland."

Al had heard of Crotone, located in Calabria, Italy's southwest peninsula. The town harbored chemical and ammunition manufacturers that, like the rail sheds in Messina, had proven resistant to high-level bombing attacks.

At midnight, the Liberators launched. As planned, they flew just above the waves. George shifted from his usual navigator's position in the lower nose of *Oregon Grinder* to the bomb bay.

There he crouched on a narrow catwalk above the open bomb bay doors and looked down at the white caps of the Tyrrhenian Sea. Every few minutes, he called off the plane's estimated height above the water to Al.

The four-ship formation swept into an unexpected cluster of low stratus clouds. Al lost sight of the other bombers. His grip on the control wheel tightened to a point where he felt as if he were strangling it.

"You see anything, Sorey?" Al said.

"Not a damn thing."

"George, what's our elevation?"

"Hard to see now. Maybe fifteen feet."

"Shit. Way too low. Hold 'er steady, Sorey. No quick moves up or down, left or right. Let's try not to ram anybody."

Oregon Grinder thundered through the leaden darkness, barely above the sea. Al kept his gaze glued on the attitude indicator, making sure he held the bomber straight and level.

As suddenly as they'd penetrated the clouds, they popped out, but found themselves still cloaked in lightless gloom.

"You see any of the other birds?" Al said, addressing Sorey.

"Negative, Pops."

"That's why I hate this follow-the-leader crap on bombing runs. Now there's nobody to follow. Hell, all we can do is abort and head back to Benghazi. George, give me a heading."

George responded. *Oregon Grinder* climbed and turned back toward North Africa as a sliver of brightness materialized low on the eastern horizon—dawn.

"There," Sorey said after several minutes, "about three miles ahead of us."

"I see," Al responded. Well in front of them, two other B-24s appeared to be on a track toward Benghazi. "Looks like we weren't the only ones to call it off."

"Well, Major Appold's on his own," Sorey said.

Just then the command channel came alive. Appold.

"Flight leader here. Too much fog and low cloudiness over the target. Sorry I lost ya. We're going for the alternate. Over and out."

"Guy's nothing but determined," Al said. He hated having to bail out of the mission but knew he had no choice. "Good luck to him and his crew."

Oregon Grinder and the two other Liberators landed in Benghazi at midday. After a quick debrief, the crews headed to their tents for much-needed sleep. They'd been without for almost twenty-four hours.

Evening had settled over Benghazi by the time Al awoke. He walked to the operations tent and learned that Appold had successfully carried out his raid on Crotone, the alternate target.

The intelligence officer on duty, a small lieutenant with a marshmallow build and big glasses, gave Al a brief summary. "That son-of-a-gun major blew apart a train with a five-hundred pounder on his run to the target, then put his other five bombs directly into a munitions factory. He blew it to hell. We won't be returning there."

"Something to be said for low-level attacks, I suppose," Al mumbled.

"Probably won't become SOP, though," the intel officer responded.

"Geez, I hope not." B-24s had not been designed for nap-of-the-earth missions.

Al strolled out into the darkness and plodded toward the mess tent, drawn by mystery smells, a veil of cigarette smoke, and the chatter of fellow airmen.

Someone fell in beside him. A deep baritone voice he didn't recognize said, "I hear you're from Oregon."

"What?" Al turned to see a tall lieutenant walking next to him.

"You're *Oregon Grinder's* commander, right?"

"Yeah."

"I was attending the U of O when I decided to join the Army Air Force. My motive—can't stand those fascist bastards in Europe."

Al stopped. "A fellow Oregonian, huh?" He extended his hand. "Al Lycoming. Glad to meet you."

"Brian Flavelle." He gripped Al's hand. "But I'm from New Jersey."

"Jersey? And you ended up at the University of Oregon? How in the hell did that happen?"

"I wanted to study forestry. Oregon seems to have a few of those . . . forests."

Al laughed. "So I've heard."

"Anyhow, sir, I wanted to ask—you were on the mission to Sicily with Major Appold, right?"

"Yes."

"And had to abort?"

"Clouds and fog. Never made it to the primary target."

"I want to try again."

"You're kidding."

"No. And I'd love for you to come along."

"I don't know, Lieutenant. One nighttime run making like a seaplane when you can't see crap is enough for me. I prefer dropping our loads from twenty thousand feet in the daylight, not twenty feet in the dark."

"I know, I know. But I'm not planning a nighttime mission. If we go in at evening twilight we can avoid those wee-hour mists that screwed up Appold's raid."

"You keep saying 'I.' Is this a bee you've got in *your* bonnet, or is this coming from on high?"

Flavelle cleared his throat. "Well, it's kind of my idea, sir. But

I'm planning on taking it to our group commander, K.K. Compton, and General Ent, and see if they'll sign off on it."

"General Ent?"

"Uzal Ent. He's the bomber force commander."

"What is it with this rooftop-level flying business? It seems to give you guys a hard-on."

Flavelle shrugged. "It worked at Crotone. Why not Messina?"

"So you haven't cleared it yet?"

"I was planning on hitting up Compton and Ent tomorrow. So how about it? You want another shot at Messina?"

In truth, he did. As much as he hated low-level missions, he hated not completing an assignment even more.

"Yeah," he sighed, "sign me up. I didn't join the Army Air Force to sit on my butt and wring my hands when things don't go right."

"That's jake, sir. I'll let you know tomorrow if it's a go or not." He popped to attention and snapped off a sharp salute. "Thank you, sir."

Al returned the salute. Flavelle strode off into the darkness, and Al continued his journey to the mess tent.

Well, at least we might be able to return to England with an attaboy from the bomber chief.

Messina (Sicily), Italy
April 2, 1943

With the blessings of General Ent and Colonel Compton, Lieutenant Flavelle led raid number two on the Messina rail sheds. The four-plane flight repeated the route Major Appold had followed, refueling in Malta, then circumnavigating Sicily to the west and north. Only this time they flew in daylight and reached the IP in evening twilight.

Skimming the wave tops, Al and Sorey in *Oregon Grinder* followed Flavelle as he turned into the bomb run.

This time, no fog or mist obscured the target. They crossed over the north coast of Sicily, skipped over a low, forested ridge, then barreled toward the Messina rail yard at tree-top level.

"Straight ahead, got 'em in sight," *Oregon Grinder's* bombardier announced, his voice steady and unexcited. Al liked the guy, First Lieutenant Kenny Brightman, a Georgia Tech engineering student who came across as serious and quiet but highly professional. Kenny rarely missed his target. He proved excellent at calculating in his head the vectors involved in bombing. He seemed almost as good as the Norden bombsight, the technological marvel employed on high-level missions over Europe.

"Let 'em go when you're ready," Al said. Hugging the ground negated using the Norden. Here it would be all seat-of-the-pants, Kentucky windage. Al expected Kenny to excel.

Al and Sorey held the Liberator steady, the roaring chatter of its quartet of Pratt & Whitney engines reverberating through the fuselage and accompanied by the creaks, rattles, and clanks of the speeding beast. The edge of the rail yard flashed beneath them. Ahead, a half dozen bombs arced from Flavelle's plane and erupted in bright flashes as they smashed into the sheds.

Almost simultaneously, Kenny announced, as calm as ever, "Bombs away." *Oregon Grinder*, freed of its bomb load, leapt up, leaving its own trail of explosions in its wake.

"Rammed the bombs right down their throats," Staff Sergeant Billy Cummings, the tail gunner, yelled.

"Good shooting, Kenny," Al said.

"Whoa, shit, look out," Sorey screamed.

Al saw them, too, a flight of German Junkers Ju 52s dead ahead, flying directly at them.

"Transports," Al said. "No weapons." But transports or not, the enemy. "Gunners, get ready. Junkers coming up on our nose. Open fire when you see them."

Flavelle didn't break formation, but headed straight for the tri-motor German planes.

"Damn," Sorey yelled, "must be forty of them."

The Liberators charged directly into the German flock, which scattered in all directions as the American fifty calibers opened up.

But one of the Junkers didn't break off and continued on a beeline for the bombers.

"What's with that bastard?" Al shouted.

A stream of tracers from at least two of the Liberators lanced into the German transport. Trailing smoke and shedding parts, it crashed into the Sicilian countryside.

"Maybe the pilot was a wannabe fighter jockey," Sorey said.

"Think we discouraged him," Al responded. "Let's head for home."

Benghazi, Libya
April 4, 1943

As Al and Sorey performed their preflight walk around *Oregon Grinder,* preparing for their return to England, a jeep rolled up to the bomber and stopped. A short but handsome man, an Army colonel wearing a set of neatly pressed khakis, dismounted and walked toward the pilots.

Al and Sorey sprang to attention and saluted. The colonel returned the salutes.

"Gentlemen, I'm K.K. Compton, commander of the 376th

Bomb Group. I just wanted to come by and thank you for a job well done with the attack on the Messina rail sheds. We've been trying to knock them out for a long time, and you, along with Lieutenant Flavelle and a couple of other Liberando birds, did it in five minutes. Oh, and General Ent sends his regards and thanks, too."

"Our pleasure, sir," Al said.

"I'll make sure Colonel Baker knows his Traveling Circus flyboys are up to the job. Glad to have you as part of the team. I like your skills."

"But there won't be a lot more demand for low-level bombing, will there?"

Colonel Compton smiled, an enigmatic grin. "Have a good flight back to England, gentlemen."

After Compton departed, Sorey said, "Part of the team? He likes our skills?"

Al ran the words through his mind. He didn't like what they suggested. "I have a feeling we're not going to be in England too long."

Sorey shook his head. "I sure as shit hope that doesn't mean we're going to be returning to this godforsaken sand box."

3

Benghazi, Libya
Late June 1943

Al and George sat on the hard desert ground, their backs resting against *Oregon Grinder's* left landing gear tire. They sipped warm English beer that, because of its warmth, did nothing to ward off the oppressive heat of the late afternoon.

Al spit his beer onto the sand. "Jesus, you'd think they could find some ice to store this stuff in."

"Come on, Pops, we're lucky to have beer, let alone chilled beer." George took another pull from his bottle. "Besides, it's safer to drink than the water."

Al swatted at a small swarm of the omnipresent flies that plagued the jury-rigged Benghazi air base. He hated the desert. Hated being back here so soon after their visit of a few months earlier. Hated the flies, the scorpions, the jerboas—hopping rodents. Hated the suspended dust that wafted in on winds called *ghiblis* and coated everything in a fine, gritty powder. He especially detested the virtually inedible meals of pressed ham and dried cabbage boiled in alkali water.

"I know, I know," he muttered, responding to George's comment on the safety, or lack thereof, of the water. "How many guys in the infirmary now?"

"Lots. Too many. Most with dysentery."

"The runny, bloody shits," Al groused.

"Trouble is, we're gonna need all the airmen we can get soon. There's something big afoot."

"Yeah, that's obvious. So what's the scuttlebutt? Where? When? Why?"

"How should I know? You're the commander."

Al shrugged. "I'm a junior officer, not brass. You've been in the Army longer than any of us. You must have connections, ways of picking up on the jungle drums."

In contrast to the bewilderment often professed by George, he always seemed to have a good handle on what was happening.

"Look around us, Pops. There are scores of Liberators here. There wouldn't be that many for some sort of minor action, so there has to be a major raid in the offing."

Al could make out through the dusty haze at least a dozen other B-24s parked haphazardly alongside the runway. Among them sat *Hell's Wench*, Lieutenant Colonel Baker's aircraft, *Utah Man*, *Tupelo Lass*, *Honky-Tonk Gal*, *Thunder Mug*, and *Jersey Bounce*.

He knew many others squatted nearby. They had arrived from England about a week ago, the entire 93rd Bomb Group, the Traveling Circus.

"How many aircraft you figure altogether, from all the bomb groups?" Al took a tentative sip of his beer. *Yep, warm, but better than dealing with dysentery.*

George crinkled his face in a show of concentration. "Let's see. In addition to us there's Colonel Leon Johnson's Flying Eight Balls out of Shipham, and Colonel Jack Wood's Sky Scorpions from Hethal. There were a couple of groups here already, the Liberandos and Pyramiders, who've been chasing Rommel's *Afrika Korps* back and forth across the desert for months. So, all totaled, I guess there's gotta be over a hundred and fifty Liberators here."

Al attempted to whistle, but his dry, cracked lips only produced something that sounded akin to a soft fart.

"The Sky Scorpions," he said, "they're new to this game, aren't they?"

"Yep. They're driving Liberators fresh off the dealer's lot, and a lot of the pilots and crews haven't even been shot at yet. But they'll learn fast. I've heard there are a bunch of missions to Sicily coming up. It won't be long before the Army and Marines hit the beaches there, so I'm positive the brass will wanna soften up the defenses before that happens."

"But that can't be why there are five bombardment groups here, can it?"

George shook his head. "No, that wouldn't make sense. Look, what don't you see here? B-17s. There are no Flying Fortresses, just Liberators. Why just Libs? Because they've got a longer range and carry more bombs than B-17s. So Sicily wouldn't make sense. Too close."

"What about mainland Italy?" Al took another swallow of his tepid beer.

"Maybe, but I was thinking something even farther away, like Austria or the Balkans. They've got munitions and aircraft factories in Austria, and oil refineries in the Balkans. But it's gotta be something special."

"Why do you say that?"

George took a pull from his own beer, then answered. "Think about it. Before we left England, what were we doing over the past two months? Flying training missions up and down the East Anglian countryside at treetop level. Scattering horses and cows, scaring kids, and pissing off farmers. Treetop level, like fighters making strafing runs. And what did we do on our TDY here last spring? Two rooftop-level raids on Messina."

"Well, two tries, one raid."

"Point taken."

"But come on, B-24s were never conceived to do that. We're supposed to be dropping bombs from twenty or twenty-five thousand feet."

"Says the guy who I heard almost got drummed out of the Army because he shaved the top off a haystack in western Kansas."

"Accidentally, not deliberately."

"And clipped a radio station broadcast antenna in New Mexico?"

"What the hell, Rabbi? You aren't going to become one of those ... those ... what do you call those lawyers?"

"Prosecuting attorneys. No. I'm trying to make a point. That the plane *can* be flown at low level."

"No way. Not safely. Look, my little, let's call them indiscretions—and I should have kept my mouth shut about them— occurred on training flights. No bombs, light on fuel, half a crew. Driving a B-24 with a full load is like trying to steer a dragon. It's not very damn responsive. Let's leave the nap-of-the-earth stuff to Spitfires and P-40s."

"The brass may not feel that way. Besides, we kind of proved a point by blowing up the rail sheds."

"But that was with four planes. You put dozens of Libs together barreling along at two hundred miles per hour at tree- top or wave-top level, and you're asking for trouble. I'll say it again, Liberators aren't P-40 Warhawks." A B-24, *Sweet Adeline* from the Sky Scorpions, settled onto the runway after a training run. It ground to a stop in a roiling brown cloud of dust and sand. Al and George watched it, then resumed their conversation.

"So why would the brass feel they have to fly bombers at kite-level?" Al asked.

George shrugged and tossed his empty beer bottle on the ground near *Oregon Grinder's* nose wheel. "To avoid radar detection? Or maybe to put a big load of bombs on a target very precisely? Maybe both. So we have to think about what kind of facility would warrant that sort of attention."

"A factory in the middle of a city where we want to avoid killing civilians and blowing up their homes and businesses?"

"Makes sense. Or maybe a target so important and so well defended the planners think we'll get only one crack at achieving total surprise."

"Yeah," Al groused, "attacking so low we'd have to navigate using road signs would certainly achieve total surprise. It would sure stupefy me."

George laughed, almost choking on his beer.

Al went on. "All kidding aside, it would be just too damn dangerous. Think about it. Down near the ground you've got all kinds of turbulence. Thermal, mechanical, prop wash from other aircraft. In close formation, how would you keep from getting tossed into each other? You know that happened in England during training, right? A couple of planes collided. Only two guys survived." He tipped his bottle to his mouth, took a final swig, and pitched it next to George's dead soldier.

"And another thing," he went on. "Think of the antiaircraft fire. It'd be point-blank range for flak gunners. They'd have a field day. Like blasting metal ducks in a shooting gallery. We might as well be sporting big red and white bullseyes on our planes saying 'Aim here.' And if we get hit, we go down. We'd be so close to the ground already we wouldn't have a chance to maneuver. Or even bail out."

"So, all those minor contingencies aside," George said, "you think it's doable, then?"

Al snorted a chuckle.

"Sure," he said, "just like those B-26 pilots did in England about a month ago. A squadron flew a low-level raid into Holland. Nobody came back."

"Ah, but I remind you again, we pulled it off in Sicily."

"Yeah, damnit. We probably should have fucked it up."

The men fell silent. In the distance, the clatter of *Sweet Adeline's* engines faded as it taxied toward its bed down site with the Sky Scorpions.

"Got a cigarette?" George said.

Al pulled a pack of Lucky Strikes from his shirt pocket, flipped one loose, and extended it to George. He plucked one out for himself, then lit both with an engraved Ronson lighter his wife had given him before he deployed.

"Last smoke for the condemned?" George asked. Gallows humor.

"I just don't know," Al said. "I just don't know if I'd be up to it, this low-level crap. You know, what if I shit my pants, close my eyes, and slam into the ground screaming like a baby."

George extended his arm, resting a hand on Al's shoulder. "That's not you, Pops. We've all seen you in action. Unshakable nerve, steady hands. The guys wouldn't want to fly with anyone else."

Al remained silent.

"Look," George continued. "We've all got the same heebie-jeebies. Every mission. But we come through every damn time, because we're the best trained in the world, because we believe in each other, because we care for each other like brothers."

Al nodded. "Okay," he said softly. "I guess if you guys got my back, I got yours."

That evening, Al rested on the cot in his tattered tent. A sea breeze off the Mediterranean kicked in, but managed to lower the temperature only slightly while at the same time boosting the humidity to tropical levels. Adding to the oppressiveness, a repulsive odor wove its way into the Circus's encampment: an amalgam of stench from the oil drum crappers mixed with the fetor of aviation fuel seeping from a rusted storage tank, probably something the *Afrika Korps* left behind. It happened occasionally when the wind was just right. Or wrong.

Darkness descended over Benghazi. Only the distant, muffled sound of a BBC newscast reached Al's ears. Memories of the Glen Island Casino seemed a million miles away, a million years away, and in a different universe.

Had he ever really been there, dancing in a tight embrace with the woman he loved to the music of the Glenn Miller Orchestra? Or had it all been merely a titillating dream designed to bring peace to a soul imprisoned in the reality of a spartan wartime existence?

No, absolutely not. After the dinner and the dancing, after leaving the casino, the night had morphed into something more than a dream. Something titillating, yes, but not a fantasy, not something imagined. It had erupted in a genuine explosion of breathless passion, tangible and real, vivid in his memory: him pawing at her skirt, slip, panties, garter belt, bra—how could it take so damn long to undress a woman?—before they both climaxed in an anvil chorus of gasps and moans.

To his amazement, his heart rate increased merely recalling the moment. The memory grew so intense he could virtually feel Sarah's presence, her smooth skin, soft lips, warm breath. He closed his eyes and extended his hand to the side of his cot, hoping Sarah might materialize to grasp it, to let him know the bond between them remained firm and eternal. But no such touch came. He knew it wouldn't, of course, knew he was being foolish, knew most of all he didn't want to admit that loneliness, despite his being among thousands of men, sometimes overwhelmed him. As it probably did everyone.

Thoughts of Sarah spiraled away and he sank into a blue funk, dwelling on the darkness of the immediate future. So many challenges. One, for instance: it seemed hopeless to think he might get through twenty-five missions and return home. Even after the sorties he'd flown out of England, and the two special missions he'd gone on out of Benghazi, he'd made it only halfway to the magic number. And now there apparently loomed on the horizon some sort of deadly fool's errand from which he and many others might never return, though no one seemed to have a clue—or if they did, weren't talking about it— what that operation might be.

Low-level bombing in a B-24 Liberator? No, it couldn't possibly be that, could it?

If so, why not just walk into the enemy's camp tugging a five-hundred pounder in a little red wagon?

He fell asleep with visions of Sarah and him gliding across a dance floor as the muted trombone section of the Glenn Miller Orchestra oop-pahed its way through "Tuxedo Junction."

4

Kalamaki, Greece
Late June 1943

Luftwaffe Hauptmann Egon Richter landed his single-engine Messerschmitt fighter, a Bf 109, at a German air base near Kalamaki, Greece, in the late morning, well before the daily peak of the searing summer heat. The base sat roughly six miles south of Athens. It had been a civilian facility before the RAF took it over in 1940, and before German forces claimed it in 1941.

Egon taxied his plane to a hardstand where a *Kübelwagen,* a light military vehicle, waited for him.

"*Oberstleutnant* Rödel wishes to speak with you," the driver of the vehicle, a young staff sergeant, said.

Egon nodded. He knew of Gustav Rödel, but did not know him personally. Rödel, deemed one of the "fast burners" in the *Luftwaffe,* had become a wing commander at the age of twenty-seven. He had almost eighty kills to his credit, a remarkable number of enemy planes shot down in just under four years. As a commander, his popularity among pilots soared, for he believed in leading from the front, in the cockpit of a fighter, not from behind, at a desk in a headquarters building.

Egon turned over his flight equipment to a ground crew and climbed into the *Kübelwagen.*

"Headquarters is just south of here," the staff sergeant informed him. "We'll be there in a couple of minutes."

Leaving a trail of dust behind them as the vehicle jounced along an uneven dirt road, they reached headquarters, as promised, in short order. The sign over the entrance to a three-story villa announced *Jagdgeschwader 27.* 27th Fighter Wing.

Egon thanked the staff sergeant and entered the building. He found *Oberstleutnant* Rödel's office on the second floor. He knocked.

"*Herein.*"

Egon entered.

Rödel rose from behind a desk where he'd been sitting.

Egon saluted. Not the Party salute, but a traditional military salute, common in the *Luftwaffe.*

Rödel returned the salute. "Ah, *Hauptmann* Richter. Welcome! Please, take a seat." The wing commander, dressed in military shorts and a short-sleeved military shirt, gestured at a chair in front of the desk. With a youthful, slightly rounded face, he appeared to Egon more like a big brother than a commanding officer. He guessed they must be very close in age. One big difference, however: the Iron Cross that hung around Rödel's neck. It helps to have shot down over six dozen enemy aircraft.

"Thank you, *Geschwaderkommodore.*"

Rödel waved his hand dismissively. "Gustav will do." He examined a stack of papers on his desk and pulled out several sheets. An electric fan rotating erratically in a corner of the room sent one of the sheets flying, but Rödel grabbed it out of the air before it could get away.

"The heat," he said, "always the heat. I think it's worse here than in North Africa."

Egon knew the 27th had previously supported the *Afrika Korps*. When the wing evacuated from Africa, its three component *Gruppes*, or groups, redeployed to France, Italy, and Greece. Egon's orders had assigned him to a new fourth group now in the process of being established at Kalamaki.

Rödel studied the paper he'd snatched from the air. "You come bearing an excellent recommendation, *Hauptmann,* one from *Generalmajor* Adolf Galland."

"General?" Egon couldn't hide the surprise in his voice. "*Meine Gott,* he was a major when I knew him."

"He's a shooting star, my friend. One of the *Luftwaffe's* best. He's got *Reichsmarschall* Göring's eye. Hard not to when you've got over ninety victories."

"Over ninety?" Again, surprise threaded his voice.

"Legitimate kills, too, not pencil whipped. He's a fighter pilot's fighter pilot. He hates his staff job, by the way. No more combat."

"He loved flying and fighting," Egon said. "That's all he wanted to do when I knew him in northern France. He couldn't wait to mix it up with the Spitfires and Hurricanes."

"The Battle of Britain."

"Yes."

"And you? Did you love it?"

Egon looked out a side window of the office. A man with a stick prodded a donkey pulling a wooden cart along a cobblestone lane.

Egon turned to face Rödel. "The first time I went after a bomber I fired from about a mile away and nearly peed in my pants."

Rödel rocked back in his chair and laughed heartily. "We all did, *Hauptmann,* we all did. If you didn't, there's something wrong with you." He studied another sheet of paper resting on his desk. "General Galland knows a fighter pilot when he sees one, and he saw one in you. You proved him right on the Eastern Front." He tapped his forefinger on the paper.

The fan sputtered to a sudden stop and the lights in the office dimmed, then blinked off.

"Damned electricity," Rödel said. "Two or three times a day it goes out. Our engineers are trying to show the Greeks how to construct a reliable system, but so far it's proved futile. Anyhow, the Eastern Front. You were there for the Battle of Stalingrad last winter. Over a dozen kills. Now here you are with twenty-two total. An Iron Cross beckons."

Thirty seemed to be the magic number for the award. Egon shook his head. "It doesn't matter. My victories came in a losing cause. Stalingrad was a disaster for the *Wehrmacht*." He stopped speaking abruptly, fearful his commentary had overstepped the bounds of what a junior officer should voice.

Rödel steepled his fingers beneath his chin and appeared to be lost in thought. After several moments he spoke. "Yes, I know. I also know it's sometimes natural to question our leadership. I have to admit, *Der Führer* declaring war on America after Pearl Harbor was, shall we say, at best, ill-timed. How could we possibly fight Britain, the Soviets, and America all at once?

"Yet we must. We fight for our country, our families, and our brother pilots. We fight to stay alive." Rödel paused, leaned forward, then spoke in an almost conspiratorial whisper. "But we do not go into battle for ideals devoid of integrity and honor. We are warriors and soldiers, *Hauptmann*, not state-sanctioned terrorists and executioners."

"Yes, sir."

Rödel fixed his gaze on Egon, not in a threatening way, but in a manner that suggested a bond between commander and commanded.

"There is an unwritten law," he said, "that I like to remind all my pilots of. Once you have defeated your opponent, shot him from the sky, victory is yours and the engagement is over. You do not fire on men in parachutes, you do not strafe men on the ground or in the water. You maintain your honor as a *Luftwaffe* officer. Do I make myself clear?"

"Perfectly, sir."

The fan whirred back to life, the lights flickered on.

"Good," Rödel said. "You'll do well here, I have no doubt. And let me tell you something else, Egon, if I may call you that . . . I need you."

"Sir?"

"You're a proven fighter pilot, battle-tested and experienced. We're losing too many men with such credentials these days. We're replacing them with youth and enthusiasm, not know-how and skill. We're getting aviators who know how to fly but not fight. We are getting kids with half the training we got. I fear we're feeding them into a meat grinder."

Egon nodded. He'd witnessed the same thing all too often of recent. He understood the vaunted Third Reich couldn't keep up with the demand for pilots. Losses had begun to exceed replacements on a regular basis.

"I need you to take these new flyers, as many as you can, under your wing," Rödel continued. "Lead them into battle. On their initial combat missions tell them to stick to you like a shadow and do exactly what you do. Maybe we can keep a few more alive that way."

"Yes, sir."

"You've a family, Egon?"

"A wife and a daughter."

"They mean the world to you, yes?"

"The universe."

"I want you to go home to them after all this is over, I truly

do. And I want to send as many of the young men that are now
joining us home, too. If you can help them fight, win, and
survive, you will have done your job as a *Luftwaffe* officer
honorably."

"You have my promise, sir."

"I don't doubt it. Now let me tell you why we're here, what
our mission is."

Rödel rose from his chair and walked to a large-scale map
tacked on the wall behind him.

"The fighter group here at Kalamaki has been formed
specifically to defend the Romanian oil refineries at Ploesti." He
pointed to Romania on the map. "Ploesti is about thirty-five
miles north of Bucharest."

"I haven't heard of Ploesti," Egon said.

"I understand. But you'll hear much about it in the future.
The refineries there supply nearly a third of the overall
petroleum needs of the *Wehrmacht*. In simplest terms, it's the
lifeblood of our tanks, trucks, battleships, submarines. More
importantly to us, the *Luftwaffe*, Ploesti supplies *all* of our aviation gasoline. Without it, the *Luftwaffe* would cease to exist."

"I assume Ploesti is heavily defended."

"General Alfred Gerstenberg, the commander of air
defenses there, has made it perhaps the most heavily fortified
target in all of Europe. He's got well over two hundred antiaircraft guns ringing the city, and hundreds of batteries of
lighter cannons, plus tethered balloons, flak towers, and count-
less machine guns."

"A bastion of death."

"I wouldn't want to be in an American bomber attempting to
penetrate it. It would be like trying to storm a castle when you're
bare naked."

Egon couldn't imagine flying in a big, slow box into that
kind of firepower. He coveted being a fighter pilot, controlling

something nimble and quick . . . which prompted his next question.

"Fighters?" he asked, meaning around Ploesti.

"About seventy Bf 109s and 110s."

"Have the Allies attempted any kind of an attack there yet?"

"Once, about a year ago. But it seemed kind of a half-assed raid, apparently unorganized and haphazard. About a dozen B-24s dropped bombs, but not very effectively. Damage was minimal. But it certainly put us on alert, gave us the incentive to create the fortress that we have."

Rödel pointed to the map again. "Now that the Allies have taken over North Africa, that opens up new avenues of attack for them. Across the Med, over Yugoslavia or Bulgaria, and into Romania. It's just a matter of time. We don't have any specific intelligence on when or precisely where, but we know they're coming. It's our job to help Gerstenberg."

Rödel returned to his chair, but didn't sit.

"So that's our mission in brief. Let's get you to your quarters now. I know you must be tired. We've found some decent villas here in town for our officers."

Egon stood. "Thank you, sir."

Rödel popped to rigid attention and extended his right arm in the Party salute. "*Heil* Hitler."

Egon, stunned, failed to return the salute.

Rödel lowered his arm and smiled an apology. "I had to make sure. The Black Coats are not welcome here, but you *will* be visited by them." The Gestapo. "They've managed to weasel sympathizers into every unit, usually at lower levels, clerks and errand boys. So, be careful of what you say and how you say it."

"Well, when they come," Egon said, "I'll be able to tell them my wing commander snapped off a sharp Party salute."

"Believe me, there are other elements of the Party I'd rather snap off," Rödel mumbled, a sharpness in his words, "but you didn't hear that."

"Hear what, sir?"

Rödel nodded his approval. "And the jokes, be careful. Our black-coated friends have no sense of humor. What's worth a snicker among us pilots is worth a trip to the guillotine in the eyes of the Gestapo."

Egon had heard the rumors. The story of a woman in Germany who apparently had told the wrong joke in the wrong place—treason—and ended up paying for it with her head.

Hitler and Göring stood on top of a Berlin radio tower. Hitler says he wants to do something to put a smile on Berliners' faces. Göring says, "Why don't you jump?"

As the Reich suffered loss after loss, gallows humor had become more rampant.

Two friends, Luke and Karl, met in Munich. Luke had purchased a new car. He popped the hood to show Karl the engine.

"But Luke," his friend exclaimed, "it doesn't have a motor."

"No matter. I'm not planning on visiting any foreign countries, and in Germany, everything is going downhill."

And another:

"Have you heard? Switzerland has added a Minister of Naval Affairs, and they don't even have a seaport."

"So what? Germany has a Minister of Justice."

Rödel's admonitions brought home to Egon the extent to which his country had come undone. Though the *Luftwaffe,* and indeed many units of the *Wehrmacht,* carried on with a proud tradition of integrity and valor, they did so in service to a brutal police state.

Still, the army, navy, and air forces fought fiercely and would continue to battle those powers that had mounted an offensive to bring Germany to its knees. Allied bombs fell on military and civilians alike. That assault would be challenged until the bitter end.

Egon understood his duty and embraced it, for the sake of his wife and daughter if nothing else. The assault on the German people would not stand. He would bring down every single British and American fighter and bomber he could.

They are my opponents ... but are they my real *enemy?*

That remained the question that conflicted him.

5

Benghazi, Libya
Mid-July 1943

Al, accompanied by Sorey, his copilot, filed into a threadbare briefing tent along with the other pilots and copilots from the Traveling Circus. The fliers—over seventy in all, Al estimated—appeared a ragtag group, more like refugees than military men. In deference to the intense African heat, many wore shorts, khaki shirts with the sleeves rolled up—though dozens showed up bare-chested—sandals, pith helmets, and dusty utility caps.

A desert wind shook the tent and sent tiny clouds of dust and sand slithering across its bare floor. The men seated themselves in several rows of folding chairs that had been placed in front of a low, makeshift wooden stage—a briefing platform.

Someone shouted, "Ten-hut," and Lieutenant Colonel Addison Baker, the Circus's commander, entered the tent and strode to the platform. The awaiting aviators stood at attention.

Al had met Baker several times but didn't know him well. Tall and square-jawed, he seemed a serious, responsible leader. Al guessed his age to be in the mid-thirties. He'd heard Baker had served in the Ohio National Guard and had owned a service station in Detroit, Michigan, before being called to active duty in 1940.

Baker walked to the front of the platform. "Seats," he said. He nodded at a sergeant on the platform who parted a curtain revealing a large map of North Africa, the Mediterranean, and southern Europe. Baker faced his audience.

"I know you're wondering what all the low-level flying practice has been about. And I know there's been a lot of speculation and rumors about the reason for it. Here's the no-bullshit skinny. It's about an operation that's been dubbed 'Tidal Wave.' Gentlemen, on August first, twelve days from now, we're going after what's been called 'the taproot of German might.' Specifically, the oil refineries and storage facilities of Ploesti, Romania. There are seven principal complexes there that crank out about ten million tons of oil every year, including ninety-octane aviation fuel, the highest quality in Europe. Most of it goes to the Nazis."

He stepped to the map. The sergeant handed him a long wooden pointer.

"Here's the target: Ploesti in southern Romania, just a short distance north of Bucharest." Baker tapped the map with the end of the pointer. He shifted it to indicate North Africa. "And here we are in Libya. We would have liked to be able to launch from Crete, but the Krauts beat us there, and seem reluctant to lease any of their airfields to us."

A chuckle or two arose from the assembled airmen.

Baker continued. "Here's the attack route." Using the pointer, he traced the proposed course over the map as he talked. "From Benghazi we'll head north over the Med to the island of Corfu off the west coast of Greece. From there we'll turn northeast, fly over southern Albania and Yugoslavia, then on into Romania. After we drop our bombs, we'll return home by pretty much the same route in reverse. In all, it'll be a twenty-three-hundred-mile roundtrip."

Someone in back issued a low whistle.

Someone else said, "That's at the extreme end of the Lib's operating radius."

Baker walked back to the front edge of the briefing platform. "I know it is, gentlemen, and I'll be frank. I've heard it said about this raid that coming back is secondary. Ploesti is that important. And not all of us *will* make it back, especially if we've suffered battle damage. A little bit of good news, however. We're getting auxiliary fuel tanks installed in the bomb bays, so we'll have a little extra range."

"And be flying incendiaries," a voice said.

The room fell silent.

Al stood, and broke the silence. "So where does all this low-level practice figure in, sir?"

"Good question, Captain. All five bombardment groups will cross the Med at low level to prevent radar detection. We'll climb to ten thousand feet at Corfu, then stay at that altitude over Albania and Yugoslavia. Depending on the weather, we might have to go a bit higher crossing the Pindus Mountain Range along the Albania-Yugoslav border, but at this time of year the weather should be okay.

"We'll drop back down to three to five thousand feet in Romania until we reach the IPs. From there to the targets we'll hug the terrain."

"Why low-level, sir? I gotta tell you, it sounds like suicide."

"The bombing has to be precise. Most of the targets are inside concussion walls. We've got to make absolutely certain we get our bombs inside those walls, otherwise we're just blowing up buildings and making craters. We also want to minimize civilian casualties. Remember, they're Romanians not Germans."

Al sat, leaned toward Sorey, and whispered, "Full bomb load, excessive fuel load, low-level flying that'll burn fuel like crazy—this is madness. None of us will get home."

Sorey whispered back, "The brass don't have to fly these missions. All they have to do is come up with these stupid-ass plans."

Outside, a B-24 cranked up its engines. The mechanical roar momentarily drowned out conversation among the men in the tent. Once the Lib had taxied away, Baker resumed his briefing.

"I'll go over the detailed attack procedures in a minute, but I want to touch on air defenses first. There have been no recent intel reports about antiaircraft defenses, but information from sources deemed reliable indicates the total number of heavy and medium flak guns is under one hundred."

As soon as Baker spoke the words, Al's bullshit meter pegged. If Ploesti was indeed the "taproot of German might," there'd be a lot more than "under one hundred" antiaircraft guns defending it. Even a second lieutenant could figure that out. He glanced at Sorey and rolled his eyes.

Sorey leaned toward Al, shielded one side of his mouth with his hand, and spoke softly. "Even the weather guessers do a better job than the damn intel weenies."

Baker, on the platform, continued. "Specific info on balloon defenses is not available, but recent reports put the number at less than a hundred. They're tethered by ordinary German-type three-millimeter cables. Another defensive tactic is expected to include smokescreens in the event of an attack. Also, we have reports that efforts have been made to camouflage the refineries by altering their vertical appearance, making them harder to identify."

"What about enemy fighters, Colonel?" a lieutenant in the front row asked.

"There are six airfields around the refineries. Before we

launch, we'll get you updates on the number of aircraft located at those fields. It's been reported that about half the fighters are manned by Germans, half by Romanians. But none has been in combat for at least a year, so they aren't likely to be at their peak efficiency.

"Okay, there is some good news in all of this. It's estimated"—the word rang in Al's ear—"that the defenses of Ploesti have been built around the idea of attacks coming from the east and northeast. Also, the gun layout has been devised for high-level assaults. We'll be doing neither. We'll be attacking from the west at low-level."

Al stood again. "You mentioned earlier there are seven major refineries, sir, so I assume that means seven primary targets. Yet we've got only five bomb groups. Does that mean some groups will be tasked with hitting more than one target?"

"Sergeant," Baker said, and motioned for the enlisted man on the platform to help him remove the large-scale map from the briefing board. Behind it sat a smaller-scale map of the area around Ploesti. Baker moved back to the front of the platform.

"Yes, Captain. Five bomb groups, seven targets. Here's how it will work. The overall attack force will be led by Colonel K.K. Compton's Liberandos. He'll go after this refinery, we'll call it Target White One." With the pointer, Baker tapped a spot on the east side of Ploesti.

"We, the Circus, will be right behind the Liberandos. We'll go after Target White Two. It's the Concordia Vega Refinery, but you don't have to remember that name. Since the target is just a bit northwest of White One, we should hit Two about the same time the Liberandos unload on One.

"Part of our group, a segment led by Major Ramsey Potts, will simultaneously attack White Three, a little southeast of One." He tapped the map with the pointer again.

"The third bombardment group, the Pyramiders,

commanded by Killer Kane, will have responsibility for hitting the highest priority target of this raid, Astro Romana, or Target White Four. It's the largest refinery in Ploesti." He indicated the target with the pointer.

Al chuckled softly at Baker's use of Colonel John Riley Kane's nickname, Killer Kane. Kane didn't care for the name but had let it stand. The tag actually had been given to him by the *Luftwaffe*. In its intelligence summaries, he'd been labeled "Killer" because of his determination to always go full-throttle and drill through Axis defenses to his targets.

A tale circulating among Army Air Force crews was that once during a spirited attack by a swarm of Messerschmitts, the *Luftwaffe* pilots had got on Kane's command frequency and drowned out his orders to his own pilots with taunts. Incensed, Kane bellowed back, "Get the goddamn hell off the air, you bastards." Stunned, the Messerschmitt pilots shut up. Kane flew on, blasted his target, and returned home safely. Killer Kane.

Baker continued his briefing. "On the right of the Pyramiders will be Colonel Leon Johnson's Eight Balls, the fourth bombardment group, going after White Five. Johnson's deputy, Lieutenant Colonel James Posey, will peel off and lead a force to Blue Target, just south of Ploesti.

"Finally, the Sky Scorpions, led by Colonel Jack Woods, will climb the foothills of the Transylvanian Alps and take out a refinery eighteen miles north of Ploesti. That'll be Red Target.

"All of these strikes will come, if not simultaneously, then within a minute or two of each other. The bastards won't know what hit them. By the time they get their ack-ack going and their fighters up, we'll be high-tailing it for home."

Al looked around the tent. He could tell by their expressions that the pilots and copilots hadn't quite bought into Baker's optimism. They realized the gravity of the undertaking, and knew the risks. They all understood the mission could go either way. It could turn out to be a colossal success or a stunning failure.

As a concept, a plan, it seemed tilted toward success. It certainly contained a massive element of surprise. But as Al well knew, as soon as a plan begins to be executed, it starts to fall apart. A failure to remain undetected, a small error in timing or navigation, the loss of a key leader, and everything goes to shit. Deep within Al's gut, a tiny alarm went off and wouldn't stop buzzing.

Baker continued to talk. "I want to go over the IPs with you. These will be the key navigation points for executing our attack. The third or final IP will be the most important. That'll be where we make the final turn into our bomb runs. The first two IPs were chosen to get us lined up for a straight shot to the final one.

"The planners tried to choose clearly recognizable features for the IPs, making it as easy as possible for us to pick them out. All of the IPs are small towns. The first is located here"—he smacked the map with the pointer—"a place called Pitesti. About twenty-five miles east-northeast of Pitesti is a little larger village, Targoviste. That's IP number two. It's got an easily recognizable landmark, a big ole monastery that sits on top of a hill. Can't miss it.

"From IP number two we'll continue east-northeastward to a hamlet called Floresti. That's the final IP. We'll turn there and follow a set of railroad tracks that leads directly into Ploesti. After a three-minute run, it'll be bombs away.

"The groups will be spread out as we attack, each heading for its assigned target or targets. We should be able to hit them pretty much simultaneously. That will maximize the element of surprise, that and the fact we'll be blasting in from the west where we're least expected. I think we can pull this off, gentlemen, I really do." He paused. "Questions?"

A number of the men had lit cigarettes. A gray-white layer of thin smoke, spurred by puffs of wind that had snuck into the tent, drifted out through the rear exit in a translucent veil.

A captain stood. "I assume there'll be a lead navigator for the entire attack force, so if we stay together, it should be pretty much follow-the-leader as far as making the final turn, right?"

"Correct. Once we hit that first IP, we'll fan out into multiple attack waves according to our specific targets. Thus, when we pass over that last IP, each group will make its turn into the final bomb run in proper sequence and position. And brother, if you're on the ground, I'm guessing it would be a pretty damn impressive sight—a five-mile-wide attack force of Liberators screaming toward you at over two hundred miles per hour, skimming the ground."

A chuckle of agreement rippled through the assembled aviators.

A crusty old major standing at the side of the tent raised his hand. Al had heard the guy had flown in the First World War but been busted back in rank a couple of times. He didn't know why.

"Beg pardon, Colonel," the major said, "but since we'll be flying in tight formation and dropping bombs from smokestack level, how in the hell do we keep from blowing the shit out of ourselves or anybody on our wing?"

"Good question, Major. The planners actually considered that."

Again a soft chuckle arose from the audience.

"The bombs will be on delayed fuses. The five-hundred pounders, for instance, will have a forty-five second delay. That should give everyone time to skedaddle off the targets before the bombs go off."

"So you'd damned well better not be forty-five seconds late, I guess," the old major growled.

"The penalty would be severe," Baker said. He looked out over the assembled pilots to see if anyone else had questions. No one did.

"Okay, several final items," he said. "First, we'll be maintaining strict radio silence prior to the attack. No chatter between planes. That will prevent the enemy from using Radio Direction Finders to discover us. Second, British engineers have just finished constructing a dummy target layout for us in the desert on a plateau a little ways south of here. We'll send a couple of Libs over it tomorrow to check it out, then turn the rest of you loose to start practice bombing runs a day or two after that. And third, the camp goes on quarantine starting tomorrow. No one comes in, except replacement aircraft, or leaves until after the attack."

Baker turned and started to leave, then spun back to face the men. "Captain Lycoming," he said, looking at Al, "I'd like to see you in my office in five minutes."

Al and Sorey exchanged a quick glance, and Al shrugged. *No, I don't know why.*

The briefing over, Baker departed the tent as the crews stood at attention.

6

Benghazi, Libya
Mid-July 1943

Al, responding to Colonel Baker's summons, walked the short distance to a large Quonset hut where senior officers and mission planners worked. Baker's desk stood in a corner. Al walked to it, saluted the colonel, and sat.

"Tomorrow," Baker said, "I'd like you to take *Oregon Grinder* and accompany Colonel Timberlake and his Lib on a dry run over a plat of the Ploesti refineries. The Brits have laid one out for us in the desert. The front of each target is purportedly marked by a furrow of lime mixed with the engineers' urine . . . no water was available"—Baker shot Al a quick eye roll—"and I just want to make sure those markers are visible. They'll come up fast when you're skimming along the sand at over two hundred miles per hour."

"Yes, sir. Should I take my whole crew?"

"No. All you'll need is your copilot, nav, bombardier, and radio operator. That should do it. Given your low-level expertise with haystacks and radio antennas, you're a perfect choice to help out here." Baker grinned, a sardonic commentary.

Al hung his head in mock chagrin. "I'm never gonna live that down, am I?"

"Probably not. But look what an asset it's become. It's why the colonel asked for you to be his wingman tomorrow."

"Colonel Timberlake helped plan this, didn't he? I mean Tidal Wave."

"He had the lead. Best man for the job."

"I know. I enjoyed serving under him when he commanded the Circus."

Baker nodded. "Ted Timberlake's Traveling Circus. England. Africa. Return to England. Now back in Africa."

"Sir, so if Colonel Timberlake took the point in planning Tidal Wave, why isn't he leading the attack force? Why Colonel Compton?"

Baker leaned forward and lowered his voice. "Don't bring it up to Colonel Timberlake, because he's really pissed off about it. He's been pulled off the mission by higher-ups. He knows too much. He'd be a huge liability if he were to be shot down and captured. Can't risk it. So now he's terrified his men will think he's chickened out."

Al shook his head. "That would never happen. His men know him too well."

"Anyhow, better not to talk about it." Baker leaned back in his chair. "You mentioned the men. That brings up another thought. I'd like a gut reaction from you. Are the guys ready for this? It's a damned dangerous undertaking. I don't have to tell you that. But since you're a little older than most of them, Pops"—he winked at Al—"and have been around awhile, you may have a little better handle on if the crews are up to the task. What's your take on it?"

Al paused for a moment to sort through his impressions

before responding. He knew Baker wanted an honest assessment, and he wanted to get it right.

"These are tough men, sir," he said, "and I don't mean in a brutal way. I mean in a manner that makes them determined, tenacious, and fearless. They went through a lot before joining the Army. The Great Depression. Joblessness. Foreclosures. They come from hard-knock backgrounds. Farming. Fishing. Factories.

"Look at my own crew. My copilot, Lieutenant Sorenson, was a commercial fisherman in Oregon. Back-breaking and dangerous work. My tail gunner, Sergeant Cummings, picked cotton in South Carolina, some days from before sunup to after sunset. My waist gunner, Sergeant Hamilton, was a riverboat deckhand on the Mississippi. Labored in jungle-like heat day after day in the summer. My top turret gunner, Master Sergeant Gallagher, slogged through blizzards and dust storms on a South Dakota farm. Yes, sir, Colonel. You give these guys a job and they'll get it done. You bet they're ready. Apprehensive? Sure. A little scared? We all are. But we're ready to go."

Ready to go? Yes. But Al wanted to bring them home, too. In truth, he loved his crew, loved them like brothers, though his position of command prescribed he remain at arm's length from them when it came to genuine closeness. As much as he wanted to get them back to the States, he knew the realities of war often dictated other outcomes. Most of the crew were mere kids when they climbed aboard *Oregon Grinder* for the first time, but after a dozen combat missions out of England, they had matured rapidly into men. His men, men he wanted to preserve, to keep safe, and return them whole and healthy to their families and friends.

"Thank you, Captain. I appreciate your candor." Baker stood. Al followed suit.

"See you on the flight line at oh-seven-hundred," Baker said.

"Oh, and please, try not to hit any camels tomorrow. The Bedouins really don't like that."

"Yes, sir," Al responded, "no camels."

As he walked toward the exit, he noticed a group of officers, several of whom he knew casually, examining a large Michelin roadmap spread out on a table. He stopped and snuck a peek over their shoulders.

"Romania?" he said, looking at the map. "What are we gonna do? Attack by land, too?" He meant it as a joke.

A major built like a fireplug turned and addressed Al. "No, Captain. We're designing your nav charts. For this mission, your high-level aeronautical charts are useless. Since you guys are going to be scooting along just above the wheat fields, the Michelin maps are really the best thing we've got. You'll be able to navigate using highways and railroads. Some fun, huh?"

"Yeah, I've been warned not to take out any camels." Al continued toward the exit, shaking his head. *Only in the Army: sand castles, camels, and Michelin road maps.* Alice in Wonderland had materialized in Libya.

"Camels?" the major called after him.

———

Early the next morning, *Oregon Grinder,* with Colonel Timberlake's Liberator on the left, roared toward the desert target at over two hundred miles per hour, skimming just above the dunes.

"Should be on-target in fifteen seconds," George, the navigator, said over the interphone from where he crouched in what was the bombardier's usual position.

"Don't see anything but sand," Al responded. "Sorey, you see any white lines?"

"Negative."

Al swept his gaze from side to side in a frantic search for the white lines of lime that were to serve as the guides for the practice bomb runs.

Ten seconds.

The bellow of the B-24's four engines reverberated through the cockpit.

"George," Al screamed, "you got anything?"

"Negative."

Al glanced to his left, at Timberlake's Liberator. Its copilot looked back at Al, shrugged his shoulders.

Five seconds.

A white line. Target. Too late. Come and gone.

"Well, that didn't work worth a shit," Al said to Sorey. "Didn't see the damned lines until the last second." He pulled *Oregon Grinder* up and rolled it right, away from the Brits' target layout.

———

Back on the ground in Benghazi, Timberlake, Baker, and Al discussed the problem.

"Refineries are huge things, right?" Al said. "They've got tall stacks, big storage tanks, cracking towers?"

Timberlake and Baker nodded.

"So get something vertical for us to line up our bomb runs on. Put some poles in the ground, stick some rags or shirts—you know, something that flutters or waves—on top of the poles. We should be able to spot those and get set up perfectly."

"Great idea," Timberlake said. "I'll make sure that gets done this afternoon, then we'll make another recon run tomorrow morning."

"We've got a detailed sand-table model of Ploesti, too," Baker said. "We've used it to make oblique sketches of the targets so the crews will recognize them on a ground-level approach, but the drawings won't help us on the practice targets. The stuff the Brits have built have the right width and depth but not the height. Let's hope the captain's pole idea works."

The following morning, Al and Timberlake hurled their B-24s over the desert again. The rising sun, low on the horizon, cast long, slanting shadows that raced across the Sahara in tandem with the Liberators as they charged toward the dummy refinery layout.

"Fifteen seconds," George announced once more.

"Crap, crap, crap," Al muttered. No poles came into view. *Why can't I see anything?*

Then they were over the target. For the second time in two days they'd flown directly over the Ploesti mockup without being able to pick it up in advance.

Al radioed Timberlake. "What the hell happened? I thought there were supposed to be easy-to-spot poles set up for us."

"Hold on, *Oregon Grinder*. I'm checking."

The static-filled reply came a minute later. "The poles were up, topped by pennants. But some Bedouins came by in the middle of the night and swiped them. They love colorful cloth."

"Unbefuckinglievable," Al muttered to himself.

"We'll try again this afternoon. The engineers are going to nail shredded petrol tins to the tops of the poles. Maybe the Rag Heads will leave 'em alone."

Trial run number three proved successful. The Bedouins had left the strips of tin in place. When Al returned to Benghazi, he found Baker waiting for him in the simmering late afternoon heat.

"Good job, Captain. I appreciate your help. We'll begin group practice runs tomorrow with wooden bombs. A few days before the raid we'll perform two mock missions with the entire task force. On the final one, we'll use live five-hundred pounders."

"A full dress rehearsal?"

"For the big show."

A private from the operations hut darted up to Baker. "Sir, sir." He stopped and saluted. The two officers returned the salute.

"What is it, Private?" Baker asked.

"There's a problem."

"Tell me."

Al noticed half a dozen "crash trucks" and at least two ambulances jouncing toward the runway.

"There's a replacement Lib coming in with no hydraulics."

"No brakes, then," Al said.

"Yes, sir," the private responded. "I mean no, sir. No brakes."

"Well, I hope to hell it doesn't end up in the Med," Baker said. "Where's it coming from?"

"Marrakesh, I think, sir."

"Must be a replacement bird direct from the States, then," Baker said. "We weren't expecting any. Didn't think we had enough pilots available to put anyone on a ferry mission. Everybody's been assigned to combat units."

"Hope the guy's experienced enough to get the thing down and stop it before it goes in the drink," Al said.

Baker shook his head. "Don't count on it. Probably a rookie. At best maybe he can get it off the runway and stick it in the sand. Then all we'll have is a plane with a busted landing gear and bent props. At worst, as you said, it'll go for a swim. Damn.

We don't need this right now. Not when we're trying to get every single Lib we have battleworthy."

The two officers walked closer to the landing strip. The private returned to the ops hut. Heat waves arose from the runway in a scintillating vertical dance. The vehicles dispatched to assist the crippled plane and its crew after it got down had virtually disappeared in a shimmering mirage at the far end of the strip.

"Gonna be tough to land in these thermals," Al said. "That Lib's gonna be bouncing all over the place. Not what you want when you need all the runway you can grab."

A black speck materialized on the western horizon. Then the distant mechanized growl of a four-engine bomber flooded over the encampment. More men appeared along the edges of the runway to watch the landing. Or more likely, the crash landing. At least it would provide a diversion to the boring day-to-day life at the desert air base.

The speck grew larger, materializing into a B-24. It made a straight-in approach, but obviously not to land. It roared along the length of the runway just above stall speed, the pilot likely checking out the landing strip.

"They've got the gear down," Baker said.

Al knew without hydraulics the landing gear had been lowered manually. Assuming the gear had locked in place, the next challenge would be to get the Liberator down as close to the beginning of the runway as feasible. The pilot would need every inch of the landing strip he could get in hopes the plane would stop—or could be stopped—before becoming a Mediterranean submarine.

The Liberator circled out over the Med, then banked inland and set up for a landing. Al tracked the aircraft carefully, knowing the trouble it faced. The pilot made an extremely low approach, lower than Al would have ever tried, but he knew the goal was to get the Lib on the ground as near the beginning of the runway as possible.

The plane skimmed over a sand berm at the terminus of the runway. Two MPs sitting in a jeep on top of the berm dived for cover as the bomber passed over them so low it snapped off the jeep's whip antenna.

"Holy moly," Al said.

"Those guys will have a story to tell," Baker said.

The B-24 flared and appeared to be doing well until a thermal caught it, lifting it upward, away from the runway. The pilot didn't lose his cool, however. He stayed with it and hammered the craft onto the surface as the thermal's force relented. Still, he was almost halfway down the landing strip. He'd lost valuable distance.

"Not gonna make it," Baker said.

"He'll be in the water," Al added.

The massive Liberator sped down the runway at over a hundred miles per hour, a twenty-ton race car with no brakes.

"Gonna be a big splash," one of the spectators yelled.

Suddenly, an object flew out of the open waist gunner's window. Before anyone could comprehend what was happening, the object blossomed into a parachute, probably tethered to the waist gun mounts. The same thing happened on the other side of the aircraft.

With two parachutes fully open and twisting in the wind—in effect, drag chutes—the bomber decelerated with startling rapidity. The chutes collapsed onto the ground as the Liberator taxied to a stop well short of the end of the runway. The waiting vehicles swarmed around it.

"Wow," Al said. "Now there's a pilot I'd wanna fly with."

"Let's go see if we can sign him up for Tidal Wave," Baker said.

The two men walked toward the B-24. Painted in the desert

tan of the African-based Liberandos and Pyramiders, the name on the bomber's nose proclaimed *Winter's Witch*.

The crew exited through the bomb bay doors on the underside of the aircraft, the pilot last to leave. He removed his utility cap as he approached Lieutenant Colonel Baker and Captain Lycoming.

"I'll be damned," Baker said.

"Holy shit," Al exclaimed.

"Sorry, gentlemen," the pilot of *Winter's Witch* said, "I know you were expecting a guy."

Lithe but solidly built with short brown hair, a mischievous glint in her eyes, and an easy, confident smile, the pilot clearly did not fall into the male category.

7

Elliniko, Greece
Mid-July 1943

After returning from a training mission, Egon Richter lay on his bed in a tidy villa in the small town of Elliniko near Kalamaki. The villa, owned by an elderly couple, looked like most of the other homes in the village: walls of whitewashed conglomerate stone, a roof of red clay tile, and windows framed in blue with blue shutters.

The couple, George and Vasiliki Kostopoulos, cooked and laundered for Egon and three other *Luftwaffe* pilots, *Leutnants* fresh out of flight school, who billeted in the home. Each pilot had a private bedroom, but they shared a bathroom and ate together in the dining room.

George and Vasiliki went about their business quietly and without complaint, but Egon knew deep down they hated having "boarders." He made every effort to treat them in a civil and respectful manner. Occasionally, one of the younger officers might snap at them or curtly order a task to be performed, and

Egon would then remind him that while they, the Germans, were indeed the conquerors, they were also guests in someone's home. The young flyers generally accepted the rebukes with grace.

Egon found it not difficult to be compassionate, for he knew that if, God forbid, his parents ever fell under the iron fist of an occupying force, he would want them treated with respect and kindness. His number-one priority would always be, however, to make sure that never happened, to make certain his home and family never fell to an enemy.

Despite that resolve, the fear it could happen gnawed at him day in and day out. The Third Reich remained under ceaseless assault from all sides: the Russians pushing the German *Wehrmacht* back from the east, the Allies preparing to invade Italy from the south, the Brits and Americans carrying out relentless bombing of the Fatherland from the west. He sensed the German dream had begun morphing into the German nightmare.

Even if that happened, he and his fellow pilots would fight until their last breaths, shooting as many Allied bombers and fighters from the sky as they could, though at times it seemed a Sisyphean exercise. An appropriate metaphor, he thought, considering their Greek base. Sisyphus—the mythological Greek condemned for eternity to push an immense boulder up a steep hill only to have it roll back down whenever it neared the top.

Egon stared at the white ceiling of his bedroom and recalled the day he'd been recruited into the *Luftwaffe* by his longtime friend, Otto. He and Otto had been schoolmates growing up. They'd played together, hiked together, hunted together, labored in vineyards together, even discussed their adolescent love lives with one another.

At the time, their future had appeared glorious—like a

golden-hued horizon at dawn that promised a carefree day filled with successes and celebration.

On a hot September afternoon in 1938, Egon responded to a sharp rap on the front door of his home in Zell, a small town perched on the right bank of the serpentine Mosel River in west-central Germany. Egon descended the steps from the main floor of the house, an end unit of four multi-story attached homes built of field stones, to answer the knock. His six-year-old daughter, Christa, scrambled down behind him.

A smiling *Luftwaffe* major, Otto Meyer, stood at the door, the autumn sunshine backlighting him as if illuminating a mythical god. He did, in fact, look magnificent in his blue-gray officer's tunic with a silver eagle embroidered above the right breast pocket. A silver-piped peak cap, also blue-gray with a *Luftwaffe* eagle adorning the peak, rested at a jaunty angle on his head.

"Otto, *mein Gott,* how long has it been?" Egon exclaimed. They shook hands for the better part of ten seconds, a robust greeting.

"Almost three years," Otto replied, his voice a rich baritone that seemed to echo off the stone walls of the small entrance.

"What a surprise. Come, come." Egon gestured at the stairs.

Otto started toward them but halted abruptly. His gaze fell on Egon's daughter. "Oh, my. Who is this? Don't tell me it's little Christa." He clicked the heels of his knee-length black leather boots together and bowed ever so slightly. "Christa, you've become such a beautiful young lady." He extended his hand to her.

Christa took it, blushed, and, as she'd been taught, curtsied.

Egon nodded his approval. "This is my old friend, Herr"—

he corrected himself—"Major Otto Meyer. We've known each other since we were your age."

Christa laughed, the sound a melodious complement to the balmy afternoon. "My age? You were ever that young?"

Egon grinned. "Yes, but we grew up." He shook his forefinger in mock reproach at his daughter. "But don't you." He wished his daughter, the pride of his being, might forever remain unchanged: blond pigtails framing her unblemished, tanned face, white knee socks adorning her tiny legs, and a blue jumper topping a freshly ironed blouse. Best of all, she possessed a smile that could melt the winter ice on the Mosel.

"Please, Otto, come upstairs. We'll have some coffee and cake, yes?"

"Of course. That would be wonderful."

Egon closed the door. The aroma of late-blooming roses mixed with the vague, earthy smell of Mosel River mud flats pursued them into the house.

Otto removed his cap, rested it in the crook of his arm, and followed Egon and Christa up the stairs to the main floor—the living room, dining area, and kitchen. The windows of the home sat wide open, ushering the afternoon warmth into the often-chilly interior of the old stone building. Outside, a horse-drawn cart bearing a huge wooden vat, perhaps six feet in diameter and filled with freshly picked grapes, clattered along the cobblestone street.

"I almost forgot," Otto said, "it's harvest time, isn't it?" The steep hillsides of the Mosel Valley gave sustenance to acre upon acre of some of the finest vineyards in the world, mostly Riesling.

"How could you forget? We broke our backs almost every autumn in those damned vineyards helping out." He turned from Otto and called out to his wife, "Inge, come see who's here. Grab a bottle of *Zeller Schwarze Katz*. We must toast!"

Inge peered into the living room, spotted Otto, and uttered a small cry of joy. She rushed to him, threw her arms around him, and hugged him tightly. She appeared fresh and prim. Her dark brown hair, tied up in a bun, accentuated her high cheekbones. A calf-length calico dress, bright yellow, clung to her slender figure.

"*Ach, mein Gott, Otto. Mein Gott.* It's been so long. It's wonderful to have you back."

"I'm happy to be back, dear Inge. And to see how your lovely daughter has grown." He lowered his voice to a stage whisper. "I think she might end up more beautiful than you."

They all laughed while Christa looked on in apparent puzzlement.

"Sit, sit," Egon said. "We'll toast to your return. Will you be here long?"

"A few days." Otto lowered his muscular frame into an over-stuffed sofa, placed his hat on an arm of the couch, and brushed back his long, dark hair with a sweep of his hand. Egon had never thought him a handsome man, but he possessed a commanding, erudite presence that both men and women found attractive.

Inge brought the wine, a bottle with the iconic black cat of Zell prominent on the label. They lifted their glasses in saluta-tion, then conversed, catching up on their lives.

"You haven't married?" Inge asked after a while.

"No opportunity," Otto replied. "It's been a busy time."

Egon nodded. He understood the rise of the Third Reich had not been without numerous challenges. "As I recall, you volunteered for the *Wehrmacht* in . . . when was it?"

"Thirty-three."

"And now you fly airplanes?"

"Some of the best in the world. It's, well, exhilarating." He grinned, then sipped his wine. "I didn't want to go into the army with all the damned SA goons, so I volunteered for pilot training as soon as I could. Best decision I ever made."

"What do you fly?" Egon asked.

"It's called the Messerschmitt Bf 109, the fastest fighter in the world." His green eyes glistened with pride as he spoke.

"How fast?" Inge asked.

Otto shook his head. "Very fast," was all he said. Egon understood that information must be classified. Otto shifted in his chair to look more directly at Egon. "It's certainly faster than your steam locomotives, those iron dinosaurs." He issued a soft chuckle.

Egon worked for the railroad, the *Deutsche Reichsbahn-Gesellschaft*. He understood his key management position there had so far kept him from being conscripted into the *Wehrmacht* or asked to "volunteer" for the SS.

"Yes," he said, "certainly faster."

"I'd like to talk to you about that," Otto said. He turned toward Inge. "Do you think we might have some coffee and cake now, my dear?"

Inge stood and nodded, understanding Otto wished to speak to Egon alone, at least briefly. She motioned for Christa to follow her. They disappeared into the kitchen.

Otto took another sip of wine. "So good," he said. "There's nothing like *Schwarze Katz*." He placed his glass on a low table fronting the sofa and leaned forward, closer to Egon, who sat across from him in an armchair. "You know our military buildup is going to continue, yes?"

"I suppose. But to what end? The last thing we need is another war."

"There will be no war, my friend. That's exactly why we must continue to strengthen our armed forces. Look what *der Führer* has accomplished. All peacefully, I remind you. The Saarland has been returned to us—"

"Rightfully so," Egon interjected, "through plebiscite."

Otto continued. "We reclaimed the Rhineland without a shot being fired. Then with the *Anschluss* we reunited Austria with the German Reich."

"Not everyone in Austria was happy with that."

"But most were," reprimanded Otto softly.

"And now Czechoslovakia? You don't believe the Czechs will resist if we move on them?"

"With what? Horse-mounted cavalry and hunting rifles? I think not. Besides, it won't come to that. Even as we speak, Herr Hitler is meeting with Chamberlain in an effort to avoid war and allow us to protect our citizens in the Sudetenland and restore order, at least there." Otto leaned back on the sofa.

"Chamberlain?" Egon asked.

"The British prime minister, Neville Chamberlain. He and *der Führer* will work out a solution that doesn't involve bombs and bullets. We know the Brits have no stomach for conflict. All will end well, my friend."

"But when? And after Czechoslovakia, what? There seems to be saber rattling toward Poland, too. It worries me."

"All we want in Poland is access from East Prussia through the Free City of Danzig—mostly German, I remind you—to the rest of Germany. Not an unreasonable request, I think. Our country has suffered enough under the oppression of that damned Treaty of Versailles, wouldn't you agree?"

Egon swirled his glass of wine in a shaft of sunlight, examining the amber clarity of the liquid. "I do agree, Otto. I can't deny I've felt a modicum of pride in the restoration of our national integrity. But we seem to be treading a fine line between capitulations and combat."

"That's because we are strong. No one wishes to challenge the German *Wehrmacht*. Certainly not the Brits. They stood aside in Austria, they'll stand aside in Czechoslovakia. And the

French? The French are more interested in their croissants and cheese."

"What about Russia?"

"Faah." A derisive sound from Otto. "That thug Stalin has been slaughtering his senior officer corps as if they were hogs to be butchered. He's more worried about internal threats than anything else."

"America, perhaps?"

"They're perfectly comfortable in their isolationist cocoon. Oh, and do you know what their air corps consists of? Mostly biplanes, relics of the Great War."

"So you foresee no armed hostilities?"

"Not as long as we continue to strengthen our military." Otto again leaned toward Egon. "And that's why we need men like you, my friend. I know you as a gentleman of integrity, intellect, and physical skills. Ha, one of the best hunters I've ever seen. You put even me to shame."

A wasp buzzed into the room through one of the open windows. Egon tracked it with his eyes as it penetrated the interior of the house. He stood and followed it back toward the window where it flew in seemingly confused circles. On its third pass by the window, Egon's hand became a blur of motion as he swatted the insect back into the outdoors.

"There," said Otto, "reflexes like that. That's what we want in the *Luftwaffe*. Come, old friend, come and fly Messerschmitts with me. It'll be the time of your life. You'll never regret it."

Egon smiled. The thought of soaring like an eagle, roaring through the heavens in a machine capable of traveling hundreds of miles per hour, had sudden appeal to him, a great adventure in life offering vast new horizons.

Inge, trailed by Christa, re-entered the room. Inge carried an ornate silver coffee pot and porcelain cups on an oaken tray.

Christa wobbled behind, carefully balancing a large platter of cakes and pastries.

Egon and Otto stood. "Otto wishes me to join the *Luftwaffe*," Egon said, and flashed a broad smile. He couldn't help it.

"Oh, my." Inge placed the tray on the table in front of the sofa. "But wouldn't that take you away from here, away from home?"

Otto answered. "It would, but not for long. Initial officer and pilot training might keep him away for more time than you'd like, but after that, leave is generous and none of the bases are that far away."

Inge's face twisted into a topography of concern. "But . . . but what about war? Isn't there that possibility?"

"*Nein, nein,* my dear," Otto responded. "That's why we need fine men like Egon. To keep the *Wehrmacht* powerful, to make certain no one will challenge us, to make sure there is no war."

"Oh, I don't know. I just don't know." Worry continued to etch her face.

"As an officer's family," Otto continued, "you'll be well taken care of. Financially, medically, socially. When he becomes a senior officer, and that will happen swiftly, you'll be able to join him. It will be a carefree existence for you and little Christa."

"Well, it sounds wonderful," Inge said. The fear she initially expressed seemed to drift into the background.

Egon, taking her words as approval, nodded at Otto. "Yes, I'd love to join the *Luftwaffe*."

Otto flashed a broad grin in return. They performed a toast to Egon's new career, then sat. Inge poured coffee, Christa passed around the plate of goodies, and they began a pleasant hour of conversation. The aromas of strong coffee, dark chocolate, and fresh raspberries filled the room.

Christa got restless toward the end. She stood. "May I go play with Else? She has a new dolly."

Egon placed his coffee cup on the table. "No, I'm sorry, Christa. I've told you before, stay away from Else and her family. Have nothing to do with them."

"But why? She's my best friend."

"Because I said so. It's, well, an adult thing. It's just not proper."

Christa stomped her foot, whirled, and fled from the room in a flurry of tears.

"The children don't understand," Inge said.

"Sometimes I'm not sure *I* do," Egon muttered.

Otto raised his forefinger to his lips. "Shh," he said, "remember, the walls have ears."

Egon shook his head. "This isn't Berlin or Munich, Otto. There are no Party bosses around here, or leather-coated Gestapo lurking in the shadows."

"Still, it's wise to keep your thoughts to yourself. I'm not asking you to join the SS, just to become a discreet *Luftwaffe* officer. It's for your own good. Understand?"

Egon nodded.

"Well, I must be going." Otto stood. "*Vielen dank* for a most pleasant afternoon. You'll receive a letter shortly regarding the details of your in-processing to the *Luftwaffe,* Egon. Congratulations. I'll be so happy to have you as a brother officer." He turned toward Inge. "So wonderful to visit with you again, my dear. We'll do so more often in the future." Once again he clicked his heels together and bowed slightly.

"I'll look forward to it," Inge said.

"Please tell Christa *auf Wiedersehen* for me," Otto said. "Perhaps when she's older she'll understand the virtues of racial purity, of the true superiority that dwells within Aryan blood." He retrieved his cap and moved toward the stairs.

Egon, remaining silent and wondering what exactly

comprised Aryan blood, accompanied him down to the front door.

"Oh, I almost forgot," Otto said, "this Saturday Mercedes is going to be testing some of its racing automobiles on the Nurburgring. I'd love to have you and Inge accompany me to watch. Can you imagine, autos that go almost two hundred miles per hour? Would you like to go?"

"We'd love to, Otto."

"Wonderful. I'll pick you up around nine a.m."

"We'll be ready."

Otto placed his cap on his head, adjusted it, and stepped into the sunlight. He surveyed the cloudless sky, children playing tag in the street, couples strolling hand-in-hand, bicyclists bouncing over the cobblestones, and birds fluttering from window sill to window sill. He pivoted to face Egon. "A great time to be German, yes, my friend?"

"It is indeed."

Otto snapped erect, shot his right arm into the air in the Party salute. "*Heil* Hitler."

Egon hesitated, then returned the salute, but merely nodded rather than verbally acknowledge Hitler. Otto lowered his arm, turned, and walked toward a waiting staff car.

Something bothered Egon about *der Führer*. There seemed a darkness about the man, a shadow that no one could peer behind. Egon could make no sense of the fact that people he'd known for years, people he'd done business with, dined and drank with, had suddenly been labeled pariahs, untouchables. Yet he knew better than to challenge that notion, for it could bring a knock on your door at midnight and perhaps a trip to Dachau. He didn't want to go to Dachau, or any other internment facility. He wanted to fly the fastest airplanes in the world.

Besides, Otto could be right, there might be no armed conflicts. *Der Führer* had, in fact, resurrected Germany from the ashes of the Great War and once again permitted it to flex its national muscle. Indeed, Hitler had accomplished much, all while other countries stood aside as mute spectators, bowing to the growing might of the Third Reich. Germany had once again become a nation to be respected.

Egon smiled to himself. Yes, midnight knocks aside, it *was* a great time to be German.

———

But Otto had been wrong about the absence of war and paid for it with his life. He'd gone to his Valhalla two months ago over Bremen, Germany, his Messerschmitt fighter blasted from the sky by an American B-17 Flying Fortress.

Egon closed his eyes and pictured he and Otto as small boys, exploring the steep-sloped, vineyard-draped hills above Zell, and Otto yelling, "Follow me." Egon always did.

But now he didn't want to, though he knew he had no choice. His devotion to duty had already determined that.

Benghazi, Libya
Mid-July 1943

"Well, yes, ma'am," Colonel Baker stammered, staring at the pilot of *Winter's Witch,* "we *were* expecting a guy. We don't get many lady aviators here."

"None," Al added. He noticed that the dozens of men who had watched the emergency landing began to gather behind her like a wolf pack.

She reached out and shook Baker's hand, then Al's. "I'm Vivian Wright," she said, "a pilot with the Women's Auxiliary Ferrying Squadron. We're called WAFS." She brushed a sheen of sweat from her forehead.

"I've heard of them," Baker said. "Welcome to Benghazi. And thanks for the *Winter's Witch.* At the moment, we need every aircraft we can get our hands on. Oh, and that was some mighty nice flying you did there. Glad you got the *Witch* down in one piece."

"Me, too," Vivian said. "But first things first. Not to be indelicate, but I gotta pee. There's no place on a B-24 a woman can do that. You got a lady's room?"

Baker laughed. "We don't even have men's rooms, ma'am."

"Vivian," she corrected.

A small crowd had gathered to watch the conversation between Vivian and the two Army officers.

"Okay, Vivian," Baker said. "Look, all we've got for toilet facilities are empty fifty-five-gallon drums sawed in half with jury-rigged seats on them. And they're out in the open. But I'm sure Captain Lycoming here can arrange some privacy for you."

"Sir?" Al, at a loss for words, stared at his commander.

"The lady needs some privacy, Captain. Help her out."

"Yes, sir." He had no idea what to do, however. He figured he must look like a dimwit standing there with his mouth agape.

Vivian stepped forward and spoke directly to Al. "I know this isn't in your job description, Captain, but it's kind of an emergency."

Al closed his eyes. *Jesus, now I'm a lady-in-waiting.* He opened his eyes and spotted a master sergeant from his bomb group in the crowd of gawking spectators.

"Sergeant Keene," he barked, and beckoned him.

The sergeant, with a massive, goofy grin smeared over his face, trotted over to Al.

"I need some help, Sergeant. The lady here, Vivian, needs some privacy to ... uh ..."

"Take a leak," Vivian said.

"I'm Ralph," the sergeant said without waiting to be introduced.

"Vivian," she said, and extended her hand. "Look I appreciate all the courtesy here, gentleman, but the needle on my overflow gauge has pegged."

"I'm on it," Ralph said, still grinning like an idiot. "Captain, why don't you escort the lady to the 'facilities'"—he pointed

toward a row of cut-down oil drums several hundred yards away
—"and I'll scare up some blankets and poles and we'll put
together a little shelter for her." He turned and darted off.

Al and Vivian strode across the sun-baked, hard-packed
sand toward the oil drum privies.

"My nose tells me we're headed in the right direction,"
Vivian said.

"Sorry. It's kinda primitive out here."

"Don't apologize. I've been in plenty of Army camps. This is
nothing new to me."

"Long day?" Al asked, mainly because he couldn't think of
anything else to say. A lady aviator seemed totally foreign to
him. "I understand you came in from Marrakesh."

"About a ten-hour flight," she said. "The guys got a couple of
tubes in the plane where they can take a leak. Doesn't work for
me. I've learned not to drink much, especially coffee, before a
long ferry, but every once in a while I just run out of storage
space." She laughed and glanced sideways at Al. "More than
you wanted to know?"

"No. I just never thought about those problems before. I've
never encountered a WAFS aviator over here."

"That's because we aren't chartered to fly overseas."

"But—"

"But here I am, right? Let's just say that little detail was over-
looked in this particular situation. Emergency, I guess. Virtually
all of the Army Air Force pilots have combat or transport assign-
ments, but I was told they needed to get this Lib to North Africa
ASAP. And I was available."

"Wow. Where'd you pick it up?"

Al caught a glimpse of Sergeant Keene and several other
men bearing armloads of blankets and poles, and sprinting
toward the latrine.

"At the Ford Plant in Willow Run. Then from there to

Bangor, from Bangor to the Azores, from the Azores to Marrakesh, and finally on to Benghazi. As you might guess, I'm anxious to get back to the States."

"Sorry, but I'm afraid you're going to be stuck here for a while, Vivian. The complex is under quarantine. That means nobody leaves until after a big mission we've got coming up is over."

"When's that? Not that you can answer precisely."

"In a week or so."

She sighed. "Guess I'd better get used to peeing in an oil drum."

She shot Al a quick smile. With a sun-bronzed, lightly freckled complexion and her brown hair styled neatly in a page-boy cut, she possessed, if not movie actress attractiveness, certainly the good looks of a girl-next-door prom queen.

Sergeant Keene arrived. "Miss Vivian," he announced, "we'll have a privacy enclosure ready for you in no time."

He and three privates went to work, pounding stakes into the hard earth at a furious rate and draping blankets over them to form a circular shield around one of the cut-down oil drums.

Vivian began shifting her stance from one foot to the other as she waited. She also started swatting half-heartedly at the swarms of black flies buzzing around her head.

"They're on latrine patrol," Al said.

"My God, some are as big as B-24s."

"Life in Africa."

"I guess I'd better get used to it."

"Okay, ma'am," Sergeant Keene said, "your little cabana is—"

She burst through the blankets to the oil drum before Keene could finish his sentence.

The following evening Al spotted Vivian in the mess tent seated with several of the crew she'd flown with in *Winter's Witch*. She motioned him over. A sergeant vacated a chair next to her and offered it to Al. He nodded his thanks and sat, placing his tray on the table.

"So, they found you some decent quarters, I assume?" he asked Vivian.

She laughed the easy laugh that seemed to come naturally to her. "Got my own private tent."

Al watched as a steady parade of airmen made it a point to plot their mess-tent courses as close to Vivian as possible. The word "ogle" came to mind. The story of her skilled landing and innovative braking technique had spread rapidly among the troops, though a female of any sort constituted a newsworthy rarity in Benghazi.

"You seem a bit of a celebrity here, Vivian. Any concerns, you know, about your, uh, security?"

"I'm a curiosity wherever I go, Captain, but it's really different here, where there are no other women at all. I guess Colonel Baker is aware of that, though. He's got an MP passing by my tent every ten or fifteen minutes."

She took a forkful of meat and chewed it for quite a while before swallowing it. "What *is* this?" she asked, reaching for a cup of water.

"Camel, I think."

She snapped a wide-eyed glance verging on alarm at him.

"Kidding. It's probably overcooked beef. Everything here is overcooked to try to avoid dysentery. It's rampant."

She sipped her water and wrinkled her nose.

"Try to stick with beer," Al said. "The water is boiled and chlorinated."

"Dysentery prevention, I assume."

Al nodded and took a bite of his own meal. Odors of greasy

meat mixed with cigarette smoke and a smidgen of aviation fuel wafted through the uncomfortable, overheated tent. A far cry from the Glen Island Casino, he thought.

"I hope you don't mind hanging out with me," Vivian said, "since I guess I'm stuck here for a while. Here's the thing: I know you're married, I saw the ring on your finger, but that puts me at ease. Over the past few years I've learned that most of you married guys are decent and safe. Not like the younger, single ones, especially the pilots, who seem compelled to show me how manly they are, if you get my gist. I'm tired of it."

"You want me as your bodyguard?"

The easy laugh again. "Well, not so much that as just laying down a smokescreen for me. I don't need the young studs buzzing around me. You see, I love flying. I love the adventure. But I don't fly all over the country—I guess I can say 'world' now —looking for romance. That's not me. I'll find the right guy someday, but not in the middle of a war. And one-night stands aren't part of my repertoire." She paused. "So, can we be friends?"

"Friends it is," he said. "Tell me about yourself. Vivian Wright from where? And how on earth did you get into flying?"

"Vivian Wright from Beatrice, Nebraska. Yeah, I'm a farm girl."

Al could see it now, supple and muscular without appearing masculine. He could picture the latent power and strength in her hands and forearms. The kind of robustness needed for horsing a B-24 around. More than some guys had.

"I saw a crop duster flying over our place one day," Vivian continued, "and said I'm gonna do that. So I did. Started out as a wing walker with some barnstormers, then went on from there. Learned how to fly. Did some crop dusting and barnstorming of my own. Then became an air racer. I flew in the Bendix Trophy Race in '38."

"That was the one that Jacqueline Cochran won, right?"

"Yep. You know your aviation history. Burbank to Cleveland. I wasn't far behind her but got forced down near St. Louis by a thunderstorm. Anyhow, after the war started in Europe I went to England and flew with the Air Transport Auxiliary. Logged time in Lancasters, Halifaxes, and even some B-17s."

"Jesus. You've probably got more time in heavy bombers than I do."

"I don't know. Maybe. All I know is I've logged thousands of hours of flying time."

Al whistled softly.

"So when the WAFS got cranked up in the States," Vivian continued, "I came home. That was about a year ago. Now, in a few weeks, we're going to become WASPs."

"Wasps?"

"It's an acronym for Women Airforce Service Pilots. The WASPs will be a combination of the WAFS and an organization called the Women's Flying Training Detachment. By the way, you mentioned Jackie Cochran a minute ago. She's going to be directing the WASP program."

"Someday women will rule the world."

She shrugged. "Not *my* goal. But you, what about you? How did you get vectored to aviation?"

He chuckled. "On my first airplane ride ever, the thing caught fire and crashed."

"You're kidding," she exclaimed. "It caught fire? How? Where? When?"

"1933. I caught a lift in a biplane carrying a newspaper photographer over a big forest fire in northwest Oregon. I had no idea the plane's fuselage was fabric-covered. I guess the pilot got a little too close to the fire. Some blazing embers landed on the wing and that was all she wrote. Down we went."

"Obviously you survived and walked away from it."

He shook his head. "I *swam* away from it."

"Swam? This story gets better and better."

He worked on chewing his own bite of overcooked meat, then continued his tale. "Well, the pilot managed to ditch the plane in a bay on the coast. I almost drowned, but an Indian fisherman just happened to be passing by in this ancient trawler —the thing looked barely seaworthy—and dragged me, the pilot, and photographer out of the water."

"And that adventure made you want to fly? Most people probably would have run like the wind from anything to do with aviation after that."

"It took a while, but I guess the fire—which turned out to be the biggest in the state's history, by the way—and the crash made me decide I wanted to be master of my own fate. So after I went through ROTC at the University of Washington and could see what was happening in Europe and that a war was coming, I got into Army aviation. I decided being a flyer might be the best way to exert some sort of control, as illusionary as I found out it is, over my destiny. So that's my flyboy secret."

"My, my, my. Well, let me tell you mine." She took a sip of water and swirled it in her mouth.

"Your what?"

"Flyboy secret, as you called it."

Al shoveled a final forkful of food into his mouth and shoved his plate way. "Okay. I'm all ears." He liked talking with this woman.

"I've always wanted to fly in combat."

He shot her a squinty-eyed stare. "Really? Come on. You can't be—"

"I know. Strange as it seems, it's a dream I've had ever since the war started."

"You could get killed."

"I could get killed on a ferry mission."

"You don't have people shooting at you on ferry missions."

"When I was a wing walker, I climbed from one plane to another in midair. Now *that's* dangerous."

Al shook his head. "Some people might call you crazy."

"They have. But I always knew what I was doing. And so do you guys." She leaned closer to Al and lowered her voice. "So let me bounce something off you. I heard earlier today that the bomb groups are going to be flying practice missions out over the desert for the next few days. Maybe I could—"

"No," Al interjected rather sharply, "you didn't hear that, because it's classified. And, no, maybe you couldn't ride along— that's what you were going to ask, wasn't it?—even if the *rumor* you heard was true. You're non-military and don't have a security clearance. Let's remain good friends, Vivian. Don't broach the subject to me again."

"I stand chastised, Captain. I apologize." She lowered her gaze and shifted it away from Al.

"I understand your passion for aviation, Vivian. But putting you in a bomber on even a training mission would get me court-martialed."

"I won't bring it up again."

But from somewhere deep within Al, a tiny voice, like the indistinct grumble of distant thunder, reverberated through his psyche, saying, *Yeah, she will.*

9

Zell-Mosel, Germany
Mid-July 1943

Egon and Inge fell into each other's arms, a tight, desperate embrace, outside their home in Zell. Bright sunshine played hide-and-seek with towering cumulus bubbling up over the higher ground north and south of the Mosel, the *Eifel*, and the *Hunsrück*.

"My love," he whispered in Inge's ear.

"Yes, yes," she whispered in return. "How long this time?"

"A few days. I have to get back to my base before the end of the month."

"Do you have to return?"

"Of course. It's my duty."

Tears filled her eyes. "I know, but I miss you so much. And so does Christa. It's so miserable here."

He held her out at arm's length. "You've lost weight." Her skirt and blouse, the same ones he recalled from several years ago, hung on her like well-used but fashionable rags. Her face, still beautiful, appeared drawn, approaching gauntness.

She flashed a sad-eyed smile. "I give most of what I get to eat to Christa."

"You've got to take care of yourself, Inge, or you can't take care of Christa. The rationing, it isn't enough?"

"Enough to survive on, I suppose."

"How much?"

"Five pounds of bread each week. A half-pound of meat. A half-pound of lard. But it's all meaningless when there's nothing to ration. We stand in line all day merely to get bread. That's where Christa is now, at the bakery, waiting, waiting, waiting, just for a single loaf."

"Can you barter for things?"

"This is wine country, not farm country."

"Yes, it's hard to subsist on grapes."

"Last week we dug for potatoes and searched for beechnuts in the forest. We didn't get much other than filthy and tired."

Potatoes, it seemed, had become a diet staple for the German people. Beechnuts, Egon knew, could be used to make cooking oil. He realized his wife, his daughter, indeed all Germans, teetered on the brink of famine.

As if to confirm his thought, Inge said, "I can see the day coming when I'll have to tell Christa that our only meal today will be two slices of bread and an apple."

Egon expelled a long, slow breath. Frustration and anger.

"Let's go inside," he said. They climbed the stone steps to the living room. Inge sat on the sofa. Egon walked to the window and looked out. Blackout curtains flapped in a warm breeze. The town seemed quieter than it used to, not much traffic on the streets, only a handful of people on the sidewalks. But then he remembered virtually all of the young men in the area had been called to duty by the *Wehrmacht*.

He examined the homes and buildings. There seemed to be

minimal damage, only a scattering of pock marks on walls where pieces of shrapnel had hit.

"Not much bombing here?"

"What's to bomb? The vineyards?"

"It's been bad in the bigger cities. Thousand-bomber raids, carpet bombing, in Köln and Bremen. Now the enemy is going after Berlin and Hamburg."

Inge stared at him. "I hadn't heard. I thought we were winning the war."

"No."

"But—"

"You hear what the Reich wants you to hear, not what's really happening."

Tears clouded her eyes again. "Oh, Egon, how did we get here?" Her voice cracked as she choked out the question.

He sat beside her, draped his arm over her shoulders, and pulled her close. "It's not where anybody thought we were going," he said softly. "After Hitler grabbed Poland, France, Norway, the Low Countries, it all seemed so easy. We—the German people— joined in a victory parade, but it turned out to be a march of lemmings over a cliff."

She wiped the tears from her eyes and stared at her husband. "How does it all end?" she asked, her voice barely above a whisper.

He wanted to tell her if they were lucky, the country would surrender. But he knew it wouldn't. *Der Führer* would never allow it. Besides, as a *Luftwaffe* officer, he couldn't say, or even think that. He and his brothers-in-arms would fight until the end. But certainly not for the Reich, and certainly not for Hitler. They would, as *Oberstleutnant* Gustav Rödel had said, fight for each other, for their families, for their homes.

In truth, he didn't have an answer for his wife's question, at least an honest one. The war would continue. At best, the *Wehrmacht* would protect Germany's borders. At worst...

"It ends when our enemies relent," he said. But he knew they would relent only after they had brought Germany to its knees.

Christa burst into the room. "Papa!" She dropped a large loaf of brown bread she'd been carrying, her prize from the bakery, and dashed to Egon. She leaped onto the sofa beside him, threw her arms around him, and nestled into his body as if she were a baby bird sheltering in its mother's feathers.

"Oh, Christa, I've missed you so much." He hugged her with protective fierceness.

"You're home, you're home. Can you stay, *Vater*, can you stay? Until Christmas?"

He stroked her blond hair. "I can stay a few days, my dear, not longer."

"Oh." The single word came riddled with disappointment.

"I hear you've been helping your *Mutter*. In the woods. I'm so proud of you, Christa."

She smiled. "But we got so scared last week."

Egon shifted his gaze to his wife but addressed his daughter. "Scared?"

"Yes," Christa answered, "we saw a huge wild boar. It came so close to us. I wanted to run, but *Mutter* kept me still."

Egon fixed his gaze on Inge. "You didn't tell me."

"You've got enough to worry about. Besides, he didn't bother us."

"Too bad you didn't have a gun. You would have had meat for the rest of the year."

"We've enough. Well, not that much, but a little."

"How so?"

"Christa," Inge said to her daughter, "take the bread into the kitchen, please."

Christa slid off the sofa, picked up the loaf of bread she'd dropped, and carried it into the kitchen.

Inge slid close to Egon and whispered, "If she mentions that her pet rabbits keep disappearing, just tell her they probably get scared when they hear the bombs going off nearby and run away."

"Oh." *So, a slice of bread and a forkful or two of potatoes and rabbit. German wartime cuisine . . . on the best of days.*

Later, toward evening, Christa laughed and chattered in the kitchen as Inge assisted with her Saturday night bath. A large iron drum filled with water heated over the wood-burning oven served as the tub.

Her bath completed, Christa, wrapped in a thin cotton robe, darted into the living room. In mock surprise, Egon threw his forearm over his eyes. "Oh, my," he exclaimed, "it suddenly got so much brighter in here."

Christa laughed politely. An old joke. She hesitated for a moment, then said, her tone almost demure, "*Vater*, could we dance like we used to when I was little?"

"Of course, my dear." He stood from where he'd been sitting in an armchair sipping a glass of *Zeller Schwarze Katz*.

She placed her bare feet on top of his flight boots, he wrapped his left arm around her lower back, held her left hand high in his right, then waltzed her around the living room as he hummed "*An der schönen blauen Donau*." "Blue Danube."

She truly had made the room so much brighter.

Inge walked in, wiping her hands on a towel, and smiled broadly as she saw her husband and daughter dancing. She stepped to the window, closed the exterior shutters, and pulled the interior blackout curtains tightly together.

"But maybe the bombers won't come tonight," she said.

But they did.

They'd just fallen asleep when the air raid sirens sounded.

An eerie wailing punched through the otherwise quiet darkness. Egon awoke first, Inge an instant later.

"Get Christa," she said, urgency permeating her voice.

He dashed to Christa's room, shook his daughter awake. "Come," he said, "air raid."

She sat up, rubbing her eyes. He took her hand and helped her from the bed.

They met Inge at the top of the stairs to the street. "This way," Inge said. She carried light jackets for each of them. "We'll go to the Schmitts' cellar. Follow me."

They scrambled down the steps onto the sidewalk. People from other houses nearby scurried along the walkway toward a larger home two blocks away.

The thrum of large bombers overhead joined the moan of the sirens. Christa stumbled over an upraised stone in the walk and sprawled to the ground. Egon yanked her back up as several people pushed past them.

The whistle of falling bombs cut through the night.

"Hurry," Egon said. He tugged Christa along, following Inge.

They reached the entrance to the cellar as the first explosions erupted in blinding brightness, red and orange novae blossoming in a nearby intersection. Stones, chunks of concrete, and shards of metal sprayed in all directions.

A piece of shrapnel zinged by Egon's head and cratered into the side of the Schmitts' house as he and Christa, on Inge's heels, ducked into the home's cellar.

"Jesus," he yelled, "I almost got killed at home."

The ground vibrated with earthquake ferocity as explosion after explosion rocked the tiny town. In the cellar, the virtually continuous detonations made conversation impossible. Several candles flickered in the darkness, revealing dozens of oaken wine barrels, racks of empty bottles—that jingled and rattled in counterpoint to the bomb blasts—burlap sacks filled with potatoes, and stacks of empty wicker baskets, tall and conical, used for harvesting grapes. The odors of stale wine, old wood, and damp earth filled the *Keller*.

After ten or fifteen minutes, the bombing relented. Half a dozen women, mostly elderly, continued to finger their rosary beads and mutter the Pater Noster.

"Why on earth were they bombing us?" Inge asked. "There's nothing here."

"Probably after the railroad tracks by the river," Egon suggested. "It's the damn Brits and their nighttime bombing. They only missed by half a mile or so. Sometimes the bastards are five or ten miles off. Their navigation systems are shit, never designed for night operations."

Inge shushed him. "There are children in here," she whispered. "Watch your language."

They waited in the cellar for another fifteen minutes, but no more bombs fell. They ventured back into the street. Except for a building in flames near the river, smoldering craters pockmarking the street, and shattered windows here and there, damage appeared minimal.

Egon and Inge returned home, fell into bed, and slept restlessly for the remainder of the night, Christa snoozing between them.

The next few days passed uneventfully with Egon visiting old friends, taking his turn standing in line at the bakery and butcher shops, and answering questions from residents, mostly the women, about why the *Luftwaffe* wasn't doing more to stop the bombing.

"Because we're running out of fuel, aircraft, and pilots," he wanted to answer, but didn't. "Because we have a fool for a leader," he wanted to tell them, but didn't. "Because we're outnumbered," he wanted to explain, but didn't. Instead he said, "We're doing our best. Don't give up hope." He wondered if *he* had.

It came time for him to return to Greece.

"I'll take a bus to Frankfurt in the morning, then catch a flight back to Kalamaki," he told Inge.

"Why not a train?"

"Too dangerous. The Allies want to cripple our rail and river traffic."

His words proved prophetic.

That night, the air raid sirens sounded again, and he, Inge, and Christa sheltered in the Schmitts' cellar once more. But this time the bombs fell farther away. Still, the earth shook, the wine barrels rattled, and dirt and dust tumbled from the cellar's ceiling.

"They're going after the double-decker rail bridge in Bullay, I'll bet," Egon said. Bullay stood a little over two miles northwest of Zell on the twisty Mosel. Egon could have taken a train from Zell to Bullay to Koblenz, where the Mosel joined the Rhine, but he realized that option had likely just been taken out of play. At least for the time being.

"Glad I planned on the bus," he whispered to Inge.

In the candlelit semidarkness he could see tears in her eyes.

After they returned home, he and Inge slept in a silent embrace, Christa nestled into Egon's back, clutching him in an iron grip of an intensity he thought impossible for such a young child.

The next morning at the bus terminal, Christa continued to hug him with animal ferocity. "Please come back, Papa, please, please, please."

He bent and kissed her, holding her for a long time. He

didn't answer, because he knew his daughter had asked for a promise he couldn't make.

Inge blinked back tears. Egon knew she understood why he hadn't answered.

He drew her into his embrace with Christa, and had trouble letting go. How ironic, he thought, that the most intense love seemed to flourish amidst the worst violence.

But it is for that love I continue to fight.

He finally released his wife and daughter, and they him, and he stepped onto the bus. He took a seat next to a window and looked out. His small family stood with downcast countenances in a flood of summer sunshine.

As the bus pulled away, a small, drifting cloud dimmed the brightness. Egon waved, then turned away to stare straight ahead as the shadow of the cloud darkened the road.

10

Benghazi, Libya
Late July 1943

Al lined up *Oregon Grinder* for its final practice run, with wooden bombs, over the dummy target in the desert. He skimmed low over the sand. The Liberator bucked and shook and rattled in mid-day thermals as he and Sorey fought to keep the craft under control. The B-24s on either side of them, three to the left, two to the right, bobbed and jerked in the heat as they roared toward the plat, the mockup, of Target White Two, Ploesti's Concordia Vega Refinery.

Oregon Grinder sat just off the right wing of *Hell's Wench*, Lieutenant Colonel Baker's aircraft. Three more waves of Liberators followed Baker, the Circus's commander.

"I got the pole in sight," Al said into his throat mike. In the distance, looming out of the weaving heat mirages, shiny, shredded petrol tins topping the pole marked the aiming point for the target.

"Got it, too," Kenny Brightman, the bombardier, responded calmly. From his kneeling position in *Oregon Grinder's* nose, he'd use a "ten-cent" converted gunsight, not the sophisticated high-altitude Norden bombsight, to aim the faux weapons. Al knew his experience over Messina would help.

"Dune!" Sorey yelled.

A sand dune materialized in front of *Oregon Grinder*, appearing like a sudden, unexpected ocean swell. Simultaneously, Al and Sorey yanked back on their control wheels. A brief rasping sound, like the brush of rough sandpaper over metal, mingled with the bellow of the bomber's four turbocharged engines.

"How we gonna explain scratch marks on our belly?" Sorey shouted.

Al shrugged and leveled the plane out seconds from the marker pole.

"Hey, you guys, we're a bomber, not a torpedo plane," Kenny snapped from his position low in the nose. Al had never heard him perturbed before.

"Get ready to toggle," he said.

The edge of the practice target flashed beneath the Liberator.

"Bombs away," Kenny called.

Oregon Grinder sprang up, suddenly four thousand pounds lighter, as the wooden bombs plowed into the sandy target.

"Looks like we nailed it," Sorey said.

"Concur," Al responded. He spotted something in the distance. "Hey, look. Target of opportunity, ten o'clock on the horizon."

Sorey spotted it, too. "Oh, no, sir. Don't even think about it." He shot Al a wide-eyed glance. One that said, *Let's not press our luck.*

"Naw, come on. How about a low-level pass, waggle the wings in celebration?" A string of camels attended by a weary-looking Bedouin tribe plodded across the rolling dunes ahead of the bomber.

"Sir, we can't come back with camel hair stuck in the paint scratches."

Al radioed Colonel Baker. "Sir, how about a victory flyby? We got some spectators at ten o'clock."

"See 'em. Sure, but we'll do it at five hundred feet, not fifty."

Al decided his commander knew him all too well.

"Yes, sir. Lead the way."

Hell's Wench banked slightly left. The remainder of the bombers followed, three waves, falling into V formations like migrating geese. They waggled their wings as they zoomed over the startled nomads, who struggled to control their animals that suddenly had become bucking broncos. The camels leapt into the air, kicking and twisting and shedding their cargos as the Liberators powered overhead.

"Raghead friends forever," Al said.

"Looks like the Pendleton Roundup down there," Sorey said.

"Ever been?"

"No. You?"

"Nope."

"After the war then, let's make it a point, Pops. You and me. Pendleton Roundup. We'll remember our bombing runs in the desert."

"Deal."

After they landed back at Benghazi, Al strolled with Colonel Baker toward the operations hut.

"Good job today, Captain," Baker said. "Tight formation, bombs on target."

"Thank you, sir. I think we're ready."

"I hope so. We'll find out for sure Wednesday and Thursday."

"Full dress rehearsals, right?"

"Thursday with live bombs."

Baker placed his hand on Al's arm, bringing him to a halt. "Captain, there are a couple of things I need to tell you." He pinched his lips together in a fleeting frown of concern.

"Sir?"

"We haven't been able to verify it yet, but a Romanian pilot we captured a few days ago claims Ploesti is the most heavily defended target in Europe."

"That wouldn't surprise me, sir. The guys have kinda been thinking the same thing, that the intel guys are full of shit. As usual."

Baker chuckled. "Okay, we're singing from the same sheet of music then. I think it's only right to pass on to my senior pilots the same info we're getting. I'm trying to minimize any surprises, and I know there'll be plenty. The point here is, the flak over Ploesti could be a hell of a lot more intense than the official intel summaries are suggesting."

"Colonel, I'm a believer in the old adage that a plan begins to come apart the instant it's launched. I know things aren't going to go smoothly, but I think we can handle whatever's thrown at us."

Baker nodded, but a flash of concern flickered in his eyes. It caused Al to wonder if they really would be able to handle "whatever is thrown at them."

"So, the other thing is," Baker said, "I want you on my wing when we attack. En route, we'll fly in boxes of six with each box having two V formations of three. I want you in the lead box with me. Lieutenant Colonel Brown, my deputy, will be in the second box. Other than Colonel Brown, you've got as much experience as any of my guys. That's why I want you and *Oregon Grinder* up front. You jake with that?"

"Yes, sir."

"See you Wednesday."

After Wednesday's run over the practice target with the full attack force, but still with wooden bombs, all that remained was the following day's big show with live five-hundred pounders. On Thursday, under a searing North African sun, one hundred and fifty-four Liberators lifted off from the five airstrips that comprised the Benghazi complex.

Oregon Grinder circled just offshore out over the Mediterranean, waiting for the additional planes belonging to the Circus to join up. Planes from the other bomb groups—the Liberandos, the Pyramiders, the Flying Eight Balls, the Sky Scorpions—did the same.

Al had heard that more planes would likely join the force for the actual raid. But that would depend on the mechanics who had been working non-stop through the desert heat and dust to get more ships battleworthy. Particularly hard hit had been Killer Kane's Pyramiders, badly beat up from operating in the desert for over a year, first in Palestine, then Egypt, now Libya.

In a discussion with a ground crew sergeant, Al had learned that the Pratt & Whitney engines powering the Liberators had a normal lifespan of about three hundred hours between major rebuilds. In the wind-driven grit of the desert, the engines of the Pyramiders could make it through only sixty. Now the mechanics under Colonel Kane's command labored around the clock to get more of his B-24s fit for battle. Reportedly, thirty-two of them had been deemed unfit for combat just a week ago.

The planes continued orbiting while the groups formed up. After a long wait, the attack force leader, Colonel Compton, gave the signal to head for the replica refineries. In keeping with the name of the operation, a tidal wave of B-24s surged toward the targets.

Al glanced at Sorey as *Oregon Grinder* skimmed over the

desert, its shadow racing along the ground in tandem with it, as though an appendage of the thundering bomber.

"You okay, Sorey? You've been kind of quiet this morning."

"Just tired, Pops. Need a little more sleep."

"We'll have a couple of days off before the attack. We'll all be able to catch up on our Zs

then."

"Looking forward to it."

Al turned his attention to the bombardier in the aircraft's nose. "Ready to blow our sand-castle refinery to kingdom come, Kenny?"

"Roger that. Take me there."

"Ten minutes."

The Liberators spread out into attack formation, a five-mile-wide force of heavy bombers roaring over the Libyan desert barely above the tops of the dunes. The prop washes of the planes kicked up truncated rooster tails of tan sand. An impressive sight, Al thought. Would it have any damn relevance three days from now over Romania?

"Target coming up," he announced.

The bomb bay doors of the wave of attackers in front of him yawned open.

"Two minutes."

Al and Sorey held the big bomber steady, fighting the thermals bubbling up from the desert.

"One minute."

The lead wave had already reached the facsimile target, and their bombs, on delayed fuses, smashed into the sand.

Then *Oregon Grinder* thundered over the faux refinery.

"Bombs away," Kenny announced, serene as ever.

Two more waves of attackers quickly followed.

Al turned to look behind him. The desert as far as he could see to either side erupted in red and orange fireballs, explosions of billowing black smoke, and towering geysers of sand. The mock-up refineries disappeared.

"Woo hoo," he yelled into the interphone.

Various other cheers reverberated through the system.

Arriving back at Benghazi, the bomb groups celebrated by making unauthorized low-level passes of the complex, clipping the tops of palms and ripping up tents. They knew they wouldn't be disciplined.

On the ground, vigorous handshakes, lots of back slapping, and shouts of triumph replaced the miasma of doubt and apprehension that had hung over the men since learning of their mission. A sudden optimism flooded Benghazi.

Al joined in the celebratory atmosphere, although a shadow of doubt—cast by what Colonel Baker had told him about the Ploesti defenses—still hovered over him.

He spotted Sorey walking slowly.

"Hey, Lieutenant," he called, "get some sack time. Nice job today, by the way."

Sorey nodded.

Al looked more closely at his copilot. Peaked and red-eyed.

"Maybe you'd better let the docs look you over."

"I'll be fine. Just need the rest."

Al hoped. The last thing he needed would be to lose his copilot, especially with additional aircraft poised to come on-line. Competition for crew members would become intense, especially with dysentery still rampant. It seemed not beyond the realm of possibility there could be more planes than healthy airmen come Sunday.

Colonel Baker approached Al. "Good flying today, Captain."

"Thank you, sir."

"Two minutes. That's all it took us to destroy the targets. Two minutes. Can you believe that? If we can do that in Ploesti, and if we can maintain the element of surprise and stay in tight formation, I don't care how much ack-ack and how many Messerschmitts they throw at us, they won't get very damned many of us."

Al grinned; he couldn't help it. "We've got a chance, sir." *Did they?*

"One more thing," Baker said, "the Pentagon, or more specifically, General Arnold, has just ordered two more of our top officers in addition to Colonel Timberlake not to fly on the raid. General Brereton and Colonel Smart. They know too many secrets. Bad business if they were to get shot down and captured."

Al knew both men. They'd been heavily involved in planning Tidal Wave, especially Jacob Smart, the prime architect.

Baker continued. "So there'll be some crew shuffling. Among other things, General Ent will take Brereton's place in Colonel Compton's command ship, *Teggie Ann*. He'll be riding in the jump seat."

"Any changes in my crew?"

"No. Keep 'em healthy and on a short leash. Don't let some other aircraft commander Shanghai any of them. There may be a lot of that going on in the last few hours before takeoff."

"I'll lock 'em up if I have to, sir."

"Do what you have to, Captain. Just don't tell me about it." Baker gave Al a squinty-eyed once-over and departed for the ops building

Al strolled to the mess tent to grab a late lunch. He found Vivian, decked out in khaki slacks and a white blouse, sitting alone, sipping coffee that looked blacker than the inside of a cave at midnight.

He sat beside her. "I hear they use that stuff for motor oil."

She examined the coffee closely, shook her head. "No way. Too damned sludgy. It'd destroy a good engine." She flashed a quick smile. "I heard it went well today."

"It did." He wondered if she had any idea what *it* was. She probably did. With nothing to do but sit around and listen to guys chatter and brag and show off, she had to have a pretty good notion of what the attack force was going after and how they were going to do it. Which, of course, dictated her quarantine.

"Listen," she said, "I've been thinking—"

"Uh-oh," Al muttered. He had a pretty good inkling of what the thrust of her next words would be.

"Hey, hey, give me a chance. Look, I know you guys are up to something big—daring and dangerous. How about you let me ride along as a nurse?"

"A nurse? Come on, Viv, you're a pilot, not a nurse."

"I could pack some bandages and morphine. I might be able to help. Really."

He rolled his eyes.

"I'm serious," she said.

"So am I," he growled, getting a bit miffed at her apparent cavalier attitude. "I get you're bored, I would be too, sitting here in the desert day after day with nothing to do, but this is the real deal coming up, Viv, not war games. Planes are going to get shot down, men are going to die, so quit trivializing what's about to happen. Women don't go into combat. Don't you the hell get that?"

She remained quiet, merely staring at him. Then she placed her cup on the table, stood, and stalked out of the overheated mess facility without uttering another word.

Al stood, too, and went in search of a sandwich.

Less than seventy-two hours to go.

11

Benghazi, Libya
July 31, 1943

The orb of the sun, splashing the sky in an explosion of crimson and salmon, poked above the eastern horizon. In the quiet warmth of the desert dawn, Al pushed into the infirmary tent to visit Sorey, who'd been placed there the previous day.

The tent, medium-sized and tan with a large red cross emblazoned on its exterior, housed several dozen cots. It had been oriented to allow the afternoon sea breeze to waft directly through it, promising at least the *hope* of a modicum of cooling. Al found Sorey near the middle of the structure. He lay on a cot with a thin sheet covering him. A small board held his left arm steady for the continuous drip of intravenous fluid that came from a bottle suspended on a pole next to his "bed." He smiled as Al approached.

"Hey, Pops," he said, "thanks for dropping by."

"So the runny shits finally got you, huh?" Sorey's normally ruddy complexion had abandoned him and been replaced by the pale pink shade of a baby's.

"Doc says I'll be good to go, no pun intended, by the end of the day. Says it's not a serious case. Just gotta get rehydrated."

"I hope so, partner. You know we got a long trip planned for tomorrow. Could be airborne for twelve or fourteen hours."

"Wouldn't miss it for the world. I'll be in that right-hand seat even if I have to strap on a diaper."

Al wrinkled his nose. "If it comes to that, I may switch you with the tail gunner."

Sorey forced a dry chuckle, then said, "You know no one can fly that beast better than you and me."

"I know that. That's why I want you well." Al didn't add that somewhere deep within himself he continued to harbor gossamer doubts about his courage. The latent fear of flying a heavy bomber at tree-top height into a rampart of flak hid behind his facade of command. To assuage his concern he wanted a man he knew and trusted in the seat next to him.

"I'll be ready," Sorey said. "Promise."

Al patted him on the arm. "Good. I'm counting on you. You probably heard three of our top officers have been forbidden to fly the mission. And between more and more Libs getting patched up for combat and so many guys down with dysentery, we're skating on thin ice to have enough pilots."

"Hey, you know what might help," Sorey said softly.

Al leaned closer. "What?"

"Got a drag?"

"Sure." He lit a Lucky Strike for Sorey and handed it to him.

Sorey took a long pull on the cigarette and closed his eyes.

A youngish-looking corpsman rushed up. Al thought the kid probably belonged in high school, not on a combat air base. "Sirs, I'm sorry. No smoking in here."

Al pulled himself erect and faced the young man. "Corporal, looks like the lieutenant's IV bottle is about empty. Why don't you rustle up a new one for him, okay?"

The corporal's gaze darted from the bars on Al's shoulders, to the bottle, to the cigarette, and back to Al. "Yes, sir. But the cigarette . . ."

"I'll take care of it. Let's take care of the patient first."

The kid sighed and nodded and marched off.

"Put the cigarette out before he gets back," Al said to Sorey. "I'll check on you again this afternoon to see how you're doing."

"No need. I will have blown this joint by then."

———

True to his word, Sorey walked into Al's tent late that afternoon.

"See, I told you," Sorey exclaimed, spreading his arms in a ta-da display.

Al greeted him with a hearty handshake, but remained unconvinced his copilot was fit for combat. He appeared pale and lethargic.

"I know I look like something the cat dragged in," Sorey said, "but give me a good night's rest, a warm English beer, and a sloppy American burger, and I'll be ready to boogie."

Al knew that Sorey, with his fisherman's experience doing battle with the Columbia River Bar and Pacific Ocean, could claim to be as tough as they came. He figured he probably would be "ready to boogie."

Al glanced at his wristwatch. "Colonel Baker wants to meet with the guys in about ten minutes. I'll cover for you. Get your beer and burger and hit the sack. Rise and shine is at oh-two-hundred tomorrow. See you then."

"You got it, Pops."

———

Lieutenant Colonel Addison Baker, bronzed and slender, stood shirtless on a raised platform beneath the relentless Libyan sun. An easel of paper maps, flapping gently in a busy breeze, stood to his immediate right. Members of the Traveling Circus, some bare-chested like their commander, most wearing pith helmets or utility caps, gathered around him.

He reviewed the essentials of the mission for the umpteenth time. Mostly he emphasized the importance of maintaining radio silence, of staying in formation as opposed to making solo runs—much easier for massed antiaircraft artillery to bring down just one target than a bunch—and of correctly identifying the IPs.

"One, two, three," he said. "One, two, three. Pitesti, Targoviste, Floresti." Each time he spoke a name he pointed to it on the map. "We don't have to remember the names, just the features. Once we hit IP number one, it's a straight shot to two and three. Two should be easy to recognize with that ancient monastery on a hill. At number three we turn and follow the railroad tracks into Ploesti.

"Quite frankly, it should all be academic, gentlemen, since Colonel Compton and his flight of Liberandos will be leading the way. They know where to go. The only thing the rest of us have to do is hold formation and follow the leader. Once we make the final turn for our bomb run, all we gotta do—well, all *I* gotta do—is ID the target, drop our bombs, and beat feet for home. If all goes well, we'll be outta there in just a few minutes."

He paused for a moment, stepped from the platform, and stood with his men. He looked at the ground and swatted away a fly circling his head before looking up again, clearing his throat, and beginning to speak softly. The men pressed forward so that they could hear him clearly. Al sensed an earnestness in Baker's voice he hadn't heard before, caught a determination in his gaze he hadn't previously seen.

"We're going on one of the biggest jobs of the war so far, men," Baker said, his voice husky with emotion. "I'll be honest, it will get rough. But our final practice run a couple of days ago proved we can pull it off. If we hit our targets in Ploesti like we did those in the desert, we might just cut six months off this damn war. Whatever the cost, it will be worth it. I know we can do it."

A navigator in the crowd piped up. "Sir, what'll happen if you and *Hell's Wench* don't make it to the target?"

"Nothing like that will happen," Baker said firmly. He paused for effect, then raised his voice. "Gentlemen, I'm going to take you to this one even if my plane falls apart."

Al hoped the colonel's words wouldn't prove prophetic.

Another question came from the group of assembled airmen. "What do you think our chances are of staying undetected, Colonel?"

Baker furrowed his brow, shook his head. "Don't count on totally surprising the Germans, fellows. Look, once we get in the air, they'll hear us all the way to Cairo, not that they'll know for sure where we're headed. A low-altitude attack is probably our best bet at catching them off guard. They won't be expecting that."

"Then why maintain radio silence?"

"Good question," Baker said. "I'm sure the Krauts will know when we depart Benghazi, and they'll be on alert, but they won't know *exactly* where we're headed. They might guess Ploesti, but they can't rule out Italy or Austria, either. If they can't pick up our radio transmissions, they can't track us."

Baker handled a few more questions before dismissing the group. "Okay, it's chow time. Eat hearty and sleep well, though I know that'll be impossible. We'll gather for a final briefing tomorrow morning, oh-four-thirty."

Al walked with the men as they moved toward the mess tent

in relative silence, many likely lost in private thoughts or, perhaps, prayer.

After dinner, Al sat on the edge of his cot, reading letters from a stack that rested beside him. The letters had finally caught up with him after being routed, via an APO address, to RAF Hardwick in England, where the Circus had previously been stationed, then to the Benghazi complex. Most of the missives had been posted in the spring, several months ago. They came from his family, his friends, and most importantly, Sarah.

Under flickering lights powered by a stuttering electric generator, he read through them one by one in chronological order until he came to the most recent, a letter from Sarah postmarked May 29.

From outside, the frequent roar of B-24 engines being tested rode through the encampment on a muggy Mediterranean breeze. Rumor had it that as many as two dozen more Liberators, in addition to those that had flown the final dress rehearsal, might be combat-ready by tomorrow morning.

Al held the envelope containing Sarah's letter in his hand for a moment before slicing it open with his pocket knife. He hated unsealing it, since it marked the last of his available mail. He compared it with having to read the final chapter of a novel you really loved—you hated for the book to end.

He pulled the letter from the envelope, unfolded it, and read the first line. His heartbeat stumbled. He reread the line, then sprang to his feet and whooped so loudly he scared himself.

He startled the officer in the cot next to him, *Honky Tonk Gal's* bombardier, who leaped up, too. Forty-five automatic in hand, he assumed a combat stance and swept the pistol in an arc from side to side.

"What is it?" he yelled. "Bandits? Scorpion? What?"

"No, no. Nothing like that. It's okay. Relax. Look"—Al held the letter aloft—"I'm a dad!"

The bombardier lowered his gun. "Shit, you scared the hell out of me, Pops."

"Sorry." He sank back onto his cot.

"Congratulations, daddy." The bombardier extended his hand to Al. "Tell me." He nodded at the letter in Al's hand.

"A boy. Eight pounds, ten ounces, born May 26." He couldn't help grinning. He thought he probably looked like a goofy Cheshire Cat.

"You're gonna have to find some cigars."

"Yeah . . . after we get back."

"Right. After we get back."

Al noted that neither of them said *if*.

He continued to read the letter. Sarah said she hadn't mentioned her pregnancy earlier, not wishing to worry him when he likely had so many other things on his mind. But everything turned out okay. In his absence, the family decided to honor him by naming his son after him: Albert Junior.

Sarah said she calculated, counting backward, that "it" had happened the night after their visit to the Glen Island Casino. "As I recall," Sarah wrote, "things got pretty passionate that night."

"Passionate" constituted an understatement, Al thought. Descriptions such as "wild" and "urgent" came to mind. All he recalled were clothes flying off, a crash landing in bed, and an eruption of lust-filled groans and cries. At least two curtain calls followed their initial performance as their final sleepless hours together ticked toward dawn.

Al lay back on his cot and clutched the letter to his chest. Overcome by emotion, he squeezed his eyes shut and allowed tears to leak down his cheeks. A tsunami of joy, and concern, flooded over him. He couldn't help but wonder if he'd ever get to see his son, hold him in his arms, hug him, wish him happy birthday, play ball with him, see him off to college, attend his wedding, and on and on. *Goddamn this damned war. Damn the Germans. Damn the Japs.*

Al opened his eyes, rolled onto his side, and retrieved several sheets of paper and a fountain pen from a beat-up metal table adjacent to his cot. He maneuvered himself into an awkward sitting position on his thin mattress. With his knees pulled up so he could rest an old *Life* magazine on them, he used the magazine as a surface on which to rest the sheets of paper and began to write his newborn son a letter.

Dear Son Albert,

You can't imagine my surprise and joy—overwhelming joy, I might add—upon learning you had arrived in the world. I'm sorry beyond words I wasn't there to greet you. Perhaps you will understand, someday when you are older, that I was away doing something important: fighting a war against evil so you might never have to. I suppose by the time you are able to read this, the outcome of that conflict will have been determined. At this time, things seem to be going well for us, if "going well" is a phrase that can be applied to armed combat and people dying.

Son, I hope against hope that I will be able to return home and share in raising the fine young man I know you will become. If for some reason I don't make it back, know that though I may never have held you in my arms, I will love you through eternity.

Know, too, that your mother loves you as much as I. She's a beautiful, level-headed, and delightful woman who will, if I don't return, raise you with great care, wisdom, and integrity. If it comes to that, I pray that you will always respect and support her.

If I make it through the mission I'm flying tomorrow, which is perhaps one of the most dangerous ever undertaken, you will have received this letter through normal post. If I don't survive, it will have arrived from the chaplain's office in Benghazi, Libya, where I'm stationed. (I will leave this letter in the chaplain's care as soon as I complete it.)

I suppose I should say a bit about the world we live in in the mid-20th century. I'm sure you'll read about it in history books, but perhaps some insights from your father might offer you a better perspective.

We, the US and our allies—Great Britain, France, Canada, Australia, and many other smaller nations—are fighting to maintain our freedom. Freedom to choose our leaders, speak our minds, live our lives as we wish, at least within legal and moral bounds. These are liberties I hope you are able to take for granted as you grow up.

Unfortunately, the 1930s gave rise to dictators—despots and fascists —who wanted to do away with those freedoms. I'm sure you will read extensively about Germany's Adolf Hitler, Italy's Benito Mussolini, and Japan's Emperor Hirohito. Also, Russia's Joseph Stalin, though we've embraced him as an ally, is reported to have murdered and starved millions of his own people. That's not exactly the kind of leader we want as a friend.

At any rate, these dictators, whom I consider moral degenerates, rule by fear, torture, and extermination as they seek to expand their empires. We cannot let that happen. It is why I and others joined the military and pledged our lives to stop the spread of authoritarianism, to stop it

now so that you might not have to. I wonder if when you reach my age,
the world will still be beset by such concerns as fascism and despots. I
hope not. I want you, and others being born in these difficult times, to
grow up in a world free of fear and terror and war. But I must admit,
my son, based on what little I know of history, I harbor my doubts.

Al continued writing for another half hour, telling Al Junior more about his mother, life in the Army, life in the desert, and as much about tomorrow's mission as he could. Finished, he folded the letter, kissed it, and tucked it into an envelope.

Missive in hand, he trudged to the chaplain's tent through the humid darkness. He found the lights in the "office" shining brightly.

He poked his head through the tent's opening. "Hey, Chappy, still open for business?"

"Never closed. Come on in."

Al entered. Major Dawson Bills sat at a camp desk, puffing furiously on a yellowed Meerschaum pipe. A frail column of foul-smelling smoke spiraled upward from the pipe's bowl.

Al fanned his hand in front of his nose. "Holy cow, padre, whattaya got in that thing? Camel dung?"

The chaplain removed the pipe from his mouth. "Keeps evil spirits away."

"I thought you used prayer for that."

"I like to cover all the bases."

Al smiled. So did Bills. He placed his pipe on a tin ashtray, then stared up at Al with tired eyes and a hang-dog look. Slightly paunchy and crowned by a sparse wreath of unkempt brown hair, he reminded Al of an aging Friar Tuck, a character he'd seen in Errol Flynn's Robin Hood movie. The chaplain gestured at Al to sit.

"So," Bills said, "I gather you're flying the raid tomorrow."

Al nodded. "With the Circus."

"Addison Baker's group."

"Yes." He held up the envelope for Bills to see. "I've got something I'd like to leave with you, Chappy. You know . . . just in case . . ."

Bills nodded. "I know." He extended his hand for the envelope.

"It's to my son."

"Tell me about him."

Al laughed. "I don't know a thing about him."

Bills cocked his head in a questioning manner.

"I just found out about him an hour ago," Al continued. The words caught in his throat. "A letter from my wife finally reached me. She informed me I'd become a dad as of the end of May."

"That's wonderful, Captain." Bills stood and waddled to where Al sat. "Congratulations, daddy." He shook Al's hand. "May God bless you, and your wife and son."

Al looked up, his eyes slightly misty. "You think He will, padre?"

"Always."

"How many men have you seen off on missions?"

Bills returned to his chair. "Hundreds, I suppose."

"And you've prayed for their safe return?"

Bills didn't answer for a long moment. He picked up his pipe, examined it, knocked the ashes out of its bowl, and placed it back on the ashtray. Finished, he spoke in soft, measured tones.

"We both know not everyone makes it back from bombing raids. All I can do is offer up prayers that God will grant you courage and wisdom, and that you will carry out your mission as you've been trained. I can't promise my words will bring you and your crew home." He paused and let his message hang in the air.

"God doesn't care?" Al's question sounded harsher than he'd meant it.

"Oh, He cares, all right. But you've got to understand, He didn't cause this war, man did. And as men, we suffer the consequences of that."

"But we're the good guys."

"In the end, I have no doubt we'll prevail. But there's still a price to be paid, on both sides."

"I guess, Chappy, I was hoping you could put in a good word for me."

Bills sighed and leaned forward on his desk. His words came out quiet and soothing. "Of course I will, Captain. But you've got to understand something, I'm in sales, not management." He flashed a wan smile at Al.

"I accept that," Al said, though he'd hoped for a different answer.

Bills stood and walked to Al. "If you'd like, I'll pray now."

Al nodded.

They knelt together on the hard ground covered by the tent's tarp. Bills draped his arm over Al's shoulders and reminded God that Al was a good man who wanted nothing more than to see his son. He prayed that God might grant Al courage, wisdom, and clarity on his mission; that he might lead his crew to victory, though Al noted the term victory didn't necessarily include safety. The chaplain concluded his petition to the Almighty with words of thanks and an amen that Al joined in on.

They stood. Bills shuffled back to his desk where he retrieved Al's letter, then walked to a makeshift set of shelves sitting in a dark corner near the rear of the tent.

"I trust I'll be giving this back to you tomorrow," he said. He held up the envelope before placing it in one of several stacks containing what Al guessed must be several dozen other letters and packages.

Al stared. "The packages, what's in the packages, if I may be so bold?"

"Photos, high school rings, family keepsakes, medals, a few bundles of cash, even a camel whip, one airman told me."

"It looks like more than a hundred letters."

Bills nodded, a deep sadness etched in his corrugated face.

"But I don't suppose you'll be returning all of them," Al said, instantly regretting it.

"No," Bills responded softly, "I won't."

Al ducked out of the tent. "Thank you, Chappy," he called back.

"Godspeed, Captain."

A scorpion scuttled across the sand, fleeing the shaft of light that fled from the tent as Al stepped out.

12

Benghazi, Libya
July 31, 1943

After leaving the chaplain's quarters, Al strolled away from the lights and noise of the encampment into the desert a short way. A vast canopy of flickering stars draped across the sky, stretching from horizon to horizon. He knew other men had gazed up at them in the past, as he did now, perhaps on the eve of other great battles, and tried to divine their place in the infinite universe, their reason for being.

He stared at the heavens for a long while, feeling his tininess, his fleeting impermanence, and unimportance in the cosmos. But at the same time, he sensed something else: that he actually might find meaning, a purpose to his temporary existence, in the mission tomorrow. Maybe, he thought, the raid would present a chance not many men got—to plunge a dagger into the ever-beating heart of evil. It was an effort that might well be forgotten in fifty years, or a hundred, but for the here and now, he envisioned it as offering a chance to validate his being. And test his courage. *I hope Al Junior will remember.*

He trudged back to his tent where, realizing any attempt to fall asleep would be futile, he lay on his cot listening to the distant, calming wash of the Mediterranean on the barren shores of the Libyan desert. But tranquility proved elusive. The rattling bellow of twelve-hundred-horsepower engines being tested punctuated the stillness at regular intervals as maintenance crews, continuing their desperate round-the-clock sprint to resuscitate as many B-24s as possible, labored through the night. The attack, now only hours away, would require every bomber that could fly, though Al knew some might be barely airworthy.

His thoughts gradually drifted from Liberators, bombing missions, and the Mediterranean to another ocean and another time—to an era devoid of being deployed to faraway lands, free of concerns over piloting planes and dropping bombs, and absent of fears over never seeing or hugging your newborn child.

He paged back through his well-worn memory book to the first kiss he and Sarah had shared, three, maybe four years prior to their marriage. They'd been strolling along a beach on the Oregon coast when a sudden spring shower swept in off the Pacific. Sprinting just ahead of the fuzzy gray curtain that swallowed the April sun and pursued them with furious sneezes of wind, they found shelter in a shallow depression hewn into a rocky cliff. A cave-let, Sarah called it. Shivering, they embraced, Sarah forcing her tiny body unashamedly against his. The redolence of salt spray coating her hair teased his senses. Tentatively, they pressed their lips together, then let them linger. Seventeen seconds, Sarah told him later, seventeen seconds. However long it was, it became an epiphany for Al. With the assurance of youth, he knew from that point on they would be together forever in a bucolic world, one that didn't include Liberators and Messerschmitts, thousand-pound bombs and eighty-eight-millimeter antiaircraft cannons, fear, and death.

Al wondered if he would ever have the privilege of hearing about a romantic moment such as he and Sarah had experienced from his son, not that sons shared those kinds of secrets with dads. But he knew they shared others. *Dad, my gal broke up with me. Dad, I'm having a tough time in math class. Dad, coach has me sitting on the bench all the time.*

Lord, give me a chance. I'll fly that plane 'til the wings fall off. Just let me walk away from it. Allow me to hold my son in my arms, look him in his big, uncomprehending eyes, and tell him Daddy loves him. I know you know about that, Father. Amen.

The mechanical roar of yet another Pratt & Whitney bursting to life snatched him from his reverie. He snuck a peek at his watch. Just before midnight. A little over two hours before he'd stagger from his cot to begin the longest day of his life. Maybe his last day. But he didn't wish to dwell on that possibility.

Kalamaki, Greece
July 31, 1943

Egon Richter entered *Oberstleutnant* Gustav Rödel's office where the wing commander greeted him with an earnest smile and firm handshake.

"Welcome back, *Hauptmann*. I trust your visit home was, well, if not enjoyable, at least rewarding." Rödel motioned Egon to a chair. The commander plunked into his own behind his desk. The electric fan that Egon remembered from his first visit droned softly in a corner, but seemed not quite up to the task of ameliorating the heat. Beads of sweat trickled down Egon's neck, but Rödel appeared oblivious to the sultriness, perhaps because of the time he'd already spent in Africa and Greece.

"Things are not well at home," Egon said.

"Yes. I've heard that from others."

"Food shortages, bombings, fathers and sons gobbled up by the *Wehrmacht,* Gestapo lurking in the shadows like child molesters."

Rödel hung his head. "I know, I know. I wish I could tell you things were going to get better, but . . ." He allowed his sentence to trail off, but began speaking again, a touch of emotion coating his words. "Perhaps you've heard?"

"Sir?"

"About Hamburg."

A knot formed in Egon's stomach. "What about Hamburg?"

"Four days ago over seven hundred RAF bombers attacked the city. The weather had been hot and dry for most of the month, firefighting crews had been decimated by previous raids, so the town caught fire when the Brits unloaded their block-busters. I mean homes and buildings and bridges for miles around. A firestorm, *Hauptmann,* a massive whirlwind of fire devoured Hamburg. Something out of the Bible. No, goddamn it, something out of hell." His voice rose. "Asphalt melted, people were incinerated in bunkers, sucked up by the firestorm. Tens of thousands killed."

Egon, stunned, couldn't speak.

"And you know what else? I'm hearing rumors that the German people are starting to blame us, the *Luftwaffe,* for the disaster, saying we stand by and do nothing because we're afraid to take on the Allies and their heavy bombers with our fighters."

"I got questions about that when I was home," Egon responded. "But if we're failing, sir, it's not because we're afraid to fly against the enemy. It's because we don't have the manpower, we don't have the aircraft, we don't—"

"You and I know that, Egon, but the German people don't. They've been told we're winning this war, that that's what their sacrifices have been for. They don't believe the military suffers any shortages. All they know is that their homes and businesses are burning, that their families and friends are dying. Someone has to be at fault."

"Other than our leaders."

Rödel forced a smile and leaned forward over his desk, closer to Egon. "Which we would never say in public, of course."

Egon smirked and clapped his hand over his mouth.

Rödel nodded and leaned back.

Egon decided to change the topic. Discussions of bombing and burning Germans had become too uncomfortable, too soul-rending.

"It's been quiet here, I gather?" he asked.

"Yes, and that's actually worrisome. The American bombers in North Africa haven't mounted a raid into southern Europe for the last eleven days. That's damned unusual. Something's brewing."

"What's intelligence think?"

"Nothing we couldn't figure out. There's a major attack coming soon, but no one knows where."

"Ploesti?"

"As good a guess as any. But Italy and Austria can't be ruled out, either."

"I'd love a chance to shoot down some furniture vans," Egon said, using the *Luftwaffe* slang for Liberators.

"You'll get that chance, I guarantee it," Rödel said. "But let me tell you something else, if the Americans go after the refineries in Ploesti, they're in for a massive surprise."

Egon waited for Rödel to continue.

"*Oberst* Gerstenberg has something waiting for them they'd

never expect. There's a train that runs around Ploesti tugging a string of what looks like ordinary freight wagons."

"But aren't, I gather," Egon interjected.

"There are dozens of antiaircraft weapons concealed in the cars. Their sides and tops are collapsible. In an instant they can transition from an innocent-looking boxcar to an antiaircraft battery." He snapped his fingers to emphasize his point. "It's a flak train. Plus, Gerstenberg, the wily dog, has other surprises. Like guns concealed in haystacks, in groves of fruit trees, in water towers, church steeples. When the Americans come—not *if*, I know they will—they'll never know what hit them. They have no idea how heavily defended Ploesti is."

"Well, I hope we get a turn at them, too," Egon said, his words hardened with determination. He hated the notion the *Luftwaffe* seemed to be becoming a cowardly villain in the eyes of Germans.

"We'll get that opportunity, *Hauptmann,* no question. Either before the American bombers reach the target, or after—there will always be survivors to feast on."

———

Egon returned to the villa in Elliniko in time for supper. George and Vasiliki had prepared a hearty Greek meal for their "boarders." It included fresh-baked pita bread, homemade yogurt, and roasted lamb seasoned with an abundance of garlic, oregano, and black pepper, all accompanied by a bone-dry white wine called Assyrtiko. Oh how he missed the sweet *Zeller Schwarze Katz.*

He missed so many other things German, too: bratwurst, *Leberwurst,* schnitzel, *Rouladen, Spätzle,* but he knew even people back home didn't enjoy those delights any longer, not in a land where potatoes and bread had become staples.

Egon poked at his lamb and sipped his wine, trying to be polite to his hosts. His appetite had been crushed under the weight of thoughts about fire bombings and starvation. The junior officers he sat with quizzed him about his trip to Zell, but he deflected their questions with vague answers and some outright lies. They obviously hadn't heard about Hamburg, so he let that ride, too.

"Kalamaki is getting boring," one young Messerschmitt pilot griped. "We go up every day, drill holes in the sky for an hour, then return to base. Very exciting. I want some action. Combat."

"Be careful what you wish for," Egon cautioned. He knew the fresh-faced kids surrounding him, as eager as they seemed, lacked the training he'd had when he'd met his first enemy bomber. He told them the story of that encounter, the same one he'd told Rödel in their initial meeting, about how he'd fired on a four-engined British Lancaster from over a mile away and pissed in his pants at the same time.

The youngsters laughed. Egon smiled. He realized his tale carried no meaning to those who hadn't yet experienced combat.

He stood and excused himself from the table, but remained for a moment and said, "Let me promise you one thing, gentlemen. Based on what *Oberstleutnant* Rödel told me this afternoon, you'll be yanked from your boredom very soon. And after that, we can compare stories, yes?"

"Yes, sir," one of them said. The others raised their wine glasses in silent response.

Egon retreated to his room where he sat in a tattered armchair and stared at a framed photograph on the wall, probably of George's or Vasiliki's relatives from the recent past—fishermen on an island somewhere in the Aegean Sea, he guessed.

He thought about his own little family, Inge and Christa, and the maelstrom of war into which they had been so innocently thrust. His daughter, he feared, stood to pay the heaviest price. Her carefree days of being a child had disappeared, snatched away by the terrifying wail of air raid sirens and the thunder of exploding bombs. She lived in a world where constant, gnawing hunger had replaced cookies and cake. Where medical care had come to deal not with measles and mumps and scraped knees but with shrapnel wounds and missing limbs.

Instead of laughter and joy, tears and death had come to inform his daughter's life. And he bore at least some responsibility for that, though he had no idea how to repair the damage. It would be like trying to un-break a shattered wine bottle.

All he could do, when the time came, would be to face the bombers and do his duty, to try to blunt the enemy's relentless drive toward his homeland and family. That would be his gift to Inge and Christa, his truncated purpose in life.

He fell asleep in the soft chair, borne away by a soothing memory of green vineyards and puffy white clouds that so often adorned his beloved Mosel Valley in summertime.

The next morning, Egon sat alone in the cramped planning room at wing headquarters after a brief meeting with *Oberstleutnant* Rödel. Rödel had instructed him to develop a training outline for the wing's new pilots. Six rectangular tables, several dozen wooden chairs, and four walls lined with floor-to-ceiling bookcases and shelves defined the room. Aeronautical charts and flight manuals jammed the shelving. Photographs of *Luftwaffe* Iron Cross recipients and a large color portrait of *Reichsmarschall* Hermann Göring, the Reich Minister of Aviation, hung in whatever free space remained.

Unannounced, two men whom Egon had never seen around

the airbase strode into the room. He knew instantly they were Black Coats, Gestapo, though in deference to the heat, neither man wore a coat. They appeared more like shopkeepers in white shirts and ties, though each wore a shoulder holster containing a nine-millimeter pistol.

The man who appeared to be in charge—a gangly individual with thick, brushed-back dark hair and a scar slashed across his cheek—introduced himself as *Kriminalinspector* Meyer. He took a seat across from Egon. The other man, short and stout with a shaved head and countenance that seemed a cross between a pig and a bulldog, leaned against the door frame and looked bored.

"We're from the regional office in Athens," Meyer said. "Consider this a courtesy call."

Egon nodded. He knew no such thing as a "courtesy call" existed when it came to the Gestapo. They operated with unchecked authority and used intimidation and fear as their primary "motivators."

"You're new to *Jagdgeschwader 27, Hauptmann* Richter?" Meyer continued.

So they obviously know who I am. He nodded again.

"It's okay to speak, *Hauptmann*," Meyer snapped.

"Yes, sir."

"Where are you from?"

"Zell on the Mosel." *They damn well know that, too.*

The pig-bulldog-faced man near the door farted softly. Meyer glared at him, then responded to Egon. "Zell on the Mosel. Beautiful country, lovely wines." He paused. "A wonderful place to raise a family, yes?"

"It is, *Herr* Meyer."

"*Kriminalinspector* Meyer."

"Sorry, sir. I stand corrected."

"You're familiar with the Party's 'Subversion of the War Effort' law?"

The question seemed a strange non sequitur after the mention of Zell. That aside, although not a Party member, Egon had certainly heard of the law. It stated that any words or actions deemed by the Gestapo as "undermining military morale" could be punishable by death. Included were such things as speaking out against the Party or suggesting the Reich was losing the war.

"I've heard of it, yes," Egon said. *What the hell do these guys want?*

"There are rumors that certain elements of your fighter wing harbor anti-Party sentiments and promote the mistaken belief the *Wehrmacht* is in full retreat now. It's true there have been tactical retreats, but the overall offensive of the Reich remains powerful and unstoppable."

Tactical retreats? These buffoons don't realize that the Luftwaffe knows what's happening militarily, the truth? That we got our asses kicked in North Africa and lost an entire numbered army, hundreds of thousands of men, at Stalingrad?

"I can assure you, *Kriminalinspektor,* that the dedication of *Jagdgeschwader 27* to the war effort and ultimate victory remains total. I can personally vouch that the loyalty of *Oberstleutnant* Rödel to the Reich is unadulterated."

Through the only window in the room, Egon spotted a *Wehrmacht* truck carrying barrels of aviation fuel jouncing and rattling over the cobblestone street. He wondered idly if the petrol came from Ploesti.

Meyer, ignoring the vehicle, stared at Egon with steely eyes. "You've heard no one speak out against the Party, or promote misinformation on how the war is going? Even a whisper?"

Egon knew if these guys really had heard rumors of such

"subversion," there would have been arrests by now. Their visit seemed nothing more than a fishing expedition.

"I have not."

"If you did, you would let us know, of course?"

"Of course." *I'd rather shatter a wine bottle over your fucking heads.*

"Don't take this lightly, *Hauptmann.* Non-reporting of subversive speech is in and of itself subversive. Punishment for treason can extend to family and friends. I'm certain you would never wish such a fate to befall your dear Inge or Christa."

So that's why the mention of families earlier. Anger boiled and bubbled deep within Egon. He drew a long, slow breath to control his anger. Had he not, he knew he would have knocked Meyer's rotted teeth from his mouth with a single punch. He didn't bother to respond to the Gestapo officer's not-so-veiled warning.

"You heard me well, I assume?" Meyer snapped when Egon failed to speak.

Oberstleutnant Rödel burst into the room, nearly knocking the Gestapo man by the door off his feet. "We both heard you, *Kriminalinspektor.* But since we're a combat unit actively engaged in hostilities, I must ask you to wrap up your business here and allow my squadron leader to resume his work." Rödel stood with his hands on his hips, making sure Meyer didn't miss the Iron Cross that dangled prominently over his *Luftwaffe* tunic.

Meyer glared at Rödel with disdain. "I'm here on official business."

"So are we," Rödel barked. "And this happens to be my castle and my rule. You're welcome to depart knowing you've accomplished your mission. Believe me, *Herr* Meyer"—Egon assumed Rödel used the title deliberately—"we well know who the enemy is."

Meyer stood slowly, glowering at Rödel and Egon, and lifted his right arm in a Party salute. "*Heil* Hitler."

Egon stood and with Rödel returned the stiff-armed gesture. Neither said *Heil* Hitler.

The two Gestapo agents stalked from the room. "We'll be back," Meyer muttered as he left.

"Make an appointment next time," Rödel shouted after them. "We're fighting a war here."

Rödel listened for the front door of the building to slam, then said softly to Egon, "Too bad we have to fight those bastards, too."

13

Benghazi, Libya
August 1, 1943

Al, a little surprised he'd finally drifted off to sleep, found himself uncivilly awakened by jeeps racing through the encampment blowing their horns and a duty officer sticking his head into the tent and bawling, "All right, up and at 'em, you guys. Time to go to war."

He struggled to a sitting position on his cot, bent over and shook the sand from his combat boots, examined them for scorpions, then wriggled them on. The *Honky-Tonk Gal* bombardier —he never could remember his name—in the cot adjacent to his had already dressed. He stood next to where Al sat and extended his hand.

"Good luck today, Pops, or should I say Daddy? Hope to see you back here tonight."

"You will," Al responded. "Let's plan on grabbing a beer together." Whistling past the graveyard.

"You got it, sir." The guy's voice sounded firm, but apprehension tinted his gaze. They parted with a firm handshake.

Al donned a fresh shirt, smoothed his uniform, and shuffled out into the warm, clammy darkness, heading for the briefing tent. Breakfast would follow. The camp had come alive with men, vehicles, and lights. In the middle distance, illuminated by floodlights, ground crews swarmed around the Liberators, loading them with bombs.

Al stepped into the briefing tent, found his crew, and plunked down beside George.

"Mornin', Rabbi."

"Pops."

"Ready for this?"

"Are any of us?"

Al shrugged. "We are and we aren't."

He looked around and didn't spot Colonel Baker, so figured he had a few moments before the briefing started. He stood and began working his way along the row where his crew sat, shaking their hands, giving them firm pats on the back, and handing out words of encouragement. He'd never done that prior to a mission, but this raid bore gravitas and high danger unlike any they'd ever flown. These men—boys, really, all in their twenties—would always remain special to him, and he sensed they knew that when he gazed into their eyes and recognized their commitment to him and the job at hand.

They had come from all over the US, from the Northeast, the Great Plains, the Northwest, the Deep South. Kenny, the bombardier, from Atlanta, Georgia; Tech Sergeant Bryce McGregor, "Stretch," the radio operator, from Coeur d'Alene, Idaho; Master Sergeant Maurice Gallagher, "Moe," the engineer/top turret gunner, a farm kid from Yankton, South Dakota; Tech Sergeant Blaine Witkowski, "Stumpy," a powerfully-built Pole from Passaic, New Jersey; Sergeant Richard Hamilton, "Chippy," the right side waist gunner, a former riverboat deckhand from Davenport, Iowa; Staff Sergeant Billy Cummings,

"Rhett," the tail gunner, a handsome kid from Sumter, South Carolina; and Sergeant Ned Reeser, the left waist gunner, from Burkburnett, Texas. Only twenty-one, he'd earned honors as the group's "kid."

Al reached the end of the line. "Sorey. Where's Sorey?" He swept his gaze over the other assembled crews of the Traveling Circus, searching for his copilot, but didn't spot him.

He scuttled back to George. "Hey, have you seen Sorey this morning?"

"Nope. Don't worry, though. Remember, he just got sprung from the infirmary late yesterday. He's probably still snoozing, trying to gain back some strength."

"I hope so." Al beckoned Sergeant Reeser over. "Sarge, go see if you can find Lieutenant Sorenson. I think he's three or four tents over. Tell him to get his ass up and in here."

"Yes, sir." The "kid" sprinted off.

Lieutenant Colonel Baker entered the tent and the men sprang to attention. The briefing covered pretty much what had been gone over in other briefings: the importance of maintaining radio silence, of nailing the IPs, of dropping the bombs from minimum altitude.

"Each plane will carry a thirty-five-hundred-pound bomb load," Baker said, "thousand pounders and five-hundred pounders. Most of the thousand pounders will be on a one-hour delay fuse, the five-hundred pounders mostly on forty-five-second delays."

The delays, Al understood, would prevent the bomb groups from blowing up other aircraft on the raid as they attacked from almost ground level.

Baker continued his briefing. "In addition to the bombs, each aircraft is being issued boxes of incendiaries, thermite sticks. Waist gunners can toss the sticks out during the bomb runs. They'll help ignite anything combustible around the refineries. And believe me, there's a lot of stuff to combust."

Baker motioned a bespectacled, pimply-faced lieutenant front and center. "Stormy will give us the weather now."

"Gentlemen," the lieutenant said in a surprisingly firm and confident voice, "the weather looks good. The nearest front is stuck over western Europe. Weak high pressure is centered over Poland. The target area should have only scattered clouds, cumulus with bases around four thousand feet, and maybe an isolated rain shower or two. Visibility is expected to be at least seven miles.

"En route weather is forecast to be clear until you hit the Pindus Mountains along the Albanian-Yugoslavian border. Over the mountains, scattered to broken towering cu, tops around sixteen thousand feet, are likely, and there could be a stray cumulonimbus here and there. But you should be able to thread your way VFR between cloud towers. Any questions?"

"Flight level winds?" Colonel Baker asked.

"A light headwind, ten to fifteen miles per hour going. A slight tailwind to boost you on your way home."

"Turbulence?" someone in back asked.

"Minimal, but probably some light to moderate thermal bumps over the target."

To be expected, Al thought. He looked around to see if Sergeant Reeser had returned with word of Sorey. He hadn't.

The weather guesser fielded a few more questions then turned the briefing back to Colonel Baker. Baker announced takeoffs from the five airstrips would begin at oh-seven-hundred local with the bomb groups rendezvousing over Tocra, about fifty miles northeast.

"We'll depart Tocra at oh-eight-thirty," Baker said. "We expect flight time to the target to be a bit over seven hours. With a lighter load and our ability to gain altitude and catch some stronger tailwinds after the attack, we should get home a lot quicker."

Al gave an absentminded nod in response. *Just getting home period is all I want.*

Baker wrapped up the briefing with a time hack so everyone's watch would read exactly the same.

"One last thing," he said. "Not to sound overly dramatic, but the next twelve to fourteen hours will likely be the most important of your lives. I've never worked with a finer group of men, and I want you to know it's a privilege—no, an honor—to fly and fight with you. I *will* get you to the target, gentlemen, and we'll make the enemy wish he'd never heard of the United States Army Air Force and Ted's Traveling Circus. That I promise. Dismissed."

The men stood and cheered.

As they filed out of the tent, they picked up escape kits, packets containing items that could be used to facilitate survival in case of being shot down. Included in the kits: a handkerchief map of the Balkans, gold pieces—US twenty-dollar coins or British Sovereigns—Greek drachmae, Turkish lire, pressed dates, water purification tablets, biscuits, sugar cubes, some sort of odd-looking chocolate, and tiny compasses that could be hidden in various parts of the body.

Al had just retrieved his kit when Sergeant Reeser skidded to a stop in front of him.

"Sir, I found Lieutenant Sorenson!"

"Is he on his way?"

"No, sir."

"Why the hell not?"

"He's in the infirmary."

"Oh, shit, no. Not again."

"He was taken there last night. Some guys found him passed

out in his bunk. His bedding was so full of crap they had to burn it."

Al gritted his teeth in frustration. "We need to find a copilot, really fast." He pushed his way back into the briefing tent and found Colonel Baker. "Sir, I've got a problem."

Baker looked at him, frowned. "Tell me."

"Lieutenant Sorenson, my copilot, is in the infirmary. His dysentery returned last night."

Baker shook his head. "Bad timing." He glanced at his watch. "Only three hours 'til we start engines. Do you know we've managed to get two dozen additional Libs combat-ready? There's been a mad scramble to assemble crews. We've pulled guys out of the infirmary, put guys back on flying status who've completed their mission quotas, and tossed a few rookies from the Sky Scorpions into left-hand seats. Hell, Major Jerstad volunteered to be my copilot. He's flown so many more missions than his quota he stopped counting. He should be on his way back to the States. I'm afraid you may be SOL, Pops."

"How about the infirmary? You think I could Shanghai somebody from there?"

"Doubt it. It's been raided two or three times already."

"I'm desperate. I don't wanna let you or my crew down." But deep within his psyche, a conflict ripped through Al. He knew he could easily stand down from the attack—he had a legitimate excuse now—and maybe live to see his son, but at what cost? Backing off from one of the most important raids of the war, from everything he'd ever trained for, while his buddies fought and died? The debate was short. He wouldn't do that. "I'm going to try the infirmary again. I may have to drag somebody out of there tied to an IV bottle."

He darted to the infirmary, burst in, and grabbed the first flight surgeon he saw. He explained to him the dire situation, the words tumbling out of him like a waterfall emptying a flooded stream.

"I get it, Captain, I really do, but I can't help you," the Army doc responded. "The walking wounded have already been drafted. We've got three extreme cases of dysentery, including your copilot, who can't even stand. No way they could fly. Got one guy with an impacted wisdom tooth, but he's not a pilot. Got three flight neurotics, and three who just flat refuse to go into combat. I suppose you could march 'em out of here with a .45 at their head, but you wouldn't want 'em in the right-hand seat. I'm sorry."

Feeling as if he were mired in a psychological swamp, Al trudged to the mess tent. The aroma of bacon and eggs—probably real instead of powdered for a change—biscuits and gravy, and Lucky Strikes and Chesterfields permeated the crowded structure. Despite the massed aircrews, a strange quietness blanketed the dimly lit tent as each man seemed to be dealing with his thoughts and fears alone.

Al found his crew and announced they'd probably have to stand down from the mission. Strangely, no one looked happy about it. They undoubtedly bore the same burden of disappointment he did, knowing they'd be sitting on their butts in Benghazi while their fellow airmen engaged in what likely could be one of the greatest battles of the war. Soldiers don't train to sit on the sidelines.

Al sat and George slipped a mug of coffee in front of him. "It's not as bad as usual," George said. "I think they left out the motor oil. Special treat for the warriors."

"Yeah, some warriors we're turning out to be."

George squeezed onto the bench seat beside Al. "Maybe we should tell the guys to ask around and see if any of the other crews are looking for backups, especially gunners. No point in everyone missing the Big Show."

"I suppose," Al mumbled.

The mess facility began to slowly empty as crews finished off their breakfasts and departed to preflight their aircraft. Finally, only the men from *Oregon Grinder* remained.

Al sipped his now lukewarm coffee and stared at a wall of the tent without really seeing it. How had it come to this? Grounded by a tiny bug, a bacterium or amoeba or whatever in the hell it was, that caused the runny, bloody shits.

"Damnit all," he blurted, and slammed his coffee mug onto the table.

"Damn what all?" A female voice. "And why are you guys still here? I heard wheels up is in a couple of hours."

Al looked up into the face of Vivian Wright. He'd forgotten completely about her. Dressed in freshly pressed khakis, she could have been a poster girl for recruiting females into the . . . what was it? WAFS? "Grab some chow and I'll tell you."

She returned a few minutes later with her breakfast and coffee and sat across from Al and George. Others in the crew had spread out in the now virtually empty facility, sipping coffee and puffing on cigarettes. No one had expressed interest in signing on with another crew.

Al explained their plight while Vivian ate. She finished and dabbed her mouth with a napkin.

"Well?" she said.

"Well what?" Al responded.

"The solution is obvious."

"What do you mean the—" He stopped before he finished the question. "Oh, hell no, Vivian. Don't be ridiculous. I'd get court-martialed, get booted from the Army if I pulled a stunt like that. Besides, the guys would never buy into it."

"Look, I can handle a B-24 as well as any of the men here. Probably *better* than most."

"Stop it. This isn't about just flying. People are going to try to kill us today. You've never had eighty-eight-millimeter shells bursting in your face, or a Messerschmitt diving at you with its twenty mike-mike cannon blazing. Quit with the fantasy crap, okay?"

She slammed her coffee mug onto the table. "Well la-di-da, I'm not the one sitting around pissing and moaning that I can't go to war with my buddies cuz I don't have a copilot. I'm offering you a way out. I'm serious. Try looking at me like I was a pilot instead of some doll who's worried she might get her mascara messed up. I can get you into the fight, flyboy, and you damn well know it. I'm the only ticket to Ploesti you've got left."

"Get off my case, Miss Wright. You know that would be illegal as hell. Read my lips. Women don't go into combat."

"Tell that to the Russians."

"We aren't Russians."

"No, you aren't. You're an American aircrew that's going to miss, from what I've heard, one of the most daring air raids in US history, Doolittle's aside. And Doolittle's, while heroic, was really designed to be more of a 'flag waver' than a 'shorten-the-war' mission like this one."

Al looked at George, who'd been listening to the exchange with Vivian without entering into it. "So, Rabbi, what would you do?"

"Defer to my aircraft commander."

"Thanks. You're a big help."

"This is a command decision."

Al sighed. "Bigger than that, I think."

George glanced at Vivian, then back at Al. "Okay, here's what I think. If we take her as our copilot, and we get blasted from the sky, what's the diff? We're all dead and nobody gets court-martialed. If we take her and make it back home, do you really think somebody would try to court-martial us? Hell, we might even get medals."

Al shook his head. "I dunno, I dunno. It's just so against tradition. If people ever found out—"

"Look at it this way," Vivian said. "I can't officially be part of your aircrew because officially I'm not here."

"What do you mean?"

"I can't officially, legally, ferry aircraft overseas. Therefore, I'm not here. Yet here I am. Here but not here. So I couldn't really be *Oregon Grinder's* copilot. Stick me in that right-hand seat and I'd be nothing but a figment of people's imagination. There but not there." She paused. "I'm good to go if you are, Captain."

"Jesus," he muttered.

"Crews are starting their preflights," she said.

Al looked at his crew scattered around the mess tent, then at George, who nodded. Al stood. "Guys," he called out, and motioned them back to the table.

After they'd gathered, Al cleared his throat and began speaking. "I've made a decision, gentlemen. We're going on the raid. I've found a copilot." He paused. "Vivian Ann Wright." He nodded at Vivian.

A couple of the younger crew members snickered, taking it as a joke. Sergeant Gallagher, the engineer and senior NCO on *Oregon Grinder*, rolled his eyes and mumbled, "No frigging way."

"Here's the deal, guys," Al continued. "What I'm proposing is highly, well, let's say, unusual. Out of bounds. So none of you has to go on this mission if you don't want to, if you feel too uncomfortable. But if you didn't see Vivian land that B-24 a few days ago with no hydraulics, you probably heard about it. It was quite a show. She's probably logged more time at the controls of heavy bombers than most guys getting ready to fire up their engines out there right now."

The crew had fallen silent, a few exchanging glances that appeared riddled with uncertainty.

"She's been a crop duster, a wing walker, and an air racer," Al went on. "And she *volunteered* to fly on this raid. I didn't go to her on bended knee."

Vivian stood and inserted herself into Al's pitch. "Volunteered, hell. I practically kicked down the poor captain's door. Made a total pest of myself. Look, guys, I'm an experienced pilot. I've logged thousands of hours. Yeah, I've never flown in combat, but I promise you, I'll hang onto those controls like a leech and help the captain get us to the target, Germans or no."

She stopped speaking briefly and looked around the table, giving each man a stony glare. Al could tell she'd had to stand up for herself against males before.

She continued speaking. "I know some crews are not going to return from this raid. I fully understand that. But since I'll be the first woman to fly in combat—not that anybody will ever know about it—I'd kind of like to be on a gang that does get back. That's *my* incentive. I know some of you might not be comfortable flying with me, but like Captain Lycoming said, you've got a choice." She sat.

"Well, I don't know about the rest of you, but there's no way I'm flying a mission with a broad on board," Sergeant Gallagher growled. "That's just not how things are done in *this man's* Army." He thumped his fist against his chest. "It's bad luck. We'd be dead men walkin'. Sorry." He stood and strode from the mess tent.

The tail gunner, Sergeant Cummings, the kid called "Rhett," stood, too. "I don't wanna die, either. Don't need no bad luck."

"Men are gonna die today, regardless of whether they got a woman onboard," Al snapped. "Forget your damn superstitions. Let God sort it out. We'll make our own luck. And we'll do that by having the best crew possible, working together, and sticking to our training. Pardon my being crude, but it doesn't make any difference whether ya got a flopper or not. That's not what counts, it's what's in here." He pointed his thumb at his heart. "Viv's got that. I know she does."

After a brief silence, George said, "I'm with Pops."

Then Kenny, the bombardier, spoke up. "Me, too."

One by one, the enlisted men followed suit, even Sergeant Cummings. He sat back down, though his face remained etched in uncertainty.

"But now we're short our top turret gunner," Kenny reminded everyone. Sergeant Gallagher hadn't returned.

"Hey, I'll handle the top turret," Sergeant McGregor, the radio operator, piped up. "Since we're maintaining radio silence, I'm unemployed." He grinned. "I was a nose gunner on a B-17 before I joined the Circus, so I can handle a fifty-cal."

"You got it, Stretch," Al said. "Thanks." He paused for a moment. "Okay, gentlemen, here's the deal—our special crew is our little secret. If anyone asks about our copilot, it's a 'Lieutenant Benjamin Smith,' a new kid, okay?"

Scattered "yes, sirs" and nods followed.

"I'll track down Moe and tell him the same. It's okay if he's not joining our party, I gave him that option, but he's gotta keep his mouth shut about why." He turned to George. "Get Viv a utility hat, will you?" Then he faced Vivian. "Viv, tuck your hair up underneath that hat when you get it. Oh, and try not to wiggle when you walk."

Chuckles and a laugh or two followed, including one from Vivian. Exactly what Al wanted.

He stood. "Oh, I almost forgot. One final thing. I've got a really strong reason for coming home alive from this mission, guys. I found out last night I'm a father. Al Junior. Born in May, eight pounds, ten ounces." He couldn't help but break into a jack-o'-lantern grin.

Hearty handshakes, back slaps, and shouts of congratulations followed. Vivian patted him on the shoulder and said, "You're gonna be a great dad."

George grinned and said, "So now you're a Pops for real."

The tumult quieted and Al inclined his head toward the mess tent exit. "All right, gentlemen, lady, let's go to Ploesti."

14

Benghazi, Libya
August 1, 1943

Oregon Grinder's ground crew, wrapping up loading bombs, greeted Al and his crew with waves and shouts as the airmen, and one airwoman, approached the plane. The chugging purr of the aircraft's putt-putt, the auxiliary power unit used to generate electricity for the ground workers, filled the air, joining a chorus of dozens of others around the base.

The maintenance chief, a veteran master sergeant, stepped forward. "Good to see ya, Pops. We heard you guys might not make it, that Sorey was back in the infirmary."

"We got things worked out, found a replacement, a new guy, Lieutenant Smith." Al inclined his head toward Vivian.

The chief nodded a greeting to the "new guy."

Vivian nodded back, staying in the shadows, away from the brightness cast by the floodlights being used by the ground crew. With her utility cap pulled low over her forehead, almost down to her eyebrows, her femininity remained hidden.

"Whatta we got for a weapons load, Chief?" Al asked, steering the sergeant's attention to other matters.

The chief, working bare-chested in the pre-dawn warmth, wiped the sweat from his torso with a tattered, oily-looking rag. "Three general purpose five-hundred-pounders on forty-five-second delay fuses, two GP thousand-pounders on a one-hour delay, and two boxes of British incendiaries. Should do some damage."

"Let's hope." Al turned to his crew. "Okay, mount up, guys. I'll do the walk-around."

George and Kenny wriggled up through the nose-wheel well of the aircraft into their respective positions, navigator and bombardier, in the front of *Oregon Grinder*. The remainder of the crew entered through the open bomb doors. From there they scrambled onto a narrow, corrugated steel catwalk and moved to their assigned locations.

Al performed his walk-around, literally kicking the tires and making cursory checks for gasoline and hydraulic fluid leaks.

"Looks like we're good to go, Chief," he said after he finished his inspection. "Thanks to you and your men for taking care of the old girl."

"Yes, sir, Pops. Please bring her back in one piece. Same goes for you and your guys."

"Do my best."

"I know you will. Godspeed, Captain." The sergeant popped off a crisp salute.

Al returned it. He crawled into the bomb bay of *Oregon Grinder*, sidled forward on the catwalk, then up a tall step onto the flight engineer's deck, followed by a shorter step up into the cockpit. Vivian, wearing a Mae West and a parachute harness, sat in the right-hand seat with the preflight checklist already open on her lap.

Al sat in the pilot's seat. He took a good look at Vivian, trying to discern if she evidenced any kind of jitteriness that might invalidate his decision to carry her into combat as a B-24 copilot.

She looked back at him, holding him in a steady gaze. Other than appearing a bit paler than she had earlier, she exuded a professional confidence that put him at ease.

"Scared?" he asked.

"Of course. Who wouldn't be?"

"No one in his right mind . . . or *her* right mind."

She smiled. "I'll be scared 'til we get back to Benghazi."

Well, at least she thinks we'll get back.

"Okay," he said, "I'm thinking this will be a normal flight, just like a ferry mission, until we get into Romania. Not much work for us to do until then except stay in formation. The lead navigator will get us there."

"He's flying with the Liberandos?"

"Yes, that'll be the group just ahead of us. He'll be in Colonel Compton's plane, *Teggie Ann*. Compton is the raid's leader."

"Got it."

"We'll cross the Med at about four thousand feet, then climb to ten thousand over the Greek Island of Corfu. That'll be the altitude we fly over the Pindus Mountains at."

"And they're where?"

"Along the Yugoslavia-Albania border."

"Okay. I assume we drop back down after that?"

"Correct. Three to five thousand feet once we're over the mountains and into Romania . . . until we hit the IPs."

"The IPs?"

"Initial Points. The landmarks that set us up for the bomb run." Al sensed the wheels cranking in Vivian's mind as she assimilated the information he tossed at her. She seemed to be absorbing it, not asking him to repeat things. "There are three IPs," he went on, "laid out in a straight line about equidistant apart as we come in from the southwest. At the third IP we'll make a final turn, to the southeast, and execute the attack. We'll be hugging the terrain by then, so it'll be pretty hairy. And there'll be a lotta bad guys trying to knock us out of the sky."

She didn't say anything in response, just nodded. He knew the enormity of what she'd volunteered for had to be sinking in now.

"Looks like you're ready to do—"

"Hey, what's with that guy?" Vivian interrupted, pointing through the cockpit window at an aircraft parked several hundred yards away. "That's not standard preflight, is it?"

Al squinted, trying to get a clear look through the haze of the slowly brightening dawn. Across the runway, a figure strode around and around a B-24 and appeared to be throwing small objects at it.

Al laughed. "That's Lieutenant John Palm," he said. "He drew an old clunker called *Brewery Wagon* for the mission. She gets shot up almost every time she goes out. Rumored to be a bad luck plane. He's tossing stones at her. Supposed to chase away evil spirits."

"Does it work?"

"We'll know by the end of the day." He paused a beat. "Ready to run through the checklist, Viv?"

"Ready."

"Go."

She began calling off the items on the engine pre-start checklist one by one. Al responded to each.

"Flight controls."

"Free and correct."

"Flap handle."

"Neutral."

"Fuel boost pumps."

"Off."

And on and on. Snap, snap, snap. They rolled through the list in a little over a minute.

Al glanced at his wristwatch. "Okay, let's wind 'em up."

Outside, the crew chief standing near engine number three, the one nearest Vivian, gave a thumbs up. Al and Vivian ran through the start procedure and the big Pratt & Whitney coughed, clattered, and came to life in a throaty, chugging growl, belching streamers of black smoke into the breaking day. The remaining three twelve-hundred-horsepower engines roared to life one by one until all four of *Oregon Grinder's* three-bladed props spun in dizzying unison. As dozens of other Liberators followed suit, a manmade dust storm sifted over the sprawling Benghazi complex. Operation Tidal Wave had come to life.

The Circus planes lumbered onto the runway. At the four other runways scattered around the encampment, Al knew the Liberandos, Pyramiders, Eight Balls, and Sky Scorpions would be doing the same. They'd gather over Torca, fifty miles up the coast, then set off in formation, north over the Mediterranean Sea, Colonel Compton in *Teggie Ann* leading the way.

At the end of the runway, the Liberators paused, waiting for the dust to settle. Tank trucks moved among the idling bombers, topping off their gas loads.

"We'll need every inch of runway to get *Oregon Grinder* up," Al said to Vivian. "It'll be like trying to get a pregnant hippo to skip rope. We're carrying thirty-five hundred pounds of bombs plus extra fuel in special bomb bay tanks."

"I'm good at getting hippos to jump rope," Vivian responded. She flashed Al a quick grin.

At oh-seven-hundred hours a green flare fired from the field's control tower arced into the sky—the "go" signal. Lieutenant Colonel Baker's lead ship for the Traveling Circus, *Hell's Wench*, waddled into takeoff position. Baker ran up the engines and released the brakes. *Hell's Wench,* almost at a leisurely pace, rolled down the runway and lifted off into the glowing dawn. As Al had warned, the ship used virtually every inch of the runway.

"We're up next," he said.

He and Vivian maneuvered *Oregon Grinder,* shaking, rattling, clanking, into position. They waited two minutes, then revved the engines and released the brakes. An atavistic roar flooded through the interior of the bomber and it lurched forward, only gradually picking up speed. As the end of the runway hove into view and the Libyan desert appeared, Al and Vivian pulled back on their control wheels and the bomber struggled into the air.

"Good job," Al said. "We've got thirty-seven more Circus planes following."

"How many all together, all five groups?"

"I think I heard the final count was one hundred seventy-eight."

Vivian's eyes widened. She nodded her acknowledgement.

They climbed to two thousand feet. Below them, bomber after bomber lifted off from the five runways into the brightening dawn.

"Oh, shit," someone yelled over the interphone.

"What?" Al snapped, alarmed.

"Tail gun here. Bomber down."

"Where? Who?"

"Behind us. On takeoff. Looks like a Lib crashed. Lots of fire and smoke. Might have been *Kickapoo.*"

"Roger that." He knew *Kickapoo.* It had been loaned to the Circus for the day by the Pyramiders. One of the weather-whipped North African Libs from Colonel Kane's group, it may have been pushed past its useful lifespan.

He turned to Vivian. "Make that one hundred seventy-seven," he said, his voice weary with emotion. The first fatalities of the Ploesti raid had been chalked up before they'd even embarked en route for the target.

By oh-eight-hundred, the five bomb groups had mustered their forces north of Benghazi and departed for the island of Corfu five hundred miles away. They fell into their basic defensive formation of six-plane boxes, each box consisting of two three-plane Vs with the Vs stepped up toward the rear of each bomb group.

The air fleet streamed northward over the glittering Mediterranean, their shadows gliding over the water like flying fish. The armada of thundering Liberators appeared to stretch over the sea for miles.

Vivian leaned forward in her seat and surveyed the dozens of B-24s in front of and surrounding them.

"It's like the 'Ride of the Valkyries,'" she said.

Al shot her a questioning glance.

"I'm sorry," she said. "You're not an opera fan?"

He shook his head. "More Benny Goodman and Glenn Miller."

"'The Ride of the Valkyries,'" she explained, "it's a piece from one of Richard Wagner's operas. He was German. The Valkyries are mythological female figures who choose who lives and who dies in battle." She paused a beat. "I wonder if the Germans know we're coming."

Al decided he had a warrior sitting in the right-hand seat of *Oregon Grinder,* then responded to her musing. "Let's hope they don't."

Kalamaki, Greece
August 1, 1943

"Wake up, *Hauptmann.* They're coming." Egon, through

squinted eyes, peered up into the face of the young *Oberleutnant* who had awakened him.

"Who's coming?" His words came out sleep-slurred and muffled.

"The Americans. *Oberstleutnant* Rödel wishes you in his office immediately."

Twenty minutes later, his eyes still half closed and his face unshaven, Egon stood before the wing commander. Rödel motioned for him to sit.

"There's something big underway," Rödel said. "We just received a flash message from our Signal Interception Battalion near Athens saying the Americans have been transmitting to all Allied forces in the Med warning that a large mission is airborne from Libya. Apparently they don't want friendly fire shooting them down.

"That fits in well with other intel we've picked up that a large force of four-engined bombers, probably Liberators, has been taking off from the Benghazi area since sunrise."

"Ploesti?"

"Maybe, but we don't know for sure. Could be Italy. Now that the Allies have landed in Sicily, we know the mainland of Italy will be next. On the other hand, they could be after the Messerschmitt plant in Wiener Neustadt."

"In Austria?"

"That would be at the extreme reach of their range, but possible. For that matter, we can't rule out Sofia or even Athens."

"So where does that leave us, sir?" Egon had become more fully awake. He eyed a pot of percolating coffee in the corner of Rödel's office.

"For now, on standby. I want your squadron to be able to launch on half an hour's notice. Since your ten new Messer-schmitts are equipped with auxiliary belly tanks, your planes are the only ones that have the range to chase the bombers down. As soon as we get a more accurate fix on the Americans' location and direction, I'll make a definitive call."

"Any idea how large the force is?"

"Nothing precise, but it sounds like well over a hundred bombers."

"They probably aren't going for Sofia or Athens then."

"You'd make a good intel officer, *Hauptmann*."

"*Danke.*"

"But you're a hell of a lot more valuable as a fighter pilot. Get your men ready. As soon as I get additional details, I'll contact you."

"Yes, sir."

"Grab a mug of coffee on your way out." Rödel inclined his head toward the burbling percolator. "It's going to be a long day."

15

Over the Mediterranean Sea
August 1, 1943

Oregon Grinder held steady off the right wing of *Hell's Wench*,
Lieutenant Colonel Baker's aircraft. In the right-hand seat of
Hell's Wench, Major John Jerstad, the guy who'd stopped
counting the number of missions he'd flown, assisted Baker in
holding the thirty-nine bombers of the Traveling Circus on a
steady course following Colonel Compton's lead group. Occasionally, Jerstad glanced over at *Oregon Grinder* and gave Al a
quick nod of approval. So far, so good.

Al called his navigator on the interphone. "Hey, Rabbi,
where are we?"

George responded quickly, giving the coordinates of their
latitude and longitude, then added, "About three hundred miles
south of Corfu. Lookin' good."

Al watched the deep blue of the Mediterranean Sea flashing
by four thousand feet below and thought about his son. He
wondered if he'd ever be able to take Al Junior trolling for
salmon in another ocean, the gray-green Pacific, or casting for

rainbow trout in the crystalline waters of a Cascade Mountain lake, or drift fishing for steelhead in the swirling, eddying currents of a coastal river in Oregon.

His thoughts drifted back to the stacks of letters and packages that sat in the chaplain's tent in Benghazi. Some would be retrieved by the men who had left them there, others would be dispatched to the families and loved ones of those who didn't come back. He squeezed his eyes shut. *Which am I destined to be, oh Lord? Which?* He didn't expect an answer and didn't get one.

A brief burst of gunfire interrupted his reverie. The ripping thud of twin fifty-caliber machine guns sliced through the monotonous roar of *Oregon Grinder's* engines. Al jerked upright in his seat.

Vivian yelled, "Cripes." Her arms twitched as she gripped the control wheel in the copilot's position, creating a little bobble in *Oregon Grinder's* flight.

"Test firing," Al said. "Sorry, they're supposed to warn us before they do that. But better get used to the sound. You'll hear a lot of it before the day is over."

"Sorry, Pops." The call over the interphone came from Sergeant McGregor, the radioman who'd volunteered to handle the top turret guns. "Forgot to give you a heads-up. Just wanted to make sure I remembered how to shoot down bad guys."

"Kill 'em all, Stretch."

"You got it, sir."

A call from Sergeant Cummings in the tail gun position came next. "Some Libs are starting to drop out of the formation behind us."

"The Pyramiders?"

"Roger that, Pops."

"What's going on?"

"At least three have feathered a prop and turned around.

They jettisoned their bombs and a bit of fuel and headed back toward Benghazi, I guess."

Vivian shot Al a questioning look.

"The Pyramiders have the oldest planes," he said. "They've been operating in the desert for over a year and their engines have taken a real beating. You know, the sand, the dust, the heat. We'll probably see more of them hitting the road for home."

Al's words proved accurate.

Cummings called again after half an hour. "It's getting hard to see, but it looks like four more Pyramiders have wheeled out of formation."

"Why hard to see?"

"They've fallen behind us quite a ways, sir."

"How far?"

"About two or three miles."

"Jesus," Al exclaimed over the interphone. "We're supposed to maintain five-hundred-yard visual contact between groups." Three miles meant the gap had opened up to over five *thousand* yards. A stab of concern shot through him. If the Pyramiders had fallen that far off the pace, that meant the two groups following the Pyramiders, the Eight Balls and Sky Scorpions, had, too. With radio silence mandated between groups, Colonel Kane, the commander of the Pyramiders, had no way of notifying the attack leader, Colonel Compton, the mission force had become stretched out.

Al feared the split would only grow, to the point where it became dangerous. He understood the likely cause but could do nothing about it. He assumed Colonel Kane had dropped the speed of his force to accommodate the slowest of his beat-up Liberators, those that had been operating in the desert for so long. The fact that seven aircraft had already turned back indicated how bad the situation had become. By reducing power, and thus speed, Kane probably hoped to preclude any additional abdications. Meanwhile, Colonel Compton, assuming everything to be fine, would continue to press forward at normal cruise speed. The separation between the two batches of aircraft would only grow.

"Uh-oh, look," Vivian shouted. She pointed out the windscreen to her right. One prop feathered, a Circus Liberator, banked out of formation and turned tail for Benghazi.

"Looks like we're getting hit with the same affliction as the Pyramiders," Al responded.

Over the next thirty minutes, four more Circus planes abandoned the group as engine failures and maybe even fuel leaks took their toll. The attack force had dwindled. Al ran the simple math in his head—at least twelve turn-backs that he knew of, and a crash on takeoff—down thirteen bombers and they hadn't even reached Corfu. Not a good sign.

If he were superstitious, he thought, he might have to wonder about carrying a woman into combat. But he decided not to accede to what he considered an old wives' tale.

"You're doing great, Viv," he said, deciding to give her a little unsolicited approbation.

"We should be almost to Corfu," she responded.

George joined them on the interphone. "It's coming up. We should start our climb to ten thousand in a few minutes."

As if on cue, the southern tip of the Greek island, held by Germans, hove into view. Ahead of the Circus, the Liberandos began their climb. Suddenly, without warning, one of the Liberando planes went into a series of wild gyrations. First dipping nose down, then up, then back down, as if strapped to a roller coaster. Nearby aircraft scattered away from it.

"Holy crap," Al called. "Can anybody see who that is?"

Kenny responded from the bombardier's position in the nose. "Looks like *Wingo-Wango*."

"Jesus," Al said, "I think that's Lieutenant Flavelle's plane.

Remember, the guy who took us on the successful raid to Messina a few months ago?"

"Damn," Kenny responded, "he's in big trouble."

The Liberator continued to wallow out of control, up and down, until it virtually stood on its tail. Then it rolled abruptly onto its back and plunged toward the Mediterranean in a vertical dive.

"Oh, God, no," Al yelled.

"No 'chutes," Kenny said.

Wingo-Wango hit the sea violently. A towering geyser of water shot into the air. The Liberator disappeared almost instantly into an azure grave.

The episode had taken no more than thirty seconds.

A second Liberator, *Wingo-Wango's* wingman, rolled out of formation and went after the doomed B-24.

"What the hell is *he* doing?" Al said.

"Maybe he thinks there'll be survivors," Kenny answered. "Probably gonna drop some life rafts."

"Nobody survived that crash," Al snapped. "Doesn't matter anyhow. You don't ever break a combat formation. Shit!" As much as it hurt to see a pilot he knew, one he'd flown a special mission with, go down, Al knew only Tidal Wave mattered now.

He also knew *Wingo-Wango's* wannabe rescuer would never catch up with the main force of B-24s. With a full load of bombs and still heavy with fuel, it would have neither the power nor the speed to climb back into formation. Scratch two more Liberators from the attack force.

Al called the tail gun position. "Rhett, you still got the Pyramiders in sight behind us?"

"Negative, sir. Haven't seen them for the last ten minutes."

Al slammed his hand against the control wheel. "Damnit," he shouted. Still five hundred miles from the target and the mission seemed to be coming apart at the seams. Not only had fifteen aircraft aborted or crashed already, the two lead groups had outdistanced the three trailing sections by what had to be at least four or five minutes. Without radio contact, no one knew how far behind the Pyramiders, Eight Balls, and Sky Scorpions had really fallen.

Maybe, Al thought, Colonel Compton would realize the formation had become dangerously separated and slow his pace as they turned northeast from Corfu and barreled toward the coast of Albania. Maybe.

As the Liberators climbed, Al stared down at the small island, its hilly topography a faded green and patchy brown in the summer heat. His stomach constricted into a taut ball. The territory belonged to the Germans. How could they not know the Americans were headed toward Ploesti? He had to assume even the element of surprise had now been lost.

He considered voicing his concern to the crew, but decided against it. What difference would it make in the end? They would carry out the attack regardless.

Kalamaki, Greece
August 1, 1943

A *Kübelwagen* ground to a halt in front of the alert hangar. *Oberstleutnant* Rödel, clad in a short-sleeved *Luftwaffe* shirt and khaki shorts, jumped out and strode to where Egon and his pilots sat in collapsible chairs around a folding table. Odors of machine oil, aviation fuel, and stale cigarettes permeated the stifling air of the open structure. Bare-chested in the blistering midday heat, the aviators sprang to attention as their commander approached.

"As you were, gentlemen," Rödel said. He spread open a map on the table. "Spotters in Corfu report a large force of

American bombers, B-24s, passed over the island about fifteen minutes ago. That means they're well out of our range already. They're also too far east to be going after a target in Italy or Austria."

"So Ploesti is certainly in play then," Egon said, more of a declaration than a question.

"*Absolut*. Especially since reports had them turning northeast, toward Albania and Yugoslavia, after they reached the northern end of the island. If you extrapolate that course, it carries them into Bulgaria or Romania."

"So it could still be Sofia, or maybe even Bucharest."

Rödel shrugged. "Maybe. But as you pointed out earlier, probably not with such a large force."

"Did we get a better fix on the numbers?"

"Spotters estimate one hundred sixty-five Liberators in all. But here's the strange thing. They passed over Corfu in two separate sections. About sixty in the first bunch. A little over one hundred in the second group five minutes later."

"Two different targets then?"

Rödel pinched his lips together, brushed a sheen of sweat from his brow. "Could be. Intel hasn't figured it out yet. It's puzzling. At any rate, Ploesti is on high alert now. They'll be ready for an attack if that's the destination."

"No escorts?"

"No US fighters can match the range of the Liberators. They're on their own."

"So what do we do?"

"Wait."

A few of the men groaned in protest. They wanted to fight.

"Whatever the target—Ploesti, Bucharest, Sofia—it makes no difference to us. The Americans have to come back the same way they went in. I'd guess that would be in about five or six hours. But we'll be better able to pinpoint their egress time after the attack is underway. Once we've got that, we'll be lying in wait."

Egon nodded. "No one escapes," he said to his pilots. Smiles and nods came in response.

"If the target is Ploesti," Rödel continued, "the B-24s, many of those that survive—and there won't be a lot—will be badly wounded when they return. Shot up, engines out, low on ammo, tired and injured crews, probably not in defensive formations. I want *Gruppe IV* to finish them off. Not a single Liberator gets back to Benghazi. *Verstehst du?*" His final words came out as a firm command.

A loud chorus of "Yes, sirs" followed.

16

Over Albania
August 1, 1943

Colonel Compton led the Liberando and Circus Liberators inland over Albania. Ahead of them loomed the Pindus Mountains along Albania's border with Yugoslavia. As the bombers approached the mountains, Al spotted the first of the towering cumulus, bubbling white stacks of clouds reaching skyward, clouds that the weather guesser warned would be there.

"Pindus Range?" Vivian asked.

"Yes, but it's not one long, continuous structure. It's a bunch of shorter ranges."

"Ten thousand will clear everything?" As she spoke, she swiveled her head, checking the formation of bombers. She made only minor movements with the control wheel and seemed able to hold *Oregon Grinder* in position with minimal effort.

"It's certainly nothing like the Rockies," Al said. "The tallest peaks are maybe eight or nine thousand feet, so ten or eleven thousand will keep us out of danger. We'll maintain a loose formation, so we'll be able to steer around the biggest clouds without running into each other."

"Got it."

"Okay. Take the controls for a while. I'm gonna go back and check on the gunners. Keep *Hell's Wench* on your left wing and we'll be fine."

"Roger that. I got the controls."

Al clambered out of his seat, removed his headset, and slipped on his leather flight jacket. The temperature in *Oregon Grinder* had dropped from the upper sixties to low forties since they had climbed away from the warm Mediterranean. *At least it's forty above, not forty below*, he reminded himself. Some of the missions he'd flown out of England to the continent at high altitude had been in that frigid forty below range. In that kind of iciness, not even the crews' electrically heated "bunny suits" could ward off the bone chilling frigidness.

Immediately behind the cockpit, he stopped to talk with Sergeant McGregor, usually the radio operator. He now occupied the flight engineer/top turret gunner's spot, the position he'd volunteered to take over after Master Sergeant Gallagher had elected not to fly the mission. While Al had offered all the men that option, only Gallagher had chosen it. It would not reflect negatively on Gallagher's record since he'd been given the choice by his commanding officer, but Al knew if his crew survived, Gallagher would be forever ostracized by them.

Al engaged in a shouted conversation with McGregor since the bellow of the bomber's engines prevented talk at normal levels. He thanked the sergeant profusely for stepping forward to fill Gallagher's vacancy, then pointed at some gauges on a panel in the position he now occupied.

"Keep an eye on these," he yelled. "Normally the flight engineer monitors them." He leaned closer to them to get a good look at the positions of the needles on the dials. "They all look fine now. If you see any big movements in the needles, give me a holler on the interphone and I'll come take a look."

"Got it, sir."

Al slapped him on the back. "Thanks again, Stretch."

He stepped down onto the catwalk that traversed the bomb bay. He couldn't go forward—too narrow a passage—to the nose of *Oregon Grinder* where the navigator and bombardier resided in cramped quarters. Instead, he edged along the catwalk, turning his body sideways and rubbing shoulders with bombs that carried almost two tons of destruction destined for Ploesti.

Behind the bomb racks, a myriad of cables, pipes, and wires —the arteries and veins of the aircraft—clung to the sides of the bomber. Just above the racks the wings met and were bolted together. The inboard section of each wing bore the fuel cells that fed the engines mounted on that respective wing.

The fact the fuel cells and bombs sat in such close proximity near the center of the plane made it the most vulnerable spot of a B-24. *Luftwaffe* fighter pilots knew this, of course, and preferred to attack Liberators from above, aiming their nose cannons and machine guns at the top-center of the bomber. A direct hit could shear off a wing and send the plane into a fire-wrapped death-dive.

Al grasped the craft's steel beams and cross members for support as he continued to wriggle his way aft along the catwalk. Even cruelly overloaded, *Oregon Grinder* jiggled and bounced in the updrafts generated by the midday sunshine and increasingly rugged topography below. Faint odors of fuel and hydraulic fluid floated through the air.

At the end of the catwalk, he clambered up two steps to the waist gunners' positions, each marked by a large open window and a manually operated fifty-caliber machine gun, one on the right side of the Liberator, the other on the left. A biting wind whipped through the windows into the interior of the plane.

Sergeants Richard Hamilton, "Chippy," and Ned Reeser arose from the ammo boxes on which they'd been sitting and greeted him with big smiles. Tech Sergeant Blaine Witkowski, "Stumpy," the bottom turret gunner, stood up from where he'd been sitting next to the ball turret well, waiting for the action to begin before squeezing into the turret and being lowered into position on the underbelly of the bomber.

They carried on a brief but loud conversation. Before Al departed, he reminded Chippy and Ned to try to avoid blowing off *Oregon's Grinder's* tail section when the shooting began. The waist gunners' firing breadth covered a huge swath, and with Liberators' twin vertical stabilizers extending out on either side of the tail, they often ended up taking hits from "friendly" fire—their own waist gunners.

Al's admonition drew a good laugh. He continued his trip toward the bomber's rear, dropping into a crouch as he neared the tail gunner's place of business. The plane's motions became magnified in the tail, and the fuselage oscillated constantly from side to side, up and down.

"Hey, Rhett," Al yelled, "any sign of the Pyramiders?"

Staff Sergeant Cummings twisted in his tight quarters to look behind him. "Oh, Pops, good to see you. No, negative. Haven't seen hide nor hair of them since before Corfu."

Al shook his head in disappointment. He hadn't imagined the force becoming separated, and doubted the planners had either.

He and Cummings carried out a brief exchange of small talk, then Al clapped him on the shoulder and returned to the cockpit.

Vivian had done a yeoman job keeping *Oregon Grinder* tucked in near *Hell's Wench*.

"Looks like you're a pro at flying in formation," he said after seating himself.

"First time." She flashed a confident grin. "At least I didn't ram him." She inclined her head toward *Hell's Wench*.

Al fell silent, thinking about the jeopardy the split in the bomber flights had put the raid in. He listened to the throaty roar of *Oregon Grinder's* engines, the sound as reassuring and familiar as that of a finely tuned barbershop quartet. He scanned the RPM and manifold pressure gauges. Everything looked good. He pointed at the gauges in front of the copilot's position—the cylinder head temperatures, and the oil and fuel pressures and temperatures.

Vivian nodded, moved her gaze over them, and gave a thumbs-up.

At least *Oregon Grinder* would be in top form as she went into battle.

After several moments, Vivian leaned close to Al and raised her voice to overcome the engine noise. "What's up? You seem preoccupied."

He considered not relaying his fears to her, but decided against it. As his copilot on a combat mission, she had every right to know and understand the situation. "The guys behind us, the Pyramiders, the Eight Balls, the Sky Scorpions, have dropped way off the pace. Our tail gunner hasn't seen them since before Corfu. The attack was designed for all the bomb groups to hit their targets almost simultaneously. If we don't, the element of surprise is lost."

"Why doesn't the lead group slow down, let the others catch up?"

"I don't know if Colonel Compton is even aware that more than half his force has fallen behind. Without radio contact, he can't check on them, and they can't inform him. It's messed up."

"So what happens?"

"Nothing good. Look, I'm sorry I got you into this. It's going to get rough." He thought of the violence that loomed in their immediate future, like a summer storm lurking unseen just beyond the horizon.

Vivian looked directly at him, a latent fierceness in her eyes. "I didn't think combat was going to be anything like wing walking. So tell me what to expect. Specifically. No mollycoddling."

They worked together to bank the plane in concert with *Hell's Wench* around a stack of bubbly clouds that appeared to be spitting out rain from their bases. Ahead of them, the Liberandos had done the same. Now they began to climb again, gaining a bit more altitude in preparation for topping a wall of clouds that sat atop a rocky ridge in the middle distance.

The maneuver completed, Al responded to Vivian's request. "We'll attack regardless of whether the groups are together. We'll go in first, us and the Liberandos, but we'll have a much smaller force than planned. So the antiaircraft crews and fighters defending Ploesti will be able to concentrate their fire on just us, not the entire force. That means, quite frankly, our odds of getting nailed go way up."

Vivian swallowed hard and nodded.

"Our only hope is that we've still got the element of surprise with us, that the Germans don't know we're coming. Maybe by staying low, beneath their radar beams, and maintaining radio silence we've been able to go undetected. But between you and me, Viv, I doubt it."

She nodded again but didn't say anything. Perhaps she'd heard more than she wanted.

He drew a deep breath and went on. "But it won't be us that gets the worst of it. Assuming we do surprise the Krauts, the second part of our force won't. They're likely to get cut to pieces because every bit of firepower the enemy has will be primed for them. It could turn into a turkey shoot for the Germans." He felt a wave of nausea slide through his gut as he spoke the words. He went back to the business of flying *Oregon Grinder*.

A short time later, George called over the interphone. "We're entering extreme northern Bulgaria now, Pops."

"Thanks, Rabbi. Okay, everyone, heads-up. The Bulgarians have some old Czech fighters and a handful of Messerschmitts, so they might get curious. But I doubt they'll challenge us unless they think we're going for Sofia."

Below, the terrain began to drop away and Colonel Compton led the Liberators in a snaking descent down the eastern slopes of the mountains toward the Danube River, the boundary of Romania.

"Why are we doing the serpentine?" Vivian asked.

Al had wondered, too, but thought he knew.

"Maybe Colonel Compton's realized he's lost his trailing groups. By zig-zagging a bit, I think he's trying to slow our advance, give Killer Kane and the others a chance to catch up, but it burns more fuel, so he's not gonna do it for long."

"You think it'll help?"

"Doubt it. I think the rest of the force is just too far behind. We haven't seen them for a couple of hours now." He considered calling his tail gunner again and asking if he'd spotted the Pyramiders. But he knew if Rhett had, he would have broadcast the news immediately.

"Could we orbit someplace and wait for them?" Vivian asked, obviously trying to discover a solution for what had become a dagger in the heart of the attack plan.

"No. We're about to enter enemy territory, and if we went into a holding pattern now, that would increase our exposure way too much, not to mention waste fuel we'll need to get outta here. And again, we have no idea how far the other groups are behind. We gotta keep moving."

In short order, they reached the Danube and swept into Romania. As planned, they dropped back down to near three thousand feet as they streaked across the river. They continued to barrel northeastward at almost two hundred miles per hour. The Transylvanian Alps loomed to the distant north.

Kalamaki, Greece
August 1, 1943

"Phone, sir. It's *Oberstleutnant* Rödel." In a corner of the sweltering alert hangar, a skinny sergeant who didn't look much older than Egon's daughter held a receiver aloft for Egon to see. He trotted to where the sergeant stood.

"Yes, sir, *Hauptmann* Richter here."

"Just wanted to keep you updated. We received a report from one of our long-range radar units on a mountain near Sofia. They're tracking 'many wings' heading northeastward over northern Bulgaria. That has to be the American bomber force. Almost certainly they're bound for Ploesti, but we don't have a visual on them yet. As soon as we confirm the target, I'll let you know and we'll go on hot standby. We'll have a nice homecoming present waiting for the Americans."

"Yes, sir. We'll be ready." They would be, of course. But Egon wondered how his young charges, as eager as they might be to fly and fight, would handle their first combat mission, especially flying against Liberators and their ramparts of fifty-caliber machine guns.

It could get ugly.

17

Over Romania
August 1, 1943

The Liberandos and the Circus, now past the Danube, dropped even lower, thundering over the Wallachian Plain, a flat, tan and green patchwork of wheat and corn. Puffy, flat-based cumulus clouds, like scattered cotton balls, floated above the level landscape.

"God, it looks like home," Vivian said.

Al tried to remember where she said she'd grown up . . . someplace on the Great Plains, he thought. Maybe Kansas or Nebraska.

"It looks so peaceful," he responded.

Below them, groups of peasants, probably extended families, labored in the fields. A few women, some decked out in brightly colored skirts, took a moment to look up and wave handkerchiefs at the Liberators as they roared over.

On narrow dirt roads crisscrossing the plain, hay wagons pulled by muscular draft horses trundled along, leaving long trails of suspended dust in their wakes.

In short order, the bombers dropped to near tree-top level. Colonel Compton, in the lead group, increased the speed of the force even more. Al nudged *Oregon Grinder's* throttles farther forward to keep pace.

"What's going on?" Vivian asked.

"Compton's pressing the assault. He's going as low as he can, trying to stay beneath enemy radars, and he's going as fast as he can, trying to reach the targets before the bad guys figure out exactly where we are." As deep as the B-24s had penetrated into Romania, they'd seen no signs of enemy fighters. A glow worm of hope glimmered deep within Al's psyche.

Maybe, just maybe, we got lucky and can pull this off. But he knew whatever they might be able to pull off would be at the deadly expense of the second wave of bombers, now irretrievably separated from the Liberandos and the Circus.

Al, looking down on the tranquil countryside that raced beneath him, wondered if he'd ever be able to share such serenity with Sarah and his newborn son. Or if he, husband and father, would be forced to pay the ultimate price. And if he did, would it have been worth it? Worth it so that Sarah and Al Junior might be able to enjoy such peacefulness in the future? He hoped above all, if he didn't return from the raid, that his son might never have to go on one.

His internal conflicts yanked him in multiple directions. He wanted desperately to see and hold his son and return to his wife. But he also wanted to successfully lead his crew on a mission deemed so important that one senior officer had said, "Coming back is secondary." He'd do everything in his power to make sure his men, and one woman, did come back. But most of all, as a military officer, he understood the mission came first.

He knew he'd broken a long-standing tradition of the armed forces by bringing a female on a combat operation. *But dammit, she knows how to fly and she volunteered. If the mission comes first, then that's my rationale. Without her, we wouldn't be here.*

Oregon Grinder, shimmying and shaking with its engines at full throat and afternoon thermals boiling up from the heated farmland, continued to pound northeastward. Just ahead of the B-24s, on a dusty path, a loaded hay cart with large painted wheels sat crossways on the track. Beneath it, two men cowered. They stared wide-eyed as the bombers roared over, their prop washes lifting whirlwinds of hay from the wagon.

Briefly, the Liberators flew parallel to a languid, blue-gray river. One of *Oregon Grinder's* waist gunners—Al couldn't tell if it was Chippy or Ned—hollered into the interphone, "Hey, let me bail out here. I could die a happy man."

Al saw why. A group of young ladies, some seductively slim, some curvaceously Rubenesque, all totally naked, bathed in the lazy waters of the river and smiled and waved at the planes as they rumbled over.

"Sorry," Al said to Vivian. "I apologize—"

"Don't be silly," she shot back. "Might be their last chance to —" She halted abruptly, obviously not wanting to voice any fatalism.

"You're right," he shouted at her over the bark of the engines. Into the interphone he said, "Jump! Do it now. We'll pick you up on our way back."

Two quick clicks came in return. Transmission received and understood.

"What're we looking for next?" Vivian asked.

"The first IP," Al responded. "It's a small town called Pitesti. Don't worry about having to identify it though. It's basically follow-the-leader through the IPs. The mission navigator is in *Teggie Ann* with Colonel Compton. They're the trailblazers. All we have to do is hang on their tail."

"And I'm double-checking everything," George interjected

from his navigator's position in *Oregon Grinder*. "So far, lookin' great."

"Roger that," Al said. "How far to Pitesti?"

"ETA in twenty-one minutes."

"And after Pitesti?" Vivian asked, her question directed to Al.

"We change course, get on a heading a bit north of due east. That'll carry us directly over IPs two and three. Two is a place called Targoviste. We're told it has a big ole monastery sitting on a hill overlooking the town, so it should be easy to identify.

"IP three, a village named Floresti, is where we turn southeastward and go into our final bomb run. We'll be down on the deck then, screaming in at over two hundred miles per hour to targets we've never seen, so things will happen in a confusing blur. But we made practice runs in the desert that worked out really well. Completely obliterated the mock-up refineries in two minutes. So if Colonel Compton is locked in on the target, I'm hoping we'll be in and out of Ploesti in no more than two or three minutes."

He paused and studied Vivian. She seemed adept at absorbing the information, and that gave him a modicum of comfort.

"But make no mistake," he cautioned, "there's going to be flak and, at least before we get away, Messerschmitts. Whether piloted by Germans or Romanians, I don't know. Doesn't matter. People are going to try to kill us."

To that, Vivian did not respond. She merely stared straight ahead, gripping the control wheel even more tightly.

They reached the piedmont, the rolling foothills separating the Transylvanian Alps and Wallachian Plain, and the character of the land changed. Orchards and vineyards appeared. Willow trees and poplars lined the banks of swift, clear rivers draining southward out of the Alps.

Small herds of cattle and sheep dotted the countryside. As

the bombers bellowed by overhead, their shadows sliding beneath them like great, black pterodactyls, some of the animals bolted and fled in terror. Their owners pursued them, shaking their fists at the airborne Americans who had dared disrupt their bucolic Sunday afternoon.

"Here it comes," Vivian exclaimed.

A small town flashed beneath them, a textile mill squatting by a river, apparently the village's claim to heavy industry.

The bombers banked to the right, setting up a new course. They climbed over a shallow, forested ridge separating Pitesti from Targoviste, IP number two.

"Minutes to Targoviste?" Al asked over the interphone, his question directed to George.

"Eight and a half."

Al's heart began to thump just a bit faster and his breaths came a bit more quickly as the Liberandos and Circus aircraft neared the threshold of battle. The two groups fanned out into a quasi-bombing front. In the engineer's position of *Oregon Grinder*, Sergeant McGregor cranked open the bomb bay doors. The rushing air added to the ear-jarring reverberations already rippling through the plane.

They crested the ridge and started down toward Targoviste, barely visible in the distance. The town, roughly the same size as Pitesti, perched astride another river draining southeastward out of the mountains. A set of railroad tracks paralleled the stream.

"Lotta little villages around here," Vivian noted. "Kinda all look the same." They'd passed over a number of postage-stamp-sized settlements.

Al concurred. "Sometimes difficult to tell one from another when you're blowing by as fast as we are. Except the IP markers are slightly bigger towns."

"We're still on the beam," George said. "Two minutes out."

"Think I got the monastery," Vivian said, "about forty-five degrees off our nose to the left." She pointed.

"I see it," Al said. A cluster of brownish-white structures, likely relics of the Middle Ages, crowned a low hill northeast of Targoviste. One of the buildings, larger than the rest, displayed several steeples topped by crucifixes.

"Two down, one to go," Al announced, referring to the IPs. They pressed on, still apparently unnoticed by the German or Romanian military. The glow worm of hope deep within Al brightened, just a smidgen.

"Should be a little under six minutes to number three," George said.

Ahead, *Teggie Ann* and the Liberando force rolled sharply to the right. Turning.

"What the hell," Al shouted over the interphone. "George, George, this isn't where we turn, is it? What the fuck is Compton doing?" Whatever tiny flicker of hope Al might have harbored sputtered out.

"This isn't it," George screamed back. "This isn't where we turn!"

Al whipped his gaze toward *Hell's Wench* off his left wing. Its copilot, Major John Jerstad, stared back, wide-eyed, brow furrowed. He gave an exaggerated shrug. He harbored the same confusion as Al.

Colonel K.K. Compton in the command aircraft had just set a course southeast from Targoviste, following a river and set of railroad tracks toward Bucharest, not Ploesti. Had he and his navigator miscounted, mistaking one of the mini-villages on a river for an IP? Al had no idea. He knew only that a huge mistake had just been made.

"No, no, no, this can't be," he barked over the interphone. The mission seemed to be suddenly in tatters. It had been in big trouble already with the two waves of bombers getting separated. But now the lead element of the daring raid had gone off course, turning at the wrong IP, roaring toward the wrong city.

"Call Compton, goddamnit, call him," George yelled. "Forget radio silence. He's wrong."

Al didn't hesitate. He broke radio silence, bellowing over the command channel. "Wrong turn, wrong turn!"

A chorus of other voices joined in. "Not here! Not here!" And, "Mistake! Mistake!"

The reprimands came not just from aircraft commanders in the Circus but from Compton's own Liberandos as well.

Yet Compton didn't budge. Al guessed he'd switched off his radio.

The other Liberators, now in bombing formation, had no choice but to stick on the tail of their leader, K.K. Compton in *Teggie Ann*. With very little separation between aircraft, and radio silence still technically mandated, the lumbering bombers could not unilaterally turn and correct their courses, not without the risk of triggering a chain of deadly midair collisions.

Operation Tidal Wave had just come apart at the seams without a single bomb being dropped. Al realized the American force had just sprung a trap on itself. With the Liberators roaring toward the wrong city, every German in Romania had to know the US Army Air Force had arrived.

He pounded the control wheel of *Oregon Grinder* in furious rage. Vivian leaned across the center console and laid a restraining hand on his bruised fist.

18

Near Ploesti, Romania
August 1, 1943

The Circus, following the Liberandos on their errant course, raced southeastward toward Bucharest. Only a single plane ignored the mass turn, the wrong turn, at Targoviste and continued straight, barreling toward the final, and correct, IP at Floresti.

Al cranked his head around and looked back over his left shoulder, trying to identify the lone aircraft. A patchwork quilt of sunshine and shadow, stitched here and there with a stray rain shower, lay on the plains northwest of Ploesti and made recognition difficult.

"Hey, Rhett," Al said, addressing his tail gunner, "can you make out who that is that didn't turn with us?"

"Looks like *Brewery Wagon*, sir."

Vivian glanced at Al. "Isn't that the old warhorse the guy was tossing stones at this morning?"

"Yeah. John Palm." Al shook his head. "I sure as hell hope he got rid of the bad juju, because he's gonna need all the luck he

can get now." Lieutenant Palm had stayed on course, a coura-
geous call, but maybe not the wisest, Al thought. As a lone
bomber, every single antiaircraft battery and Messerschmitt
defending Ploesti would be trained on him.

But Al's immediate concern centered on the huge mistake
that had just been made by the main body of bombers. To his
left, through the summertime haze, he could discern, just
barely, the tall stacks and dark smoke that defined Ploesti's oil
refineries. That's where they should have been headed.

He glanced into the cockpit of *Hell's Wench*, still on his left
wing. The copilot, John Jerstad, appeared to be in earnest
conversation with Colonel Baker, the Circus's commander. John
turned and looked at Al, nodded, then inclined his head toward
Ploesti.

Yes! They were going.

"Hang on, guys," Al hollered into the interphone, "we're
changing course. Get ready to fight."

Baker slowly banked *Hell's Wench* into a ninety-degree turn
and, as if performing an aerial ballet, his entire force followed.
He remained off the command channel, not wanting to broadcast their immediate intentions to the Germans.

"Where's our target?" Vivian asked.

"On the other side of the city," Al answered. "But forget
about it now. We'll drop our bombs on the first refinery we
reach. Coming in from this direction, I wouldn't know how to
identify ours anyhow." The raid had become a free-for-all. The
attack had been planned to come from the northwest with the
entire force. Now it came from the southwest with only the
Circus. Al counted twenty-two Liberators in Baker's force as they
made the turn. A far cry from the one hundred seventy-eight
that had departed Benghazi. Totally fucked up.

Flying parallel and to the right of Baker's Liberators, Major
Ramsey Potts led a separate echelon of Circus aircraft, about ten

bombers, toward the other target assigned to the bomb group. Not that specific targets mattered any longer. They'd hammer the first facility they came to.

Al spoke to his bombardier. "Kenny, first set of storage tanks or cracking towers we see, put the bombs inside the containment walls."

Click, click.

Baker, leading the attack, dropped lower and lower, pushing his throttles forward. The Circus thundered toward Ploesti, so near the ground that fields of alfalfa and sunflowers flattened in their wakes. Corn stalks snapped. Bundles of hay flew apart.

Oregon Grinder, pushed to its limits, shook and rattled like a runaway locomotive as it reacted to a multitude of forces. The Pratt & Whitneys bellowed at maximum power. The plane bounced and vibrated in violent thermals and swirling wake turbulence. Al and Vivian strained to hold the bomber straight and level.

Sweat drained into Al's eyes, making the airspeed indicator hard to read. He thought he saw in excess of two hundred fifty miles per hour. They couldn't be more than twenty feet off the ground.

Ahead of them, not far away, he spotted *Brewery Wagon,* the lone B-24 that had remained on the correct course. Hugging the earth and racing southward just west of the city, it had come under vicious antiaircraft fire.

"Jesus, look at that," he yelled.

A burst of orange and black flak blew apart *Brewery Wagon's* nose. The explosion shattered an inboard engine and set two others on fire. The bomber rolled one way, then the other, but seemed to recover. The crew jettisoned its bombs. The Liberator continued to flounder.

But *Brewery Wagon* never had a chance. The *Luftwaffe* had joined the battle. A Messerschmitt, a Bf 109, dove from above, stitching the crippled, staggering plane from tail to cockpit with twenty-millimeter cannon fire. The bomber plowed into the earth, but didn't explode. Foam flooded its engines. Good work by the aviators. Several men scrambled from the smoking Liberator, two carrying a third. Al wondered if John Palm had survived.

The thought didn't last long. Black balls of death, flak, began erupting around the Circus aircraft as they knifed toward the city. Stacks, cracking towers, and storage tanks came into sudden focus through the haze. Something else, too.

"My God, what are those?" Vivian yelled.

"Barrage balloons. They're tethered by steel cables. Hold us steady, Viv." He didn't have time to explain.

His next word: "Christ!"

Beneath them, the tops of haystacks flew open, revealing yet more antiaircraft guns. Machine guns sprouted from pits dug in alfalfa fields. A stream of bullets ripped into *Oregon Grinder,* leaving a gash of shredded metal in the thin skin of the plane just to the rear of the cockpit.

Vivian screamed.

Now the interior of the plane reverberated not only with the bellow of its engines but with the deafening clatter of its fifty-calibers opening up not on enemy fighters—they wouldn't attack with the B-24s so low and approaching the city—but on ground targets.

Streams of fire belched from the waist positions, and presumably the tail gun, though Al couldn't see it. His gunners blasted away at Romanians and Germans only yards away from the bomber.

An antiaircraft shell blew up so close to *Oregon Grinder* it rocked the plane and spiderwebbed the plexiglass cockpit. Ahead of the Liberator, pink and orange muzzle flashes, gunfire from dozens of antiaircraft cannons, bore through the dark curtain of flak already draped over the landscape. To Al, it seemed they had embarked on a death run. Still, he held the bouncing bomber on course, picking out a set of tall smoke stacks as his target. Maybe three minutes down range.

"Going for the smoke stacks," he yelled, informing his bombardier.

Again, two quick clicks in response.

"Up, up," Vivian yelled.

Al had been so focused on the stacks, he'd failed to notice a hedgerow that had materialized seconds ahead of them.

In a desperate motion, he and Vivian yanked back simultaneously on their control wheels, vaulting *Oregon Grinder* over a bushy green windbreak sheltering a country road.

Baker, in *Hell's Wench,* had done the same. Now he pulled slightly ahead of the other Circus aircraft, determined to fulfill his promise of leading them to the target.

A cacophony of noise—engines, gunfire, flak—filled the furiously vibrating *Oregon Grinder* as it thundered toward its chosen refinery, Al no less committed than Colonel Baker to reach it.

Around them, streams of smoke trailed from several B-24s whose engines had been blasted away. Still, they pressed on.

Al glanced down as he passed over a bare-chested flak gunner jamming a shell into the breech of an antiaircraft weapon. The gunner glanced up, wide-eyed, then disappeared in a flash of blood and flesh as the fifty-cals from another Liberator cut him in half.

The first Circus casualty came two seconds later. To the right of *Oregon Grinder,* a brutal explosion ripped through a B-24 as it took a direct cannon hit in its bomb bay. It instantly became a flying torch. Ruptured fuel tanks spit out gushers of fire that streamed out on either side of the Liberator. They abruptly morphed into a single blazing river roiling out behind the condemned ship.

The pilot attempted to climb to allow his crew a chance to parachute. But the bomber stalled, hanging in the air like a flaming fountain. Still, two figures tumbled from its nose-wheel hatch, though only one 'chute blossomed. Two more followed out a waist gunner's window. Then the aircraft plunged to earth, ending its life in a funeral pyre on the edge of a tiny Romanian village.

A pungent odor filled *Oregon Grinder's* cockpit. Al recognized it instantly. He glanced over at Vivian, then dropped his gaze. A stream of light yellow liquid ran down her leg, puddled on the floor. She didn't acknowledge his gaze, instead stared straight ahead, intent on holding the aircraft on the target. Her arms vibrated with the effort as she battled the shimmying plane . . . and her own fears. Al couldn't help but admire her.

"We're on target, Viv. Almost there. Hang on, hang on." He intended his words for himself as much as Vivian. The sky had become filled with what seemed a solid blanket of flak, a shroud of death. A flash flood of doom washed over Al. He ignored it. He focused instead on the stacks of the refinery coming up fast. Two minutes.

Two plane-lengths ahead, *Hell's Wench* clipped a balloon cable. The balloon, now untethered, wobbled skyward like a runaway dirigible. *Hell's Wench* shuddered. Then a series of devastating blasts from ground fire struck it, ripping into its wing, wing root, and finally the cockpit. Flames exploded from the fuel tanks.

"God, no," Al bellowed.

In the burning aircraft, Baker and Jerstad jettisoned their bombs.

Al spotted an open wheat field in front of the burning bomber.

"Go down, go down," he screamed, not that the doomed crew could hear him.

"Why doesn't he mush it in?" Vivian yelled.

Al knew. Baker had promised. Promised to lead the Circus to the target. *Gentlemen, I'm going to take you to this one even if my plane falls apart.*

Hell's Wench, fire streaming from its tanks, didn't waver. Baker aimed it between the two stacks. A figure tumbled from the nose-wheel hatch, blew back toward *Oregon Grinder,* a white parachute blossoming in the black hell. Al could see the burned legs of whoever had bailed out as *Oregon Grinder* missed him by mere feet.

Hell's Wench took another direct hit.

Oregon Grinder reached the target, barreled between the twin stacks.

"Bombs," Al yelled.

Kenny released them. *Oregon Grinder,* freed of almost two tons, sprang upward.

On either side of them, other Liberators triggered their weapons. Some bombs skipped along the ground, arcing into and through buildings like earth-bound porpoises. With delayed fusing, the weapons didn't explode immediately upon contact.

Just ahead of them, the blazing *Hell's Wench* canted over on its right wing, then attempted to climb. Al couldn't see how. Flames engulfed it. It staggered upward a couple of hundred feet. Three or four more men dived from the airborne holocaust. But the *Wench* could no longer fly. It fell off on its right wing, plunged past *Oregon Grinder* so close both Al and Vivian reflexively ducked. The dying bomber disappeared beneath them in a trail of fiery black smoke.

Colonel Addison Baker and Major John Jerstad had literally flown their ship to pieces leading Ted Timberlake's Traveling

Circus to the refineries of Ploesti. Their fate jabbed a wrecking ball of a fist into Al's gut.

A second phalanx of smoke stacks and cracking towers materialized in front of *Oregon Grinder.*

"Not gonna make it," Vivian screamed.

Al knew why. The wing span of a B-24 exceeded a hundred feet. The stacks stood only about fifty feet apart. No time to climb.

"Roll it right," he bellowed.

Together they cranked their control wheels, banking the craft to the right. The left wing lifted, the right dipped. But not quick enough. The left wing tip blew apart as it nipped a stack. But *Oregon Grinder* flew on.

"Level!" Al commanded.

He and Vivian rolled the plane back to level flight.

Vicious volleys of flak continued to erupt all around them. An exploding shell struck the craft, shaking it from stem to stern.

"Where?" Al shouted, hoping one of the gunners would respond.

"Right vertical stabilizer. About two feet missing." Al assumed the call came from the right waist gunner, Ned. He'd have the best angle of sight.

"Everybody okay?"

"Right waist here, Pops. Okay."

One by one, the crew reported. Except for Sergeant Cummings, the tail gunner.

Al feared they'd lost him. But he couldn't scramble back to check, or send anybody else. Not in the middle of a battle.

"Get it lower, Viv," Al said. "If we come out of the city too high, the fighters will nail us."

They dropped the nose and thundered down a wide boulevard mere feet above the road, eye-to-eye with rooftop gunners.

Streams of red, orange, and white tracers interlaced the thoroughfare as continuous blasts of gunfire, from both the enemy and *Oregon Grinder*, filled the space between them in what had become a great air-ground battle.

"Hell of a lot more guns here than we were briefed on," Al snapped.

Vivian only nodded.

A burst of shells caught the Liberator in the right wing, ripping apart the number four engine—the outboard engine—and taking a section of the wing with it while launching a spray of shrapnel into a fuel tank.

"Damnit," Al exclaimed. "Three engines now."

"We can fly it on two," Vivian shouted.

"We're gonna have fighters after us."

Vivian didn't respond to that statement. Instead she yelled, "Ahead!"

Al saw it, some sort of wire, maybe a radio antenna, draped across the street between buildings. Too late. They ripped into it, through it, and beyond it.

They reached the end of the street, climbed. On a parallel avenue, a B-24 in full flame, both wings sheared away, careened down a street like a speeding locomotive engulfed in a blast furnace.

"Let's get the hell out of here," Al barked.

They continued to hurdle multi-story buildings and smoke stacks as they stayed low, abusing the three engines that still functioned, but they'd lost speed. Other bombers raced ahead of them. They executed a ninety-degree pivot and struggled toward the northwest edge of the city. There Al meant to turn toward the southwest and retrace, in the opposite direction, their approach to Ploesti, now their escape route.

Al glanced back at the refineries they'd struck. Orange flames and obsidian smoke billowed skyward as the delay-fused bombs reached the end of their forty-five-second countdowns. Storage tanks exploded in mammoth fireballs, their steel tops spinning into the air like flying dinner plates.

Al wanted desperately to scramble rearward and check on his tail gunner, but had no opportunity. Black balls of flak continued to explode all around them. And he knew that the *Luftwaffe's* Messerschmitts lurked, waiting for the bombers to exit the city, waiting to feed on the cripples. Like *Oregon Grinder.*

"On the right, aircraft coming hard and low," Vivian exclaimed, pointing.

19

Over Ploesti, Romania
August 1, 1943

Al peered through the cracked plexiglass of the cockpit, trying to spot the aircraft Vivian had indicated. He saw them instantly. Five of them, big planes, hugging the ground, bearing down on *Oregon Grinder's* flight path.

"Liberators," he said. "Ours."

"Where'd *they* come from?"

In the wake of the approaching B-24s, fire and smoke billowed from a refinery on the northeast side of Ploesti. Much farther east, well away from the city's petroleum facilities, a score of bombers barreled northward, dropping bombs and triggering columns of black-gray smoke. Al realized instantly what had probably happened.

"It's the Liberandos," he said, "from the bomb group that headed toward Bucharest."

"They came back!"

"Some did. Looks like most of them are scooting *around* the city well to the east. They're hitting targets of opportunity, not refineries."

"Who the hell ordered that?" snapped a voice over the interphone. Al guessed it belonged to George.

"Dunno. Maybe Compton. Maybe General Ent. He was riding in *Teggie Ann* with Compton."

"Who's General Ent?" Vivian asked.

"Commander of all these bombers, 9th Bomber Command," Al answered. "I think the Liberandos turned around when they realized they were headed toward Bucharest. Then they saw that wall of flak over Ploesti and decided—either Compton or Ent did— it would be certain death to attempt an attack."

"All except for these guys, apparently," Vivian said. The group of five Liberandos appeared only seconds away from *Oregon Grinder*.

"Stay low, stay low," Al cautioned. "Damn, I hope they see us."

The five B-24s roared over the top of *Oregon Grinder* with only feet to spare.

"Guess they did." Vivian spoke calmly.

Oregon Grinder, already shaking like it had the palsy, vibrated even more violently in the wake turbulence of the rogue Liberandos, whoever they were.

"They deserve medals," Al said.

Flak continued to erupt on all sides of them. Al knew with their reduced speed, the antiaircraft gunners had to be licking their chops.

"Keep ridin' the treetops," he urged, "it's hard for the ack-ack guys to depress their guns that low."

Off to the left, a B-24 without a tail section splattered into a corn field and erupted in flames. Five men scrambled from the wreckage and dove into a drainage ditch as the Liberator exploded. Well out in front of *Oregon Grinder,* a Liberator with smoking engines lowered its landing gear and plopped down in a wheat field. A wing clipped a mound of earth and the bomber ground-looped but didn't burn. The crew evacuated in a matter of seconds and waved at *Oregon Grinder* as it rumbled by overhead.

Al dipped a wing, very slightly, in acknowledgement.

"God bless 'em," he said. Then, "Hey, Kenny, you see who that was?"

The bombardier responded, "Looked like *Honky-Tonk Gal.*"

"Thank you, Lord," Al muttered. The guy in the bunk next to his at Benghazi, the guy he'd made plans to grab a beer with after they got back from Ploesti, was *Honky-Tonk Gal's* bombardier.

"Pops, Pops, hey, what happened?"

"Rhett?" Al couldn't hide his surprise, and relief, at hearing the voice of what sounded like his tail gunner.

"Yeah, it's me. I guess I, well, I dunno. Took a nap."

"Took a nap?"

"All I remember is a big explosion right over my head. Everything went black. Knocked me silly. Knocked me out, I reckon. Woke up just now. Got a bitch of a headache. Cuts on my face. The plexiglass is shattered."

"Ack-ack hit the right vertical stabilizer. We only got half of it left. That's what blew out the glass in your turret and put you outta commission. Probably gave you a concussion."

"Feels like somebody took a hammer to my noggin."

"Soon as things quiet down, I'll get somebody back there to look at you."

"Thanks, Pops."

"You okay to shoot?"

"Can't see shit through the cracked glass, but I think my guns are okay. Yeah, I'm ready."

Oregon Grinder continued to vibrate and shake, but it seemed controllable, albeit unable to exceed two hundred miles per hour. Fighter bait. The fuel leak at least seemed minor, with more of a spray exiting the plane than a solid stream. Still, Al realized, their odds of making it back to North Africa had plummeted. In all probability, they wouldn't have enough gas. Not that they wouldn't fall prey to a fighter before they had to worry about that anyhow.

Al rolled the plane gently to the left and took up a course toward the southwest. They'd soon be out of the flak zone, but in what the guys called Indian Territory, the area outside of Ploesti where the fighters would be waiting to ambush them.

"More bombers, lots of them, about two o'clock, down low!" The call came from Tech Sergeant McGregor in the top turret.

Al swiveled his head to look slightly to his right.

"Holy cow," Vivian said, "is that the rest of the force?"

Two echelons of B-24s swept toward Ploesti from the northwest, charging hard from the direction of the third IP.

"It's Killer Kane and Leon Johnson," Al responded. "The Pyramiders and Eight Balls."

"Late to the party," Vivian said.

"Yeah, and they're getting cut to pieces. Shit, look at that."

The Pyramiders and Eight Balls, hugging the earth and following a set of railroad tracks, screamed toward the refineries. A freight train, or at least what looked like a freight, rolled along the rails in tandem with the Liberators. But the sides of the freight wagons had been folded back, revealing batteries of antiaircraft guns that now ripped into the attacking planes at almost point-blank range. A deadly trap.

Enfilades of exploding steel tore into the bombers as they barreled southeastward on both sides of the tracks, the Pyramiders on the left, the Eight Balls on the right. The Liberators' fifty-cals returned the fire in almost continuous streams of lead. The space between the planes and the train had become a virtual wall of red and white tracers. The locomotive tugging the flak train exploded. The cars behind it accordioned to a sprawling halt.

But the damage had been done. Almost two dozen Liberators either lay in smoking wreckage on both sides of the tracks or continued to limp toward their targets with shot-up engines and wounded crew members.

The surviving bombers thundered across *Oregon Grinder's* path, their bomb bay doors open, only feet above the ground.

"They gotta be confused as hell," Al said. "Their targets are already burning and exploding."

"The ones we hit?" Vivian asked.

"Yeah."

"What a mess."

"An understatement."

"Hey, where are the Sky Scorpions?"

"Going for a target north of Ploesti."

Oregon Grinder exited the flak zone, but Al knew the fighters would now come for them.

"Heads up, everyone," he announced over the interphone, "eyes peeled for fighters."

No sooner had he spoken than someone yelled, "Bandits, bandits. On the right, two o'clock high."

Kalamaki, Greece
August 1, 1943

In the enervating Mediterranean heat, Egon dozed off in the alert hangar, his head nodding to his chest as he sat in a rickety chair. His daydream drifted away to Germany, to the green banks of the Mosel on a summer day with a soft breeze. To a time before men soared through the beauty and vastness of

European skies intent on destroying one another with bullets and bombs.

He and Inge and their infant daughter, Christa, rested on a cotton blanket in velvety grass. While Christa giggled happily with a rag doll clutched to her chest, he and Inge sipped cold *Schwarze Katz* and nibbled on thick black bread topped with chunks of *Leberwurst*. In the center of the river, a small passenger boat slid downstream toward Koblenz and the Mosel's confluence with the Rhine.

"I wish we were aboard," Inge said. "It would be such an adventure."

Egon smiled. "Ah, yes." He stared at the vessel weaving through the narrow, serpentine valley with its steep slopes quilted in verdant vineyards. "But our life will be an adventure. A good one, I think."

Inge leaned toward him and placed her hand on the back of his neck. He turned to acknowledge her.

"A pleasant reverie, I hope, *Hauptmann*." The voice belonged not to Inge, but to *Oberstleutnant* Rödel, who stood over him, a hand resting lightly on Egon's shoulder.

Egon leaped to attention, almost too quickly. Dizziness lanced through his head and he involuntarily tilted toward his commander, who steadied him.

"It's okay, Egon. Your boredom is about to end."

"Sorry, sir. The heat—"

"Don't worry about it. It gets to me, too. Come." He motioned Egon and the other pilots to the folding table. He opened an aeronautical chart of Greece and the Ionian Sea and spread it across the table.

"The American bombers did indeed hit Ploesti. They're heading home now, although not all are following the same route they came in on. They seem to be in scattered, disorganized formations. They got shot up badly by General Gerstenberg's defenses."

"Was the raid a success, sir?" Egon asked.

"Several refineries were heavily damaged. A couple went untouched. But the Americans lost many planes. Gerstenberg estimates over three dozen Liberators went down, and many others were so badly crippled they won't make it back to Benghazi. In fact, we've had reports that a number of them are heading south toward Turkey. But I'd guess they're probably trying to make it to Cyprus rather than be interned in Turkey."

"Why would they be interned?" a young pilot asked.

"Turkey is neutral. Any belligerents—men, ships, aircraft—that end up there are out of the war and have to remain a 'guest' of the country until the fighting is over. The majority of combatants don't care for that. So it looks like most of the bombers are trying to exit on the same route they entered on, tracking over extreme northern Bulgaria, Yugoslavia, and then Albania. After leaving Albania, they should turn south just off the west coast of Greece over the Ionian Sea."

"And then it's our turn?" another aviator asked.

"Yes, but don't underestimate our foe, even wounded. Gerstenberg reports the raid was a marvel of skill and bravery. The Americans split their forces, feinting at Bucharest before attacking Ploesti almost simultaneously from three different directions. And the assault was carried out at low-level, the Liberators hugging the ground, believe it or not."

"That's something different," Egon said.

"It is. These are bombers designed to attack from high altitude. Still, the general said the pilots displayed amazing airmanship. Their planes often missed each other—sometimes on virtual head-on collision courses—by mere feet as they went for their targets. They drove through almost solid curtains of flak, flames boiling from burning refineries, and smoke so thick and black it blotted out the sun. Some of the aircraft, Gerstenberg said, pressed their attacks even after they'd lost engines or were on fire." Rödel pinched his lips together and shook his head in grudging respect.

"So my point is this: These American flyers are warriors. Don't think you're going to have an easy time bringing them down even if their aircraft are shattered and crippled. They will fight to the end . . . as we would."

"We're prepared, sir," Egon responded, although he knew some of the youngsters in his squadron might not be, despite their expressions of enthusiasm over finally meeting the enemy. "What's the plan?"

"We'll position you off the west coast of Greece just west of the island of Kefalonia. You'll be in a good spot there to intercept any of the enemy trying to make it back to Benghazi."

Rödel checked his wristwatch. "You'll be wheels-up in two hours. With the auxiliary fuel tanks on your new planes, you should have enough gas to orbit, fight for half an hour, and get back here before sundown."

Egon examined the faces of his rookie aviators. They reflected a mix of eagerness and apprehension. He knew the feeling. He'd been there himself, hardly able to contain the fervor of entering combat, but at the same time harboring gnawing doubts about his skills and bravery.

Rödel reached out and rested his hand on Egon's shoulder. "Good hunting, my friend. I know you'll do well." He paused, then nodded at the other pilots. "Gentlemen."

They responded by snapping to attention and popping off crisp salutes.

Rödel returned their salutes. "Oh," he said, "I almost forgot."

He signaled an *Obergefreiter* who sat in an idling *Kübelwagen* outside the hangar. The enlisted man retrieved a large cardboard box from the rear of the vehicle and trotted toward Rödel.

Rödel took the box and handed it to Egon.

"Your landlords, I forget their names—"

"George and Vasiliki Kostopoulos."

"Yes, yes. They came by headquarters a short while ago and brought this. 'For their boys,' they said."

Egon opened the box. "Ah, *wunderbar*."

The interior contained perhaps a dozen gyros and two jugs of iced tea.

"Greek iced tea," Rödel pointed out, "sweetened with honey."

"*Danke*. On a hot day like this, much appreciated."

"I suppose they guessed something big must be up with 'their boys' standing alert all day. And by the way, Egon, thank you for allowing them to think of you that way, 'their boys,' instead of as their wardens or something worse. It reflects well upon the *Luftwaffe*."

"Sir, I hope my squadron will live up to your approval over the next few hours."

"I have no doubt of that." He stepped close to Egon and spoke in quiet tones. "But allow me to remind you, there will be losses. I have complete trust in your abilities and leadership, but I know your pilots are inexperienced and undertrained. That's what this war has come to. The Liberator pilots you're going up against are battle-hardened and hurting now." Rödel lowered his voice to almost a whisper. "You're going into combat against a dangerous, wounded animal. Godspeed, Egon."

20

Over Romania
August 1, 1943

Al spotted the "bandits," enemy aircraft, about five miles out on his right, a pair of Romanian fighters. They looked like something called IAR-80s, not as formidable as Messerschmitts, but certainly capable of bringing down a B-24. Especially one on crutches, like *Oregon Grinder*.

"We're gonna keep hugging the ground," Al announced over the interphone. "That'll limit the gypsies to attacks from above."

The first of the Romanian aircraft dove at them from the rear, but fired from a long way out. Tracers from its in-wing machine guns followed a downward arc that petered out well short of the bomber.

"Not even close," Rhett, the tail gunner, yelled. *Oregon Grinder's* gunners didn't bother returning fire.

The second IAR-80 dove. Taking a lesson from the initial ineffective attack, this fighter screamed in much closer, loosing a stream of machine gun fire that ripped into the rear portion of the Liberator's fuselage. This time *Oregon Grinder's* aircrew blasted back. The clatter of heavy machine guns from three positions—right waist, tail, and top turret—joined the din of the plane's three overworked Pratt & Whitneys.

"Fucking gypsies," one of the gunners bellowed.

The Romanian fighter broke off its attack and climbed away from the bomber.

An odd whistling sound, undoubtedly from the shot-up fuselage, added to the discordant racket permeating *Oregon Grinder's* interior.

Al and Vivian held the vibrating plane on course, keeping it near the ground, hurdling haystacks and windrows. Al pushed the throttles as far forward as he dared. They flew underneath the bases of fleecy white clouds that speckled the summer sky. Below them, the B-24's shadow raced over the quilted farmland like a great, avenging angel.

"What's happening?" Al called into the intercom. He knew the bandits still had to be trailing them. They wouldn't make just one pass and break off.

"Getting their courage up for a second run," someone responded.

Another voice: "Looks like they may try to hit us from both sides at the same time."

"Roger that," Al said. "If they do, tail, take the plane on your right. Top turret, the one on your left. Waist gunners, make sure of your fields of fire before opening up." With one vertical stabilizer already half destroyed, he didn't need the waist positions doing any additional damage.

He turned to Vivian. "Ready?"

She nodded. Her knuckles had turned white from her fierce grip on the control wheel.

It happened fast—the rattle of six fifty-calibers reverberating through the plane as if it were an echo chamber—then a ripping, tearing, shredding sound as the fighters' gunfire ripped into *Oregon Grinder*, shaking it violently. An enemy fighter flashed by on the left, trying to climb but trailing smoke. The second fighter screamed by just beneath the bomber's nose.

The second fighter, too, attempted to climb, but had attacked at too steep an angle. Its flight attitude flattened, but too late. It pancaked into a corn field and erupted in a roiling ball of orange flame and black smoke.

"Got 'em both," Al hollered. He twisted to look back into the fuselage. He saw nothing but daylight. The IAR-80s' gunfire had minced the B-24's thin aluminum skin. "Jesus, we're a flying colander."

"But still flying," Vivian pointed out.

"Yes, yes. Everyone okay?" Al waited for the responses.

"Tail, okay."

"Top turret, okay."

"Left waist—oh, shit. Oh, no. Oh, no."

"What, what is it?" Al's throat constricted with fear.

"Chippy's hit. Oh, man, lotta blood." Chippy, Sergeant Hamilton, the right waist gunner. The puffy-cheeked kid from Davenport, Iowa, who worked on Mississippi riverboats.

"Stop the bleeding. Where's he hit?"

"Dunno. Stumpy's with him." Stumpy—Tech Sergeant Witkowski—the bottom turret gunner who hadn't seen action yet since the ball turret had remained in a retracted position during the low-level action.

"Stumpy," Al said, "what's Chippy's status?"

A long silence ensued.

Then, "He took a couple of rounds in his right shoulder, Pops. I got the bleeding stopped, jabbed him with morphine. Looks bad though. His arm's just kinda hangin' there. He needs a doc. Bad."

"Thanks, Stumpy. Keep him as quiet as you can. Elevate his legs a bit. Throw some blankets over him. More morphine as needed."

"Roger that. I'll take over the waist position, but I'll keep an eye on Chippy, too."

Oregon Grinder continued to shimmy her way southwestward, skimming over treetops and rooftops.

"She's holding together," Al told everyone, "and I'll do my best to keep her up. But make sure you're ready to bail if it comes to that. Stumpy, if we have to jump, make sure Chippy's 'chute is secure, then shove him out first."

"Will do, Pops."

Once again they sped over the sprawling Wallachian Plain, a brown and green mélange of farms and villages. At one point a grizzled farmer flanked by two youths sprang from behind an outbuilding, threw shotguns to their shoulders, and emptied all barrels at *Oregon Grinder*. The wake turbulence of the thundering bomber blew them into a pile of manure.

"If you ever wondered where the Three Stooges lived, now you know," Al said.

"Poetic justice," someone else commented.

Vivian grinned.

"Let's take her up a bit," Al said. "We should be out of range of the Messerschmitts from Ploesti and the gypsies from Bucharest. Maybe we can catch a bit of that tail wind the weather guy was yammering about."

"Don't forget about the Bulgarians," George reminded Al. "They got a few Messerschmitts. We'll be back over northern Bulgaria in about ten minutes."

Oregon Grinder struggled upward a few thousand feet and gained a little push from northerly winds. Still, the main group of fleeing Circus aircraft had outdistanced them, and no other Liberators hove into view.

As they pressed on alone, Al occasionally caught snippets of plane-to-plane radio transmissions between other Liberators. One in particular caught his attention, though he didn't know if the aircraft were ahead of or behind him, or who they were.

"Wonder if we might sit on your wing for a while? Got a bit of a problem here."

"Sure. Tuck in as close as you feel comfortable. What's going on?"

"I'm the engineer—in the copilot's seat. The copilot is flying the plane. We lost our command pilot."

"Killed? Wounded?"

"Not exactly."

Pause.

"Well, what happened to him?"

"Ever since we departed Ploesti, he's been curled up in a fetal position in the bomb bay. Won't talk or move."

"Jesus."

"So we got a butterbar flying the plane now. First mission."

"Jesus, Mary, and Joseph. Yeah, you can hang on our coattails all the way to Benghazi if you want. We'll try to assist you as much as we can."

A flight of three Liberators—*Thundermug, Let 'er Rip, Exterminator*—closed in on *Oregon Grinder* from above and behind. Al watched as they soared by on his left in an ad hoc diamond formation, punching in and out of billowing white clouds. They gave their wings a little waggle to acknowledge Al's slowpoke bomber and cruised on by.

He watched as the trio of Liberators drilled into the top of the next towering cumulus. *Thundermug*, probably with the least experienced pilot, veered slightly away from the other two bombers as they disappeared into the fair-weather stack of clouds.

"Oh my God," Al yelled.

Thundermug reappeared seconds later on the far side of the cloud, but the other two didn't. *Exterminator* exited the cumulus in a steep dive and plunged into the Bulgarian countryside in an explosive crash. *Let 'er Rip* came out minus her tail turret, which tumbled toward earth on a separate trajectory. The aircraft itself grazed a ridge line then went into a flat glide toward the ground. Four figures came out a waist gunner's window, but one wore a 'chute that collapsed as quickly as it had opened. The plane smacked into the ground, bounced, then bounced again and came apart as it erupted in flames.

Al leaned his forehead against the control wheel and closed his eyes. *Goddamn. How in the hell can men fly through walls of flak, hordes of fighters, make crisscrossing bomb runs at treetop level, then ram into each other in a puffy cloud? Does God care about this crap, or does He even give a shit? Probably not.*

Al opened his eyes, but allowed his cynical thoughts to continue their free rein.

No, of course He doesn't care. War is our folly, man's folly. Not His. It's our lunacy that leads to the whims of life and death that get played out on a fucking cosmic roulette wheel.

"We're just along for the ride," he said softly.

Vivian looked over at him. "What?"

He shook his head, not wishing to give voice to his black musings.

The terrain below became mountainous as *Oregon Grinder* exited the northwestern bulge of Bulgaria and entered Yugoslavia.

"Let's gain a little more altitude," Al said to Vivian. "We'll have to climb back over the Pindus Mountains shortly."

"Are we out of range of the Bulgarians yet?"

"I can't honestly say. But we're over Yugoslavia, so I don't think the Bulgarians will come after us here. And the Germans in Yugoslavia are probably a lot more worried about the partisans they're fighting than they are B-24s with no bombs."

Despite limping along on three engines and missing part of its vertical stabilizer, *Oregon Grinder* continued to fly steadily albeit slightly wobbly. The thrumming roar of the engines told Al they remained dependable, but he also knew the plane continued to spray fuel into the air from its shrapnel-ripped wing tank.

"Take the controls, Viv," he said. "I'm going back to check on Chippy."

He made his way along the catwalk through the bomb bay, then up to the waist positions, stunned by the amount of damage the Romanian fighters had inflicted on the fuselage. There seemed to be more daylight than metal visible. An icy wind swirled and whistled through the interior of the wounded aircraft, giving Al the sense of being as much outside the bomber as cocooned in its aluminum shell. He wondered if he might be experiencing something akin to Vivian's wing walking exploits.

He reached Chippy. Stumpy attended to him. The injured waist gunner lay on the floor, his virtually severed shoulder swathed in cloth and gauze bandages but still seeping blood. Blankets and a flight jacket covered his body. His breathing had become rapid and shallow. He appeared unconscious.

"Don't know if he's gonna make it, sir," Stumpy said, his voice strangled by concern.

Al studied Chippy, then turned to Stumpy. "Maybe we should try for Turkey, get him medical attention as soon as possible."

"We'd be outta the war then, Pops. Interned. If we made it."

Al considered where they were now, cruising over Yugoslavia. "Yeah, given our current position, to get to Turkey we'd have to backtrack over Bulgaria and Greece. Probably not a grand idea when we're already shot to shit. Enemy fighters would be on us like sharks on chum."

He knelt next to Chippy, laid his hand on the young man's forehead, and spoke, though he knew the sergeant couldn't hear him. "Sorry, Chippy. This isn't good. We'd probably get shot down trying to make it to Turkey, and we don't have enough fuel to get back to Benghazi. So I'm thinking maybe Crete or Sicily. But we still may have to dodge Messerschmitts out of Greece. We'll do our best, partner. Promise. Hang in there."

Al stood. "Keep him as warm and quiet as you can, Stumpy. We still got a chance."

"Yes, sir."

But Al read in Stumpy's expression that he didn't believe that chance amounted to anything greater than a moth flying toward an open flame.

Back in the cockpit, Al could see exhaustion had overtaken Vivian. She'd worked hard using both the control wheel and rudder pedals to keep *Oregon Grinder* flying steadily. She'd used the rudder pedals to help steer the plane now that it had more pull on one side than the other with an engine missing.

She wasn't a frail woman, but the task had been demanding. A sheen of perspiration, despite the chilliness that permeated the bomber, coated her tanned and subtly muscular arms.

"Take a break, Viv," Al said as he sank into the pilot's seat.

"I'm okay . . . but I'm glad you're back." She paused. "Look, I'm sorry about that." She inclined her head at the dark spot on the floor of the flight deck where she'd involuntarily urinated earlier.

Al pulled the throat mike off his neck and leaned toward her. "There are guys who've come back from their first mission and had to burn their underwear. Understand?"

"Yeah, but I'm still embarrassed."

"Viv, you're doing as well in that seat as any man I've ever flown with. If you were, well, a guy, I wouldn't hesitate adding you to my crew. God's honest truth."

"Thank you, Pops." She grinned. "To change the subject, what on earth happened back there, in Ploesti?"

"I can tell you what but not why. Things started to go south when the bomb groups got separated. I can only speculate that Killer Kane decided he was going to break his planes if he tried to keep up with us and the Liberandos. Remember, most of the Liberators that turned around because of engine failure came from his group."

Vivian nodded. "But we continued to push ahead at normal cruise speed, while Kane's guys reduced power to save their engines and get to the target?"

"Yep. And the two groups following Kane, the Eight Balls and Sky Scorpions, were forced to throttle back to stay in touch with Kane's Pyramiders."

"And the radio silence order didn't help, did it?" Vivian said, more a statement than a question.

"Nope. I guess security overrode tactical execution. But I have a feeling the Germans knew we were coming anyhow. The amount of firepower they unleashed on us sure suggests that."

In the distance, the Pindus Mountains appeared, the higher peaks and ridges still capped by billowing stacks of cumulus.

"Let's take her up to about ten," Al said. "That should get us over the mountains safely."

Oregon Grinder labored higher into the sky, the engines groaning, the tattered fuselage rattling, and a low frequency whistle—wind whipping through the numerous holes in the bomber's skin—reverberating through the interior.

After the plane settled in at its new altitude, Vivian returned to the subject of the screwed-up raid. "Why did the Liberandos turn at the wrong IP?" The key question.

"No idea," Al answered. "I couldn't begin to guess."

"But heads will roll?"

"Probably, but that's way above my pay grade."

"At least Colonel Baker corrected the bad turn."

"And paid for it with his life."

"I don't think I've ever seen courage like he showed," Vivian said. "I used to think it took guts to stroll out on a wing while going eighty miles per hour two hundred feet above the earth, but what Baker and his copilot did today . . ." Further words seemed to fail her. She blinked tears from her eyes.

Al had to agree. He couldn't imagine bravery like Colonel Baker and Major Jerstad had displayed. He knew without a doubt *he* didn't have cojones like that. "They got us to the target, Viv, not the one we were supposed to hit, but he led us to the enemy. Few men would have even *attempted* that."

Al and Vivian remained silent for a poignant moment. Then Al continued. "Anyhow, that's how we got there, screaming over Ploesti, then meeting up with that quintet of bombers from the Liberandos late to the party after visiting Bucharest."

"Finally going after their assigned target?"

Al nodded.

"Then, on top of everything else, here comes Killer Kane, nailing all the IPs and bringing the remainder of the force over Ploesti. Jesus, we had aircraft converging over the city from three different directions." He shook his head slowly, in amazement and disappointment, as the reality of how much had gone wrong sank in.

"It's a wonder we all didn't kill each other," someone said over the interphone. Al had forgotten the entire crew could listen to the conversation between him and Vivian.

"You know," Al added, "it's hard to believe, but after leveling our practice target in the desert in two minutes, we spent almost half a goddamned hour over Ploesti."

They crested the mountains, then began their descent toward the Albanian coast.

"Okay, everyone," Al announced, "we're going to try to make it to Sicily, get Chippy to a flight surgeon. But the Germans have Messerschmitts in Greece and may have other ideas about where we end up."

Like at the bottom of the Ionian Sea.

21

Kalamaki, Greece
August 1, 1943

Egon's ten Messerschmitts scuttled across a grassy verge toward the runway. On the ground, especially on uneven turf, Bf 109s appeared ungainly as they taxied, wobbling and hopping like drunks playing hopscotch. The fighter's awkward appearance came from a pair of long, skinny main landing gear struts, like a stork's legs, that canted the nose upward while the tail, supported by a single small wheel, seemed to almost scrape the ground. But once in the air, with the gear retracted, a 109 took on the profile of a streamlined killer shark. Egon harbored few doubts it remained one of the best fighters in the world.

He reached the runway and turned into takeoff position. With the nose pitched upward, Egon, from the cramped, uncomfortable cockpit, could see nothing but sky straight ahead. He had to constantly peer out to his left and right through the armored windscreen to make certain of his track on the ground.

He revved the engine while he held the brakes on. The roar

of the craft's 1475-horsepower Daimler-Benz motor filled the cockpit. It sounded fit, ready for combat. The plane shook and shimmied, almost as if in anticipation of going to war. He backed off on the throttle and radioed his squadron that takeoff time had come.

He slipped on his goggles, released the brakes, and shoved the throttle forward. The Messerschmitt surged down the runway. The tail lifted and leveled the plane, then the main landing wheels rose from the runway and Egon roared aloft. He looked back to check his flock. To his satisfaction, he spotted the number two fighter already screaming along the runway. It followed him into the air over Elliniko.

One by one, the Messerschmitts lifted into the clear Greek sky and fell into a racetrack pattern, waiting for the entire squadron to become airborne. Once formed up, they separated into two five-plane units, one led by Egon, the other by a young *Oberleutnant* from Hockenheim, near Heidelberg. The kid had gained a bit of air warfare experience on the Eastern Front, and was the only other pilot in the squadron besides Egon who claimed any combat skill at all. None of it, of course, had come against the heavily armed United States Army Air Force airborne battleships such as Liberators or Flying Fortresses.

Egon knew the conflict between his Messerschmitts and the Liberators would be brief but intense and, as *Oberstleutnant* Rödel had warned, deadly. Egon remained concerned that his young aviators, despite their enthusiasm and bravado, would find the learning curve of battle steep and bloody.

They flew toward the island of Kefalonia in two arrowhead-shaped formations. They pressed on to a point ten miles west of the island, climbed to fifteen thousand feet, then began patrolling in elliptical orbits, waiting for the Liberators, waiting for their prey.

They assumed the B-24s would hug the coast, thus had positioned themselves west of Kefalonia, a coastal island, so they could attack out of the sun, hopefully into an enemy blinded by the late-afternoon brilliance.

Egon had briefed his men that he and his five planes would initiate the assault, mounting an attack from above on the flanks of the Liberators. The second group of five would hang back and wait for the Americans to become preoccupied—hopefully —with the initial wave of Messerschmitts. Then they would pounce. A simple plan, but sometimes the simplest schemes fostered the best results. The bomber crews had to be exhausted, demoralized, and wounded, not to mention short on ammo and functioning engines. In other words, not up for a running battle with Germany's best fighter aircraft.

Over the Ionian Sea southwest of Corfu
August 1, 1943

Oregon Grinder labored past the island of Corfu and turned south, following the same track they'd used earlier in the day flying northward. Well ahead of them, Al could make out an ad hoc formation of about a dozen Liberators, many in various states of necrosis, limping toward Benghazi. He longed to join them—safety in numbers—but he knew they still had hundreds of miles to go traversing the Mediterranean Sea, and that *Oregon Grinder* had no chance of making it that far since her fuel loss continued unabated. Not only that, but with one engine already kaput—curious that a German-derived term applied—they lacked the power to catch up to the planes in front of them anyhow.

Al planned to limp along to the rear of the loose formation as a distant Tail End Charlie, then peel off and plough west once they reached the latitude of Sicily.

Below *Oregon Grinder*, the gentle, ultramarine swells of the Ionian Sea rolled southward beneath an azure sky speckled with ice cream scoops of puffy cumulus. All in all, it seemed a strange, bucolic setting, an ironic counterpoint to the death and destruction that Al sensed lurked nearby. The Germans were not going to allow them free passage home. The battle would continue.

"Keep a sharp eye, guys," he said into the interphone. "We're over bandit waters now."

They cruised on for another ten minutes, leveling out at four thousand feet.

The warning came over the command channel from one of the bombers out in front of *Oregon Grinder*. "Fighters at three o'clock, straight into the sun."

The loose formation of Liberators tightened up.

From his vantage point well to the rear of the incipient battle, Al spotted the Messerschmitts high and to the right in two groups of five. They didn't attack immediately, merely cruised parallel to the fleeing bombers.

"Why aren't they attacking, Pops?" It sounded like Sergeant McGregor from his top turret position.

"Don't know. Maybe they're sizing up the Liberators, figuring out how to attack."

Egon held his fighters out of gun range of the B-24s. He wouldn't launch the assault until the fuel in the Messerschmitts' auxiliary tanks had been sucked dry.

On the thick armored glass of the Bf 109's windscreen, he had taped a photograph of Inge and Christa. It had been taken at Zell's annual *weinfest* just prior to Christa's fourth birthday, before the war, before death fell from the sky, before hunger ravaged the German people. He lifted his right hand to his lips, kissed his fingertips, then pressed them to the picture. *"Liebe Inge, Liebe Christa,"* he whispered. *"Euch noch einmal werde ich wiedersehen?"* Will I ever see you again?

He studied his foe below. He'd already chosen his target, an old warhorse in the middle of the refugee flight, a Liberator with one prop feathered and trailing smoke from the number-two engine. For the other pilots in his group, he'd selected targets that appeared even more badly wounded—top turrets out of commission, tail guns destroyed, waist positions blasted out—in hopes his young warriors wouldn't be shot from the sky on their first combat run.

As always, he refused to put faces on the men inside the opposition aircraft. He viewed them only as part of a war machine trying to kill Germans. They had no backstories, no families, no hopes or dreams. They were the enemy. That was all. That was enough. Prey.

He raised his arm, signaling his fellow pilots to prepare to attack. He activated the Messerschmitt's command channel and called out, *"Jetzt."* The fighters jettisoned their belly tanks. Egon rolled his plane toward the bombers and dove at full power, targeting their flanks. His young aviators followed, two on either side of him, each aiming for their assigned bomber.

The shattering bellow of the Bf 109's engine inundated Egon's senses as he jammed the throttle full forward and plunged toward his quarry. Halfway down, without looking and using automatic reflexes honed by many battles, he reached for and grasped the switch that armed his weapons—a prop-hub thirty-millimeter cannon, two nose-mounted thirteen-millimeter machine guns, and two underwing twenty-millimeter cannons. The glow of a red light confirmed the success of his action.

Al, from his distant vantage point to the rear of the planes, watched the battle develop. The Liberator gunners, well trained and many battle experienced, waited until the Messerschmitts were within a thousand yards before opening fire. The gap between the bombers and fighters became thick with fifty-caliber tracers.

The *Luftwaffe* pilots replied with machine guns and cannons. What appeared to be the lead Messerschmitt hammered a Liberator with heavy fire, leaving it with two engines in flame and the right vertical stabilizer shot away. The bomber sank toward the sea in a trail of smoke.

Another Messerschmitt, smoking and shedding parts, screamed directly through the formation of B-24s. The pilot bailed out. The fighter exploded. A parachute blossomed and drifted toward the vast expanse of water below.

Egon raked his chosen Liberator with machine-gun and cannon fire from tail to nose. The top of one of the vertical stabilizers blew off. Both of the engines on the right wing burst into flame.

One enemy kill closer to an Iron Cross.

He snapped the 109 into a vertical climb, the g-forces pinning him against his seat, and glanced back over his shoulder. The bomber, still flying but sinking fast, followed a trajectory toward the sea.

He watched as another Messerschmitt piloted by a rookie aviator got his nose a bit low and missed a B-24 with his cannon volley. The fighter zoomed beneath the plane and came back into Egon's view with flames and smoke jetting from its engine. The pilot bailed out. The 109 exploded.

"Unerfahrenheit," Egon muttered. Inexperience.

He swiveled his head in the other direction just in time to see a second fighter plunge steeply into the sea, leaving only a vertical column of smoke in its wake.

The fucking Thousand-year Reich. It leaves its young men with only thousand-second life spans.

Egon joined his remaining flock, seven aircraft plus his own, and led them in for a second pass at the flanks of the Liberators.

Al heard as much as saw the fury of the second attack—the command channel filled with frantic radio calls from the besieged Liberators. "Fighters everywhere." "We're burning—going down." "Too many, too many!" "We're hit—bailing out." It seemed unlikely any of the fleeing B-24s would make it home. A profound sense of sadness mixed with anger wrapped itself around him and bore into his soul.

"Let's fall back even more and drop lower," Al said over the interphone. "We can't help those poor bastards ahead of us, and they can't help us. Maybe the damned Germans are so focused on them they won't notice us." He hated saying it, hated hoping that the assault on other American aircrews might save his own, but it came down to that simple fact of war, that simple fact of survival.

Oregon Grinder slid lower over the sea surface and reduced its speed to just above stalling.

"We're far enough south we can take up a course for Sicily now," George said over the interphone.

"Good," Al said. "That'll put a little more distance between us and the fighters, too." A glimmer of hope lit up deep within him. Maybe they had a chance.

He and Vivian banked the plane toward the right and set it on a westward track.

"I'm comin' home, Al Junior, I'm comin' home," he said softly.

Vivian seemed to read his lips and gave him a thumbs-up.

"You, too, young lady," he said loudly, "you're goin' home, too."

He hoped to God he could keep his promise.

"Keep a sharp lookout," he announced over the interphone. "The bandits could still spot us, but they gotta be running low on fuel."

Egon climbed away from the second engagement. He knew his fighters had to be nearing the end of their avgas supplies. As he climbed, he radioed commands to his squadron.

"Don't form back up. Attack from your current positions. It'll save fuel and confuse the enemy. Keep an eye on your fuel gauge. Once it hits half-full, break off and head back to Kalamaki."

He checked his own gauge. The needle quivered just above the half-full mark. Enough for one final pass. He picked out a Liberator with a smoking engine and launched his attack, aiming for the top of the bomber where the wings joined the fuselage, the B-24's Achilles' heel.

He triggered his weapons. The bomber returned fire, orange and white tracers screaming toward him from the waist and top turret positions. Over the yowl of the Messerschmitt's engine, a sharp "crack" reverberated through the cockpit. The armored glass on the left side of the cockpit exploded into a prism of spiderwebs. Egon rolled away from his target and climbed.

Far below, yet another 109 shot a geyser of fire and water into the air as it plunged into the ocean. Several other Messerschmitts scooted eastward, away from the conflict, low on fuel and running for home. The Liberator he'd hit shuddered and began to lose altitude, descending rapidly toward the blue-green Ionian swells.

Egon checked for battle damage beyond his maimed canopy glass. Miraculously, none. But he knew the time had come—low on fuel and low on ammo—to head for Kalamaki.

Just as he banked toward home, a call came in on his radio from another 109.

"Got a straggler down near the sea surface trying to give us the slip. Looks like he's heading for Sicily. I'm going after him."

Egon swept his gaze over the vast expanse of water below him. After several seconds he spotted his fellow *Luftwaffe* airman and the Liberator off to his right, a couple of miles distant. The Army green bomber, meaning it originally had flown missions out of England, appeared to be struggling. The Messerschmitt pursued it, the pilot setting up his attack from above and to the left of the B-24.

Egon debated joining the assault, but decided to allow one of his youngsters to claim a solo kill. He held his position and watched as the 109 dove toward the lumbering B-24.

22

Over the Ionian Sea
August 1, 1943

"Bandit, bandit!" The shout over the interphone startled Al. Vivian turned, stared wide-eyed at him.

"Where?" Al yelled. Alarm filled his voice. He thought they'd verged on a clean escape.

"High on our six, a little left. Single bandit."

Al pivoted in his seat, trying to spot the attacker over his left shoulder. Couldn't.

"I'm gonna bank right, give the waist a better field of fire." He and Vivian turned the plane to allow the left-side waist gunner a wider arc of fire. No need to shoot the left vertical stabilizer apart, too, with half the right one already gone.

The tail, left waist, and top turret positions opened up on the Messerschmitt simultaneously. The ball turret remained inactive since its gunner, Stumpy, had taken over the right waist position for the badly wounded Chippy. The rattle of the fifty-caliber machine guns resonated through the interior of the bomber, joining the clamor of the thundering engines.

"Here he comes," someone shouted over the interphone.

Oregon Grinder vibrated as violently as if a giant hand had swatted it. Shrapnel ricocheted around the cockpit as a cannon round sliced diagonally through the top of the bomber, carving a gaping hole in the aluminum top just to the rear of Al and Vivian. Al heard Sergeant McGregor scream and knew without looking the sergeant and the top turret position had been obliterated.

At the same time, a burst of machine gun fire from the fighter blew apart the number two engine just left of where Al sat. Something speared into his left upper arm, jolting it into numbness.

"Jesus," he yelled. "Jesus!"

He flexed his arm, making certain it still worked. It did. The numbness morphed into searing pain. Blood soaked his sleeve. But adrenaline kept him functioning, able to ignore the wound.

He glanced at Vivian. A piece of metal had knifed into the side of her temple. She bled profusely, but kept wiping the flow from her eyes as she battled to hold *Oregon Grinder* steady. The plane, now flying on only two engines and losing power, wobbled toward the water.

The Messerschmitt roared just over the top of the B-24. Al and Vivian leveled the wings of the bomber. Al whipped his head to the right, spotted the 109, saw that at least one of *Oregon Grinder's* gunners had nailed it. The fighter appeared fully engulfed in bright orange flames and tar black smoke. The pilot tumbled from the blazing plane, but his parachute, also ablaze, failed him. Arms and legs flailing in frantic desperation, the German plunged into the sea like a human torpedo.

Egon watched the death dive of his fellow aviator from above. A mixture of anger and sorrow flooded through him. Anger at the Americans, sorrow over the death of yet another young pilot. *Lack of experience again? Or does your luck just eventually run out regardless of how skilled an aviator you might be? Does fate overwhelm everything in the end?*

Damn this war. Damn the Third Reich. He knew the *Wehrmacht* no longer fought for the glory of the Reich, but merely for the survival of the German people.

He throttled back and studied the battle-riddled bomber. It bore so many holes in its fuselage it looked like a perforated sausage. Or a chunk of flying Swiss cheese. Only two props continued to turn. Part of a vertical stabilizer had been shot away, as had the right wing tip. A wire or cable of some sort clung to a tail fin, fluttering in the B-24's slip stream like a tattered battle standard. A filament of a battle standard, anyhow. Like the plane itself, there didn't appear to be much to it.

Another thing he noticed, the crippled Liberator pissed fuel like an *Oktoberfest* celebrant who'd swilled too much beer. He marveled the craft remained airborne. It obviously had no chance of making it to Sicily, or wherever it might be bound. It would end up in the sea. But perhaps he could hasten its demise. Another kill. More enemy dead. Revenge for his fellow aviators. Revenge for Köln and Bremen and Berlin and Hamburg. Still— he hated to admit it—he harbored a grudging admiration for the Liberator's crew. But however much he might admire them— their daring, their bravery, their skill—they remained the enemy.

He had enough ammo for one pass. But not enough gas to attack *and* get back to Kalamaki. He needed to make a decision. *Is a Bf 109 worth sacrificing if I take down a B-24 and its crew?* He made his choice and eased the Messerschmitt abeam of the Liberator just out of range of its fifty-cals, seeing if he could draw fire, seeing if he could determine which gun positions were still operable. Some, he knew, had probably been destroyed or were out of ammo. If so, he could build the tactics of his attack around that knowledge.

But the bomber didn't fire. That meant either well-disciplined gunners, waiting for the Messerschmitt to creep closer, or that its guns had burned through all their ammo. He could see the top turret had been destroyed, and that cracks spiderwebbed the armored glass in the tail position where the guns pointed down, not at him.

"Bandit, nine o'clock, level!" The call came from Sergeant Reeser, Ned, who manned the left waist gun. "And big trouble. I'm down to only about a dozen rounds." Enough for a single quick burst.

"Right waist. Nothing at all left here."

Al stared at the Messerschmitt running parallel to them over a thousand yards to the left. It seemed in no hurry to attack, so its pilot must have resigned himself to the fact he didn't have enough fuel left to make it home.

"What's he doing?" Vivian asked. Her bleeding had stopped, but the side of her face had become swollen and purple where the shrapnel had smashed into her.

"Sizing us up, figuring out the best way to bring us down. Bastard." Al's arm throbbed in nonstop waves of pain, but he refused to loosen his grip on the wheel. *Oregon Grinder's* shaking verged on violent and it continued to lose altitude. The fuel leak had turned from a spray into a gusher. He knew the old gal didn't have long to live. He considered jettisoning everything possible—ammo boxes, oxygen bottles, fire extinguishers, machine guns, even the ball turret, though that would take time

—to stay aloft, but realized it would forestall the inevitable by only a matter of minutes.

He squeezed his eyes shut, thought again about the son he'd never seen—might never see—and issued a silent, sardonic snort about the reason he'd decided to become an Army aviator. At the time he'd made his choice, he thought being a pilot might be the best way to exert a modicum of control over his destiny. But he realized now, the vagaries of war overwhelmed everything. In matters of life and death, he had control over nothing. He could try, would try, to dodge the Grim Reaper, not only for himself, but for his men and Vivian. But in the end, it all came down to a roll of the dice. He'd seen too much death to believe otherwise.

He pressed his throat mike. "Gentlemen"—he paused and shot a glance at Vivian—"and lady, I'm proud to have served with you. Words can't express the respect and admiration you've earned. You've fought bravely and honorably. I doubt there exists a finer crew in the Army Air Force. But we can't fly any longer. It's time to leave. I can keep this thing in the air for a few more minutes, long enough for everyone to bail out. Go out through the bomb bay. Make sure you take the life rafts. Hopefully there are American or British ships nearby that will pick us up."

"Won't the German shoot us in our 'chutes?" Vivian shouted at Al.

"The *Luftwaffe* doesn't have that reputation," Al yelled back. "We'll be okay."

"Sir, Stumpy here. We can't move Chippy. It'll kill him. He's barely alive now."

"Leave him here. I'll try to ditch. But the rest of you, get out!" Al knew ditching a B-24 constituted suicide, but maybe he'd get lucky. Whatever, he had no intention of abandoning a wounded comrade. He had his doubts about Rhett, the tail gunner, too. At the very least, the kid had to have suffered a severe concussion.

"Rabbi here, Pops. Kenny and I have discussed it. We've made our decision. We're sticking with you. We're a team, remember?"

"Damn it, you guys. That Messerschmitt out there will likely knock us out of the sky before I have a chance to get us in the drink. We've nothing left to fight with."

"He doesn't know that."

"He'll figure it out real quick."

"Let's make him work for his kill, then."

"Stumpy here. I'm with Rabbi and Kenny. I'm stickin' around."

"Ned here. I'm not goin' no place, neither."

Al looked directly at Vivian.

"I don't believe in jumping out of airplanes," she said. "Besides, in for a dime, in for a dollar."

Al hadn't heard from Rhett in the tail, so had to assume he might have passed out again.

"So what do you know about ditching B-24s . . . assuming we get the chance?" Al said to Vivian.

"Not much. Only what I've read and heard. Kind of like how I knew to try using parachutes as drag chutes when I landed without hydraulics."

"That worked out okay."

She shrugged. "So you think I can get lucky twice?"

"Given that we have no other options, yes."

She flashed a quick smile, then pointed out the windscreen past Al. "Our German friend is still watching us."

———

With the Liberator's top turret fifty-cals out of the game, and likely the tail guns, too, Egon decided to attack from the rear and above and shoot for the wing root, where the wing joined the fuselage. If he could sever the wing, the bomber would become a lead sled.

He peeled off and climbed, circling back to get behind and above the wounded bomber as it staggered along like a drunken dinosaur . . . a relic of the past.

He knew he could make quick work of it and maybe still have enough gas left to get back to the Greek coast. Kalamaki was out. But he might be able to at least reach land.

The fighter climbed away from *Oregon Grinder* and executed a one hundred and eighty-degree turn.

"He's leaving us," Vivian yelled, optimism and excitement infusing her voice. "Maybe he's running on empty. Or out of ammo."

"He'll be back," Al retorted. "If he were down to zero gas or ammo, he wouldn't have bothered spending time studying us. Now he knows how he wants to kill us."

"Oh." The word came out freighted with defeat and fear.

"Okay, guys," Al said, "the bandit will attack our six from above. He knows the top turret is gone, and I'm guessing he probably figures the tail guns are no threat, either." He paused, then called Rhett in the tail position once more, but again got no response, confirming his worst fear.

"So, no tail weapons. That means all we've got left are a few rounds in the left waist. But I've got a half-assed plan. We can at least go down fighting."

"Let's hear it, Pops." It sounded like George.

"Stumpy, Ned, you guys in the waist positions will have the best chance of spotting the Kraut when he comes after us again.

Holler at me when he starts his attack. He knows we're wounded and can't fight, so he'll shed speed and try to keep us under fire as long as he can.

"There's a big ole cumulus up ahead, just off to our right. Viv and I can't make any fancy turns, but I think we can make it into that cloud before he fires. It'll be risky, but we'll drop the flaps and landing gear when we get in there and see if we can dump enough speed the bastard will lose us and blow right on by."

Risky didn't begin to describe the maneuver. Even now they verged on stalling. If they slowed too much more, *Oregon Grinder* would become a cannonball. Not that it wouldn't anyhow.

Al continued speaking, but realized his voice must sound as if it were wrapped in barbed wire. "When we pop out of the cloud, we'll roll slightly right and try to give the left waist a more open field of fire. If you spot the bandit, Ned, blast him."

"Yes, sir."

Then, "Here he comes, Pops. On our six, about two miles back."

Al and Vivian pivoted *Oregon Grinder* toward the white mass of cloud.

23

Over the Ionian Sea
August 1, 1943

Oregon Grinder shimmied and rattled even more as it plunged into the towering cumulus. A thick, gray mist swallowed the plane. More than that. The bomber, half shot to pieces, had become a sieve—the swirling fog invaded the interior, as well.

In the cloud, the visibility dropped to zero. Al focused his eyes on the artificial horizon indicator on the instrument panel, making sure he held the aircraft in level flight.

As quickly as they had entered the cloud, they popped out, back into sudden, brilliant sunlight. He and Vivian retracted the landing gear, lifted the flaps, and shoved the throttles forward to keep from stalling. And, as planned, they banked the B-24 a smidgen to the right, just in case the left waist gunner, Ned, had an opportunity to fire one last volley.

Egon had seen the maneuver before. Run and hide in a cloud.

He watched the bomber disappear, but didn't pursue it. He throttled back and turned away from the cumulus. He remained on its periphery and tried to gauge where the Liberator would exit. If he guessed correctly, it would be an easy surprise kill.

"*Ja,*" he exclaimed, as the bomber burst from the cloud, a bit below him and slightly to his right. But the craft had shed speed and he found himself, much to his chagrin, virtually abeam of it —an awkward position from which to attack, since a fighter carries only forward-firing weapons.

Before he could register his foe's intention, the bomber rolled slightly right and the fifty-caliber machine gun in the waist position swung in his direction. A short stream of tracers burst from its muzzle and swept toward him.

"*Scheisse,*" he cried—shit—and jammed the stick and throttle forward, attempting to dive away from the American's ambush. But too late. At least one round smashed into the fighter's nose just to the rear of the engine. A thin stream of black, viscous liquid erupted from where the shell had struck. It slithered back along the side of the aircraft.

Oil tank. At least the volley had spared the engine. Not that it would last long without oil. He glanced at the oil gauge. The needle quivered, but didn't yet indicate a loss of pressure. He still had some fight left, time for one last pass, one final opportunity to bring down an enemy that wouldn't abandon the battle.

He yanked back on the stick, climbed, and turned, intending to counterattack. The machine gun burst that had struck his plane had been strangely brief, so he guessed that had been the bomber's last hurrah, its final rounds of ammo. For all practical purposes, it had become an unarmed Zeppelin. It would be no more of a challenge now than routine target practice.

"I got 'im, I got 'im," Ned screamed over the interphone.

The Messerschmitt had been positioned dead even with *Oregon Grinder* as it blew out of the cloud. Al had been as surprised as he guessed the 109's pilot had been. The ploy of reducing speed appeared to have worked, for the German had found himself in no position to attack. In fact, he had inadvertently placed himself in a momentarily defenseless situation.

At least one round from Ned's short burst found its mark. Sparks flew from the fighter's fuselage just to the rear of the engine. A thin stream of oil followed, snaking back along the side of the aircraft. But the wound hadn't been catastrophic. The Messerschmitt continued to fly.

"God loves fools and fighter pilots," Al muttered. A P-40 jockey had once told him that after bailing out over occupied Belgium and landing near a farm house full of resistance fighters.

The Bf 109 peeled away from *Oregon Grinder* and climbed. Al knew it would be back. And next time it would be met with no resistance. To make matters worse, there seemed not even enough time to ditch before the bandit returned.

Al's innards churned. He'd failed to get his crew to safety. He clenched his jaw in anger and a sense of defeat. The thought of never having held his child bordered on unbearable. It hollowed out his soul, leaving nothing but a dark, infinite void. He drew a deep breath and sucked in an incongruous mix of odors—fresh sea air, aviation gas, expended ammunition . . . and death.

He got on the interphone. "We're done, guys. We didn't knock the bastard down, so he's coming back for us. Everyone move to the floor near the waist gun windows. I don't think I can ditch before he returns, but in case I can, I want all of you in position to get out once we hit the water. Go out the windows. Well, assuming we don't break up, which we probably will.

Sorry. There's not much structural integrity left in this old bird. Thank you one and all. And Godspeed."

He turned to Vivian. "Get back there with the rest of the guys. I'll stay here and try to land us in the water, assuming we don't get blown to bits before I have a chance."

"No," she said.

"It's an order," he snapped.

"I'm not in the military," she lashed back. "I'm not even here, damnit."

"Vivian, please." Exasperation overwhelmed him.

"You'll need help ditching. I've got some ideas."

Oregon Grinder continued to tremble and quiver. One of its engines—of the two that continued functioning—coughed. Al knew the lifespan of the bomber had dwindled to a matter of seconds. Maybe all of their lifespans had.

Egon pulled a tight turn and brought the fighter in behind the bomber and slightly above it. He reduced his speed, intending to take his time and keep the Liberator under fire as long as he could, or at least until he'd expended all his ammunition.

The irony of the situation struck him. Yes, he'd bring the bomber down, but he'd lose the Messerschmitt, too. He peeked again at the oil pressure gauge. The pressure loss had begun to register. He knew he couldn't remain airborne much longer. He had to attack immediately, then hope the engine would keep cranking long enough to ditch.

He had no intention of bailing out. He knew how unreliable German parachute harnesses were. Constructed of hemp, many snapped or tore once the 'chute deployed, and pilots would plunge to their death. Rumor had it that nylon straps were being developed, but that didn't help now.

He eased back on the throttle a bit more. He leaned forward and framed the crippled, battle-scarred Liberator in his reflector gunsight. He again marveled at how badly it had been wounded yet continued to stay aloft, aloft but losing altitude. It seemed to bear the gashes and fractures of a thousand battles, not just one.

He yanked his head back from the gunsight, blinking. The bomber had inexplicably morphed into something else, a swirling, fuzzy memory from many years past—of a huge hog, an old boar, crippled and limping, making its way across a snowy field high in the *Hunsrück*. Steam jetted from its nostrils as it snorted and glared with malevolence at those who had come to kill it.

Egon sensed his father's presence, felt his hand on his shoulder, heard his brittle voice as if issuing from a time-warped echo chamber. The same words he'd heard on the *Hunsrück* that bleak December day reverberated through the cacophony filling the cockpit. "Don't shoot him. He's an old warrior. Let him live. Honor his service and bravery."

But Egon had decided on his response. It would be no different now from what it had been fifteen years earlier. "*Nein, Papa.* He challenged us. I will answer that. I, too, am a warrior." *Am I? Or just a murderer?*

He flicked the unexpected, unwelcome conflict from his thoughts.

No. I'm a warrior to the end.

He squeezed his eyes shut briefly to clear his vision, then sighted in once more on the B-24. He intended to walk his cannon fire from tail to nose, from between the bomber's twin vertical stabilizers forward to the armored glass that cocooned his counterparts.

He rested his forefinger on the cannon's firing button on the top of the control column as he drifted the Messerschmitt into position.

"Take your time," he cautioned himself.

Without warning, the benevolent ghosts of years past reached out to him again, like Lorelei, the mythical temptress of the Rhine. Only this time they rode the swirling currents of the air, not those of the river. A siren song mingled with the growling whine of the fighter's engine and beckoned him back to bucolic times before the inanity of war, before bombs and bullets and hunger and death. It called him back to a life filled with the tinkling laughter of his daughter Christa, the sweet, soft words of his wife Inge, the lazy summer wash of the river on the banks of Mosel Valley.

Back to a time that would never return.

Goddamn Adolf Hitler and the Third Reich.

He edged closer to the wounded, staggering Liberator, re-sighting his cannon, his finger caressing the firing button.

———

"He's back," someone growled over the interphone.

Too soon, Al thought. *We don't have a prayer of ditching before the SOB knocks us out of the sky.* There seemed only one option remaining.

"I'm opening the bomb bay doors," Al announced. "Time to bail out. We aren't going to be flying much longer. Even if the bastard doesn't shoot us down, he'll put so many shells into us I doubt I'll have any control left. Jump now. Take Chippy with you. Did somebody check on Rhett?"

"Got 'em, sir," a voice answered. "He's unconscious, but we'll make sure he goes out with the rest of us."

Al looked again at Vivian and flicked his head toward the rear, toward the bomb bay. "Go," he said. "You'll die if you stay here. We aren't going to be able to ditch."

She hesitated, then said, "Are you coming?" A palpable tremor coated her words.

"I'll put it on autopilot. I'll follow you."

She released her seat harness but didn't exit her seat.

"Go," he ordered again.

"Well?" she said.

"Well what?"

"I don't see you putting the autopilot on."

"For Christ's sake, Viv."

"We're still flying. I'm the copilot."

"We aren't going to be flying much longer."

"No one's shooting at us."

"Not yet. We aren't exactly challenging the guy."

A call over the interphone interrupted their back-and-forth. "Stumpy here. Bandit's coming up on our left. Pretty damn close."

Al swiveled to look over his shoulder. The Messerschmitt sat just off *Oregon Grinder's* tail. A slight bank to the right would allow the pilot to guide his cannon fire along the side of the bomber from rear to front, taking his time, making certain he destroyed his enemy.

Al, exhausted and hurting and no longer able to fight, surrendered to his fate . . . and found a strange peace. He studied the fighter as it crept closer and closer. Oil continued to stream along its flank, just above the air intake for the super-charger. An antenna mast and a smaller circular antenna—probably a direction finder—sat on top of the fuselage just to the rear of the cockpit. The rear side of the camouflage-painted fighter displayed a large black German cross. To the rear of the cross, a broad white stripe encircled the fuselage. Al knew the stripe signified the Mediterranean Theater.

Despite his imminent death, he wondered about the Messerschmitt's pilot, the man who would be his Grim Reaper.

Old? Young? Married? Did he have a son? A daughter? Did he believe in God? Worship Hitler?

In another time, another place, would they have sat down together somewhere on a Saturday evening and swilled beer and swapped stories about flying and showed each other pictures of their families?

Al turned to stare straight ahead through the splintered windscreen and await the cannon burst that would seal his fate.

Vivian remained in her seat.

Egon drifted the 109 ever closer to the shell-riddled Liberator. He continued to marvel that it remained aloft—so much damage. Like all American bombers, it bore a colorful logo on its nose. He didn't understand the writing, *Oregon Grinder*, but allowed a smirk to flit across his face at the image of an organ grinder in a top hat with the word "OREGON"—whatever that meant—printed on it, stuffing a fiendish-looking monkey, a cartoon Adolf Hitler, into a meat grinder.

"Ich helfe Dir," Egon muttered. I'll help you. But knew he wouldn't.

He moved the Messerschmitt forward, paralleling the crippled olive-green bomber. He caught a glimpse of a face in the waist gunner's window. Then someone flashed a middle finger at him. Apparently that was all the Americans had left with which to counterattack.

He banked the fighter to the right with a quick flick of his control column, then just as quickly snapped it back to level flight. The face in the window ducked. The obscene gesture disappeared.

Egon maneuvered his fighter into a position just off the Liberator's left wing tip, placing the Messerschmitt's right wing tip several feet below and several feet forward of the bomber's wing. The bomber didn't alter course. It pushed straight ahead, skimming just beneath the scattered, flat-based cumulus dotting the sky, while at the same time continuing to drop inexorably toward the pristine blue-green swells of the Ionian Sea.

Egon glanced at the belly of the bomber and did a double take.

"*Mein Gott,*" he exclaimed. What looked for all the world like a sunflower dangled from a shredded piece of aluminum near the bomb bay. *Had the Americans flown* that *close to the earth?*

A smidgen of the grudging admiration he held for his enemy reignited deep in his psyche.

But he extinguished it, and instead took solace in the knowledge that for this American bomber christened *Oregon Grinder,* the battle had clearly ended.

Curiously, that opened a new memory, one that again came without warning or invitation: the admonition of his commander, *Oberstleutnant* Gustav Rödel. "*There's an unwritten law I like to remind all of my pilots of, Hauptmann. Once you have defeated your opponent, shot him from the sky, victory is yours and the engagement is over. You do not fire on men in parachutes, you do not strafe men on the ground or in the water. You maintain your honor as a Luftwaffe officer. Do I make myself clear?*"

Egon fixed his gaze on the ill-fated bomber. *So, Oregon Grinder, you are an old warrior, perhaps one my father would revere. But you still fly. Your men have not parachuted, though I have no doubt they have been ordered to. And they are not in the water, nor on the ground. Do I blast you from the sky as my enemy, or pay homage to your warrior spirit?*

The conflict knotted and twisted his soul as though it had been seized by a python.

24

Over the Ionian Sea
August 1, 1943

Al held his gaze straight ahead, well aware that the German Messerschmitt sat less than sixty feet off his left shoulder. *Oregon Grinder* continued to quiver and pulsate, its engines seeming to gasp for breath. Al knew he gripped the controls of a brave lady in her final moments.

He thought about praying, but decided he'd used up all his prayers. Besides, he'd lost confidence in the efficacy of petitions to God. Too many planes had fallen from the sky. Too many good men had died. What happened, happened. It seemed, at least in this war, God had ceded control to man.

A call over the interphone: "Hey, Pops. What the hell is that bastard doing? Why doesn't he get it over with?"

"I don't know. I just don't. Maybe he's savoring his kill."

"Maybe the SOB is a sadist. Just wants us to suffer as much as possible before he blows us to Kingdom Come."

Al didn't have an answer. He glanced at Vivian and noticed tears draining down her cheeks. Yet she held grimly onto her control wheel, trying, like Al, to keep *Oregon Grinder* in the air as long as possible.

Al's forearms ached from the fierce grip he'd applied to his own control wheel. His left upper arm throbbed without ceasing where he'd apparently taken a piece of shrapnel in his bicep. Blood continued to leak down his arm, eventually splattering onto the cockpit floor where it left a pattern of dark crimson dots. He considered ramming the fighter, but knew he couldn't move the crippled bomber rapidly enough to surprise the *Luftwaffe* pilot.

No longer able to tolerate, or even understand, the specter of an enemy flying in formation with him, Al turned his head to look directly at the German fighter pilot. A young man, his flight goggles lifted, stared back at him through the Messerschmitt's splintered cockpit glass, a man who had to be no older than himself. Their gazes locked. And held. Neither looked away. Neither smiled nor frowned. Just two kids sizing each other up.

In the fighter, Egon stared at his opponent. It could have been a guy he went hunting with in the *Hunsrück,* or swimming with in the Mosel, or had a beer with in a *Gasthaus.* It could have been his old friend Otto.

He allowed the Messerschmitt to slip back a bit until he could look directly into the waist gunner's window of the B-24. A half dozen faces, all of young men about his own age, stared back at him like baby birds craning their necks from a nest. No obscene gestures this time. Merely curious looks. Without smiling, he nodded at them, then drove the fighter forward again.

Mystified, Al watched the fighter slide back and forth, still running parallel with *Oregon Grinder*. The *Luftwaffe* pilot brought the fighter forward again until he could look directly at Al once more.

This time the German pilot's face seemed to relax ever so slightly and he gave Al a barely perceptible nod. Al, still attempting to sort through his emotions, didn't return it. Instead, he continued to study his opponent, trying to decipher what the guy's end game might be.

What happened next sent a shock wave through Al, as if someone had attached electrodes to the balls of his feet. The Luftwaffe pilot stared directly at Al, then raised his right hand to his temple in a slow, deliberate military salute.

He held it there, apparently waiting for a reaction.

"Jesus, Mary, and Joseph," Al said.

"What?" Vivian asked.

"He's saluting me, us."

"Like last rites?"

"I don't think so. That's not what a salute is for."

Vivian leaned forward to look out past Al at the *Luftwaffe* flyer. "What's it mean?"

"It's a military greeting, a sign of respect."

"He's not going to shoot us down?"

Al paused before answering. The German had been too measured, too deliberate in his actions for them to mean anything other than he'd decided to call their fight a draw.

"No, I don't think he's going to shoot us down." Al, his throat tight with emotion, returned the fighter pilot's salute. They each held their salutes for a moment, then dropped them.

The *Luftwaffe* pilot gestured at himself, then pointed down, at the water. Al assumed that meant he intended to ditch, and nodded his understanding. He wondered why the German didn't bail out, but then he remembered the stories he'd heard about *Luftwaffe* parachute failures.

Al pointed at himself, then down, indicating he, too, intended to attempt a water landing. Well, crash landing. The fighter pilot nodded, then peeled away from the bomber to create some space between the two aircraft as they dropped toward the sea.

Al pressed his throat mike to make sure his crew heard. "The battle is over, gentlemen. Our German 'friend' has declared a truce. We're both going in the drink. Prepare to ditch."

Cheers and shouts mingled with the rattle and roar of the wounded bomber as it continued to sink toward the sea.

"What's the drill, Viv?" Al asked.

Another violent shake rippled through *Oregon Grinder.*

"No pressure, right?" she responded.

"Still time to bail out."

"Yeah, but nobody took you up on the offer."

"It was an order."

"Guess you've got a rebellious crew."

He stared at her.

"Or maybe a loyal one," she said.

He checked the altimeter. They continued to lose altitude. They wobbled along barely a thousand feet above the sea.

"Not much time left," he said.

"Okay, here's what I understand. Land into the wind like always. Except if the water is too rough, try to put her down parallel to the swells."

They both checked the state of the sea below.

"No whitecaps," Al said. "Doesn't look too bad. Just long, low rollers."

"Looks like a light wind out of the north," Vivian said. "So we'll have to turn to a northerly heading."

"Don't know if we've got time to do that before we hit the water."

"Let's try."

They eased *Oregon Grinder* into a long, slow bank.

"What else?" Al asked.

"Full flaps. Absolute minimum speed, just above stalling."

Al figured that meant about a hundred miles per hour, maybe ninety-five.

"But don't let the aircraft pitch up with full flaps," Vivian continued. "We want to maintain a level attitude, like trying to make a three-point landing on the nose wheel and two main wheels, rather than making a normal touch down with the main gear first."

"Roger that," Al responded. "Why?"

"If the tail hits the water first, the theory is the drag will cause the nose to pitch down and smack into the water like a torpedo. Don't want that."

"Okay. Let's leave that maneuver to the Navy flyboys."

They'd managed to get *Oregon Grinder* about halfway through the desired turn. They'd dropped to about five hundred feet above the swells. The two functioning engines began to sputter and miss, presumably on their last few sips of fuel.

"We aren't going to get all the way around to that northerly course," Al said.

"Let's level her out and get this over with then."

They leveled the wings and steadied the bomber's flight.

Al pressed his throat mike. "Okay, this is it, guys. Ditch, ditch, ditch."

Egon held the Messerschmitt about two hundred yards off *Oregon Grinder's* left wing and, in tandem with the bomber, sank toward the sea. The needle on the oil pressure gauge dropped steadily. A stream of smoke shot from the engine. In moments it would be on fire. He feathered the prop, let the fighter glide, and jettisoned the canopy.

He hoped—perhaps fantasized would be a better word—he might get plucked from the water by an Italian warship, but that seemed highly unlikely. With the Allies holding most of Sicily and about to shove Italian and German forces off the island, the Americans and Brits already controlled the seas in this part of the Mediterranean.

Being taken prisoner by the Allies wouldn't be the worst fate in the world—propaganda aside, word of mouth had it they treated *Luftwaffe* pilots humanely—but it would remove him from the fight for his country, something he dearly wanted to continue.

If nothing else, perhaps he would live to see Inge and Christa again, assuming they survived the damned war.

He glanced to his right. The bomber skimmed just above the sea, mere feet from the crests of the gentle swells.

The Messerschmitt, too, sailed barely above the surface, the water now coming up fast. Egon braced for impact. The fighter smacked belly first into the Mediterranean. The nose pitched forward, forcing a cascade of briny ocean into the cockpit. Egon grappled for his safety harness release, found it, snapped it open, yanked the tab on his life preserver inflator, and shot upward through the dark water.

He popped into a sparkling world of sunlit diamonds reflecting, refracting, shimmering on the undulating surface of the sea. Swell after swell rolled over him, filling his mouth, choking him with warm, salty water. He coughed and spit, struggling for air.

Somehow, the fighter hadn't sunk and now floated just feet from him. But its engine boiled in full flame. He feared an explosion and dog-paddled away from it in furious little strokes, at the same time trying to see if he could spot where the bomber had ditched. Perhaps they had life rafts and would pull him aboard. He feared drowning almost as much as burning.

Disoriented, he didn't know where to look, couldn't see any sign of the B-24.

Oregon Grinder's tail gave one last violent shake as the bomber stalled, then thudded into the sea. A violent rending sound mingled with the crashing rush of water surging over the craft. Al sensed the nose of the Liberator tipping forward, preparing to plunge beneath the surface of the ocean. Blackness enveloped the cockpit. Then the plane seemed to level out, but with water filling it, it began to simultaneously sink.

Al released his seat harness, made sure Vivian had done the same. Already waist-deep in water, he stood, pointed back between the seats and up, toward the top of the aircraft.

"Escape hatch," he yelled.

With the sea thundering in through the already-shredded fuselage of the bomber, the rising water lifted them toward the hatch with little effort on their part. Al sprung it open, boosted Vivian out, then followed her. They inflated their life vests and swam away from the sinking Liberator.

"Jesus," Al said. "Where's the rest of the plane?"

The nose section had snapped off forward of the wings. Treading water, he spun in a circle, desperately trying to find the rest of *Oregon Grinder.* Pain wrapped his left arm in what felt like ground glass.

"There," Vivian yelled. "Over there." She pointed fifty yards behind the submerging nose section.

A large swell attacked Al from behind, knocking his face

into the water. He held his breath, lifted his head from the sea, and looked in the direction Vivian had indicated.

The rear two-thirds of *Oregon Grinder,* more or less intact but filling with water, rode the swells. The B-24's crew spilled out the waist gunner's window into the ocean. Several men struggled to pull two inert forms—presumably the unconscious tail gunner, Rhett, and the badly wounded waist gunner, Chippy—through the window to safety before the tail section went to the bottom. One life raft had been inflated, and a second appeared in the process.

Al and Vivian, riding the swells as if aboard a slow-motion roller coaster, paddled toward the crew and rafts, or in military lingo, inflatable dinghies. Al used only his right arm to make intermittent strokes.

Egon finally spotted the dark green vertical stabilizers of the B-24 several hundred yards from where he floated. He glanced back at his sinking fighter. Despite the nose being half underwater, flames and smoke billowed from the engine. It seemed unlikely it would explode, given there couldn't be much fuel or oil left in the plane, but he couldn't be sure. He wanted to get farther away from it.

He set out with determined strokes toward the downed American bomber, wanting to put more distance between himself and the burning fighter, wanting to escape the swells that persisted in their relentless assault on him, driving surges of salty water into his nose and mouth. He sensed his life vest deflating. *The Americans must have life rafts.* He windmilled his arms and kicked harder, driving himself directly into the oncoming rollers and toward his enemy. Former enemy. Ironic —he now viewed them as rescuers.

25

In the Ionian Sea
August 1, 1943

Al and Vivian reached the remainder of *Oregon Grinder's* crew just as its tail section sank below the swells with a loud gurgle and thunderous rush of sea water.

"Did everybody get out?" Al yelled.

George paddled over to Al. "Yes. Except for Stretch, of course. No way we could get his body out of that top turret. There was nothing left of it."

"I know, I know. Fuck it all. How about Chippy, how's he doing?"

George shook his head, looked away, treading water.

"Oh, no," Al said. "Oh, no."

George turned back to Al. "The crash in the water, then pulling him out through the waist—he just stopped breathing. Too damn much trauma, too much blood loss. We got his body into one of the dinghies."

"And Rhett?"

"Got him in a dinghy, too. He's semiconscious. Loopy as a loon, but he's alive."

A big swell lifted Al, George, and Vivian several feet above the surrounding sea.

"Hey, hey, hey," George said. "What's that coming our way?"

About two or three miles distant to the west, a ship, heeled over and coming hard, smoke from its stacks flattened in the wind, bore down on them.

Al wiped the salt water from his eyes and squinted, trying to identify the vessel. He and George and Vivian sank into the trough following the swell, then rose again as the next crest reached them.

"Looks like a British corvette," Al said.

It didn't appear to have the sleekness or speed of an American destroyer, but it plowed through the sea at a determined rate, close to twenty miles per hour Al guessed.

"Lordy, I'm glad it's one of ours," Vivian said. Her left temple had turned the color of a plum, but she seemed to be functioning just fine.

"Holy shit," George exclaimed. He pointed to the left of the corvette and much closer to them at a small form stroking determinedly through the swells in their direction.

"I'll be damned," Al said, "it's the German pilot. Guess he made it down, too."

"What do we do," George said, "take him prisoner?"

"Hell no, he could have shot us down, but didn't. I think I'll give the SOB a big hug."

The German, now maybe a little over a hundred yards away, lifted a hand in greeting, or so it seemed, then continued his resolute course toward the Americans. He gagged and spit seawater as he battled his way directly into the teeth of the relentless swells, making only slow progress.

Egon's arms and legs felt like those of a rag doll. He didn't know how much longer he could paddle and keep his head above water. His life vest had totally deflated. He'd never spent much time swimming in an ocean, and the effort he'd exerted over the past few minutes had taken an extreme toll. He stopped and rested, allowing the swells to carry him up and down.

He spotted at least two life rafts among the downed American flyers, although several men remained in the water. There appeared to be at least one inert form—a deceased crew member?—the men in the raft had tugged in with them. Egon wondered if they would take revenge on him for that.

It didn't matter. That option had to be better than drowning. He gathered himself for a final, resolute drive toward the Americans. He drew a deep breath and plunged forward, like a man assaulting an enemy position. Do or die.

Al and George remained in the water with Vivian, watching the British corvette and tracking the approaching German. The British vessel had drawn close enough Al could make out the sailors on deck, rushing about, making preparations to pull them from the water. Something else, too.

"Oh, shit, no," Al yelled. Twin fifty caliber machine guns on the ship's bridge swung toward the German.

Al snapped his head around to look at the *Luftwaffe* pilot. He plowed through the water with a renewed fierceness, swimming directly toward them, almost as if in an attack mode. Al realized that was probably all the Brits saw.

He porpoised from the water, leaping, waving both arms over his head, ignoring the pain that lanced through his wounded arm. "No, no, no," he screamed at the sailors manning the gun.

The rattle of the fifty calibers reverberated across the sea surface as the Brits opened fire.

"No, you bastards, goddamnit no," Al bellowed. "Stop. Cease fire, cease fire." But the gunfire and wash of the swells swallowed his words.

A trail of watery stalagmites erupted from the ocean's surface as the gunfire swept toward the German.

———

Something with the force of a sledgehammer pounded into Egon's chest and left arm and sent a shock wave of pain surging through his body. He stopped swimming and allowed himself merely to float, riding the up-and-down motion of the swells. Sea water flowed into his mouth. The sunlight dimmed and he felt himself slipping away into a fathomless gray fog.

He attempted to kick, to move his legs through the water, but couldn't remember why, only that he'd been doing it and had a destination in mind. Now, however, he had no idea what the goal had been. The swirling grayness tightened around him, grasping at his shoulders, speaking a strange language.

———

After a short, furious swim, Al and George reached the German with Vivian not far behind. Blood pooled around the *Luftwaffe* aviator and Al realized the man had taken a likely fatal hit. He and George grabbed the officer underneath his shoulders and lifted his head from the sea.

The British ship drifted to a stop about a hundred yards from them. Al could see a life boat being lowered on a davit.

The *Luftwaffe* pilot stared at his American rescuers with incomprehending eyes as blood spread out in the water around him, an expanding dark stain.

"Hang in there, partner, hang in there," Al said. "We'll get you help."

Vivian stripped off her Mae West, ripped off her blouse, and jammed it against the German's chest wound. Not an easy task in the endless train of heaving rollers.

The German seemed to be trying to focus on the figures around him.

"Was ist passiert?" he said, his speech slurred.

Al, George, and Vivian looked at one another.

"Do you understand German?" Al asked George.

"A little. My grandparents came from Germany. I think he asked what happened."

"Tell him he got shot, but it was an accident. We'll take care of him. We're his friends."

George seemed to struggle to find the correct German words. *"Ein Unfall. Du wurdest erschossen. Wir werden uns um dich kümmern. Wir sind deine Freunde."*

"Freunde?" the wounded pilot mumbled.

"Jawohl. Deine Freunde."

Al stared into the half-closed eyes of the young German he held, realizing he seemed no different than any of the hundreds of men he'd dealt with in the American bomber force over the past few years.

"Tell him thank you for not shooting us down. For being an honorable man. We offer our respect to him."

George nodded, and spoke to the *Luftwaffe* officer in a soft but stumbling voice.

"Damn Limeys," Al muttered. "Why in the hell did they have to shoot him?"

"He was swimming our way pretty hard," George said. "They

probably thought he was going to attack us."

"Fucking morons," Al snapped.

The life boat from the corvette had reached the water and now bobbed in place as it waited for the British sailors to board it.

Al and George continued to hold the German as they rode the never-ending swells. Vivian pushed her blouse, now blood-soaked, ever harder against the jagged wound that had been torn in the pilot's chest.

"We should find out his name," Al said.

George nodded and spoke. *"Wie heißen Sie, mein Herr, dein Name und Rang?"*

The pilot stared without answering. Al didn't know if he'd heard, or even understood the question.

"Ask again. Tell him your name."

George did.

This time the German answered, though he struggled to speak. Al and George persisted in their efforts to hold his head above the water, to prevent the sea from washing into his mouth.

"Luftwaffe Hauptmann Egon Richter, *Jagdgeschwader 27,"* he gasped, then winced in pain.

"Ask where he's from," Al said, "where he lived in Germany."

They waited for the fighter pilot to answer. It took a while. Then he spoke only two words in a wheezing, whistling breath. "Zell. Mosel." His eyes rolled back in his head.

"Come on, Captain Richter," Al urged. "Don't go. Don't leave us. Hang in there. Help is coming." He attempted to make his words soothing, but knew they probably sounded desperate.

"Bleib bei uns, bleib bei uns, Egon," George whispered to the German. Stay with us.

The fighter pilot's eyes repositioned themselves and seemed

to focus on Vivian, who continued to squeeze her blouse against his chest. He attempted to lift his arms as if to embrace her.

"*Liebe Inge, Liebe Christa,*" he whispered. "*Ich liebe dich über alles.*"

Vivian, her face masked in despair, looked at George. "What's he saying?"

George shook his head. Despair. "I think he thinks you're his wife, or mother, or daughter. I don't know. He's saying how much he loves you."

Vivian's eyes welled with tears. She leaned forward and pressed her face against his. "Don't die, please don't die," she said. "You saved us. You don't deserve this."

The German's breathing slowed, coming in long, shallow gasps. He seemed to smile.

"Otto," he said, "Otto. *Ich komme, alter Freund.*"

The grayness, like a flannel mist, lifted and parted. In a shaft of brilliant light, Egon saw his old friend Otto waiting for him on a high, rolling meadow in the *Hunsrück,* a place where they'd hunted together so often as boys.

"Otto," Egon exclaimed, "Otto. I'm coming, old friend."

He strode toward his longtime companion, a man he'd looked up to and loved like a brother. Otto reached out to him. They embraced.

A large swell lifted the German and three Americans upward much higher than the previous rollers had. The *Luftwaffe* pilot tipped his head skyward and drew one last, long breath. His eyes slid shut and his head fell forward, his chin coming to rest against his chest.

"No, oh, no. Don't let him go, God." But Al knew God *had* let him go, and that his entreaty had come too late, or maybe just been ignored. War, after all, was the result of the idiocy of men, not the creation of God. Al understood, too, it could have been any one of them, himself, George, Vivian, that lay dead in the sea. Yet the vagaries, the unfairness, the cruelness of war had claimed an honorable man who, in the heat of battle, had spared his enemy.

Al squeezed his eyes shut, feeling tears track down his cheeks, mingling with the splash of Ionian Sea water and the blood of a German fighter pilot.

He opened his eyes to see George place a hand on the *Luft-waffe* officer's head and say in a soft voice, "*Sh'ma Yisra'eil Adonai Eloheinu Adonai echad.*"

"What was that?" Al asked, his voice raspy with emotion. "What did you say?"

"It's called the Shema." George continued to tread water while he held the German. "It's a sort of prayer we would say for a dying friend. 'Hear O Israel, the Lord our God, the Lord is One.'"

Al gazed at the dead pilot. "I wonder if he was a Nazi?" He paused, then said, "And I wonder if he knew he was being comforted in his dying moments by a Jew?"

"Nazi or not, I don't think it would have mattered to him if he'd known. All he knew was he was among people, fellow warriors, who cared for him."

Vivian, her eyes filled with tears, released the German and

drifted away from him on her back. "Sorry, sorry, sorry," she kept repeating.

"Strange," Al said, "here we are, mourning for an enemy as much or more as for our own."

"Maybe," George responded. "But except for him—Egon was his name, remember—we probably wouldn't be mourning at all."

The British launch reached them. Several sailors spilled into the sea to help the American airmen.

A large swell, the final one in a parade of big rollers, lifted the trio of Americans and the German fighter pilot skyward into the bright, warming rays of the Mediterranean sun.

26

Benghazi, Libya
August 10, 1943

Al settled into a creaky wooden chair in the tent of the Circus's new commander, Colonel Leland Fiegel, a spare but well-liked aviator from Minnesota. He had assumed command after the loss of Lieutenant Colonel Baker in Ploesti. Fiegel sat across from Al behind a desk that looked as war weary as some of the B-24s. The usual heat and sand of the desert had invaded the interior of the tent, but after what the Benghazi bomb groups had been through, such discomforts seemed trivial.

"I can't tell you how good it is to have you and your crew back," Fiegel said. "But I'm sorry about your casualties."

"Thank you, sir."

"Right after the raid, we thought we'd lost you. A couple of Libs that struggled back here said the last they saw of *Oregon Grinder* it was heading west, barely flying, and about to be pounced on by a couple of Messerschmitts. I gather you were trying to make it to Malta or Sicily."

"Sicily was our only hope. We were running on fumes, and quite frankly probably weren't even going to make it that far."

"According to the report we got from UK naval forces, you and a 109 shot each other down over the Ionian Sea, then a British corvette showed up and came to your rescue. Good thing, too, because apparently"—Fiegel peered at some papers on his desk—"the German pilot wasn't finished with you and was continuing his assault in the water."

Fiegel looked up from the papers.

Al drew a deep breath before speaking.

"That wasn't quite the case, sir."

"Oh. What was the case?"

Al told him, told him how the German fighter pilot had opted not to shoot *Oregon Grinder* out of the sky, how he'd been swimming toward them after ditching—but not in a threatening manner—how the Brits had opened up on him with their fifty calibers.

"Just before the Limeys opened fire," Al said, "the German raised his arm as if greeting us. I think all he wanted to do was get out of the water. He must have seen our life rafts. And the corvette. I doubt he ever thought they'd shoot him."

Fiegel sat in silence for a while, tapping a pencil softly on his desk. Finally he said, "Quite a story."

"You don't believe it?"

"You've no reason to lie. But it's probably a story that shouldn't go beyond you and me and your crew."

"Sir?" Al didn't understand. It seemed to him that the tale of a *Luftwaffe* fighter pilot who'd spared his American enemy should be a headline maker.

"While it's a great story," Fiegel responded, "one of bravery and honor and compassion, it's one that would probably be better left untold until after the war is over. Couple of reasons. First, it might give American bomber crews a false sense of hope that in similar situations there might be other German pilots who would act the same way. I seriously doubt that's the case, so it would be a dangerous mindset to harbor.

"Second, we should probably think about the German, too, or at least his family. You know, wife, children, mother, father, brother, sister, whatever. It wouldn't take much for the *Luftwaffe* to figure out who the pilot involved was, and once they did it could get really ugly for anyone connected to him, even in his military chain of command. The Gestapo and SS aren't exactly your friendly local sheriffs." Fiegel shook his head slowly, as if envisioning a firing squad or brutal prison camp.

Al nodded in agreement. "Yeah, I get it. I guess the Germans wouldn't necessarily hold him—his name was Egon Richter, by the way—in the same regard we do."

"They wouldn't." Fiegel glanced at the papers on his desk again. "Okay, just to clarify one thing, since the report seems a bit, uh, lacking in spots, you did shoot the German down, didn't you?"

"My waist gunner, Sergeant Ned Resser, a kid from Texas, nailed him with the last few rounds we had."

"So I guess the fighter pilot . . . Richter?"

"Yes."

"Richter must have decided the battle was over for both of you. You were both going down, enough blood had been shed, so why not call it a day? Truce."

"That's my take on it."

"I've heard rumors the *Luftwaffe* operates under its own code of honor, but I would never have expected something like this."

"I doubt it's mentioned explicitly in the code," Al said.

Fiegel chuckled and slid the British Navy report off to one side of his desk and retrieved another set of papers.

"On another matter," he said, "I'd like to nominate you and

your crew for Distinguished Service Crosses. What you accomplished was nothing short of remarkable. Getting your bombs on the target in Ploesti, fighting your way back to the Ionian Sea, knocking a Messerschmitt out of the sky when you were barely flying yourself. Absolutely astounding. Extraordinary. I applaud you, Captain Lycoming. You and your men." Fiegel's voice rang with sincerity and admiration.

"Thank you, sir."

"One small problem."

Al had a pretty good notion what that might be. Again he said, "Sir?"

"I've gone over all the records and orders I could turn up and haven't been able to find a Benjamin Smith, first *or* second lieutenant, listed anyplace. But you had him on your manifest as your copilot. Could you help me out here?"

Al held his voice steady. He'd rehearsed his story. He hated lying, but in this case, something less than the whole truth might be the best policy. "Probably not, Colonel. We lost our copilot, Lieutenant Sorenson, to dysentery just before Tidal Wave launched. And you know how short of crews we were. This new guy turned up at the last minute. Said he was a replacement pilot from England. I really didn't know anything about him, but we were desperate, so we kinda shanghaied the guy and jammed him into the right-hand seat. The mission always comes first, right, sir?"

"Always." Fiegel held Al in a steady gaze. "What happened to him?"

"After the raid, after the Brits fished us out of the drink, he said he should probably return to his original unit in England."

"And that was?"

"I don't recall."

"I see. And I suppose you didn't get his serial number either?"

"Sorry, sir. I guess I had other things on my mind."

"I'm sure you did." Fiegel retrieved the Naval report from the edge of his desk and studied it once more. "It says here a female, who identified herself as a nurse, was pulled out of the water along with *Oregon Grinder's* other survivors. A nurse. Really?"

"A volunteer observer."

"I wasn't aware we had any female nurses in Benghazi."

Al swallowed hard.

Fiegel continued. "Apparently she went back to England, too."

"Yes, sir."

Fiegel, looking pensive, leaned back in his chair and folded his hands in front of him. He remained silent for a short while before speaking again. "You know, there was a WAFS pilot who flew in here a couple of weeks before the raid. She's the one who landed the B-24 without hydraulics."

"I know," Al said. "I watched the landing. A lot of guys would have struggled doing what she did. She made it look like a grease job."

"But I don't suppose you would ever, not in million years, consider taking a WAFS pilot on a combat mission, would you?"

Al attempted to sound offended. "That would be highly irregular, sir."

"Yes, it would be."

"Besides, it would have been impossible." Al recalled the conversation he and Vivian had had prior to Tidal Wave.

"How's that, Captain?"

"Well, since WAFS aren't allowed to transport planes overseas, Miss Wright could never have been here. Correct? And if she were never here, she certainly couldn't have flown on the Ploesti raid. Agreed?"

Fiegel sighed. "I think what you're saying is, like the tale of the German not blowing you out of the sky, some stories are better left untold."

"At least for a long time."

Fiegel drummed his fingers on the desk. "Well, I'm afraid I won't be able to put 'Lieutenant Smith' in for a Distinguished Service Cross if we can't find him. It's a shame."

"It is, sir."

"Okay, one final item you can help me with."

Al waited. A heavy truck rumbled by on the road outside the tent, and a mini-dust storm blustered into the interior, coating everything in a fine, brown grit. Colonel Fiegel seemed not to notice. Perhaps he'd become acclimatized to such events.

"You were on Lieutenant Colonel Baker's wing when he and Major Jerstad went down in *Hell's Wench*, correct?"

"I was. And I have to tell you, sir, I've never witnessed bravery such as those two men displayed on their run-in to Ploesti. Their plane was fully engulfed in flames. Normal human beings would have bailed out. But they pressed on, jettisoned their bomb load, and as Colonel Baker had promised, led the Traveling Circus to the oil refineries before they crashed." Al shook his head in slow motion, still amazed at what he had seen. He knew he would never forget. "I could have never done anything like that, Colonel," he added.

"Few men could have. That's why I'm putting them in for the Medal of Honor."

"That should be a lead-pipe cinch."

"Maybe not."

Al stared at Fiegel. "What?"

"I've heard rumors that at high levels there are some people who think maybe Baker's actions to break formation and then hit the wrong targets, ones not assigned to the Circus, make him ineligible for the award."

Al leaped to his feet. "For Christ's sake, sir, he broke formation because Colonel Compton fucked up and headed in the wrong direction."

"Captain, take it easy. Sit down. And be careful about saying who fucked up. We don't have all the facts yet."

"Sorry, sir." Al sat. "It's just that I was there. I saw what happened. The Liberandos turned at the wrong IP and headed for Bucharest, not Ploesti. Colonel Baker had the guts to break off that goofy follow-the-leader shit we were doing and take the Circus to the right target. Yeah, we didn't hit the refinery assigned to us, but given there was more flak than breathable air over Ploesti, I think we did a hell of a job."

"You did. I don't disagree. And that's why I need your help. The more first-hand, eyewitness input I can get about what happened, the better the chances the award will have of getting approved. I share your outrage that people who didn't have their lives on the line, who weren't taking fire, who didn't have a dog in the fight, would make a technical judgment regarding the bravery of men who sacrificed everything."

"I agree one hundred percent. I'll do everything I can to help you."

"Good. I'll make arrangements to get you and your crew back to England within the next few days."

"Thank you, sir. And I know this isn't how you wanted to assume command of the Circus, but congratulations. I'm looking forward to serving under you."

"I appreciate that, Captain. See you back at Hardwick. Okay, that's all. Dismissed."

Al stood and saluted.

Colonel Fiegel returned the salute.

Al pivoted and walked toward the tent's exit.

Just as he prepared to step out, he heard Fiegel call after him, "And if you ever turn up anything on Lieutenant Benjamin Smith—initials B.S., I might note—please let me know."

Al almost gagged. *B.S.?* He'd never thought about that when he'd come up with the off-the-cuff name for his couldn't-have-really-been-there copilot.

"I will, sir," he choked out, "but I suspect that might be a lost cause."

"Why do I think you're right about that?" Fiegel responded in a subdued tone.

Al walked out of the tent into the sun, heat, and dust of Benghazi. He looked forward to his return to the green coolness of England.

27

Casper Army Air Base, Wyoming
Early 1944

Al, flying out of England with the Eighth Air Force, completed his twenty-five combat missions and returned to the States in early 1944. Promoted to major, he became heavily involved in training B-24 crews at Casper (Wyoming) Army Air Base. Sarah and Al Junior joined him there, where they remained until the end of the war.

Shortly after being posted to Casper, Al learned that Lieutenant Colonel Addison Baker, the pilot of *Hell's Wench* and commander of the Traveling Circus, and his copilot, Major John Jerstad, had both posthumously been awarded the Medal of Honor, America's highest and most prestigious military decoration.

Al also heard that despite the objections of some high-ranking officers that Baker's actions—breaking formation and bombing an unassigned target—should have disqualified him for the medal, that the words of the men who had flown with Baker and witnessed his bravery and leadership ended up overriding any opposition. To Al, Baker and Jerstad represented the very essence of what the Medal of Honor stood for.

In addition to Colonel Baker and Major Jerstad, three other individuals who had flown on the Ploesti raid received the Medal of Honor. The five medals were the most ever awarded for a single mission on a single day.

Though he had met them only once or twice, Al knew two of the other recipients, Colonel John Riley Kane, "Killer" Kane, and Colonel Leon William Johnson. Both of the colonels, Kane of the Pyramiders, Johnson of the Flying Eight Balls, had courageously led their respective bomb groups into the hell of Ploesti and murderous antiaircraft fire that awaited them there. Both of the officers and their crews survived the mission, though Kane's Liberator, *Hail Columbia,* crash landed on Cyprus while attempting to make it back to Benghazi.

The fifth Medal of Honor for the Ploesti attack, like those awarded to Baker and Jerstad, came posthumously to Second Lieutenant Lloyd "Pete" Hughes, a young pilot with the Sky Scorpions.

In addition to the five Medals of Honor awarded for Tidal Wave, all men who flew the mission received either a Distinguished Service Cross or Silver Star.

Al's proudest postscript to the raid, though he would relate it only if asked, was that every crew member of *Oregon Grinder*— the mysterious Lieutenant Smith excepted—became the recipient of the Distinguished Service Cross.

Four hundred and thirty survivors of the raid received Purple Hearts, the military decoration awarded to those wounded or killed in combat. Among the survivors, Al and his tail gunner, Sergeant Billy Cummings of Sumter, South Carolina, each received the decoration.

Al knew full well his copilot had earned a Purple Heart, too, taking a piece of shrapnel to her head, but since she hadn't offi-cially flown the raid . . .

Shortly after receiving his Purple Heart, Al boxed it up and sent it to Vivian care of the WASPs—Women Airforce Service Pilots—in Sweetwater, Texas. The WAFS, for which Vivian had been flying at the time of Ploesti, had been absorbed by the WASPs upon their formation just a few days after the Ploesti raid in August 1943.

He advised Vivian it would be okay to display the decora-tion, but also suggested she should remain vague about exactly how she'd earned it.

The cost of Operation Tidal Wave had been horrendous. Three hundred and ten men lost their lives. Over one hundred were taken prisoner after crash landing in Romania.

Forty-one B-24s were shot from the sky by withering antiair-craft fire and relentless enemy fighter assaults. Only half the bombers, eighty-nine, made it back to Benghazi in the imme-diate aftermath of the raid. Of those eighty-nine, only thirty-three proved to be combat ready the following day. Most had been too heavily damaged to be able to fly another mission without extensive repairs or maintenance.

Twenty-two Liberators landed at other locations, spots such as Cyprus, Malta, Sicily, and Palestine. Eight ended up interned in Turkey, three crashed while attempting to make it back to North Africa.

The mission marked the end of low-level bombing ventures against Ploesti. Now only high-level missions, as in the rest of Europe, appeared in the skies over Romania. Al assumed some of the men he now trained would get their chance to attack "the taproot of German might." He hoped none, however, would go through the hell he did.

A question often asked in the aftermath of the raid, one Al often posed to himself, had it been worth it? Had Operation

Tidal Wave been a success? He didn't know. How in the hell do you balance the loss of human life against refining capacity? There is no objective measure for that.

Al knew there were many who looked solely at the numbers, the statistics on the bombing efficacy of Tidal Wave that indicated only forty-two percent of Ploesti's refining capacity had been destroyed. Worse, he'd heard that after six months, the damage levied by the Americans had been repaired and the refineries put back on-line . . . churning out more petroleum products than before the raid.

Al maintained his own definition of success. Despite the mission getting colossally fucked up, the target had been hit. American airmen had, in the face of ramparts of death, exhibited remarkable ingenuity and exceptional bravery. That, to Al, defined success, and always would. Operation Tidal Wave would always remain the most memorable accomplishment of his life.

EPILOGUE

United States of America
1946 to 1973

Al, like millions of other men, mustered out of the service in 1946. He returned to Oregon where he went to work for the US Forest Service. By the early 1970s, he'd become head of the Pacific Northwest regional office located in Portland.

He kept track, as best he could, of the men he'd flown with on *Oregon Grinder*.

George, the plane's navigator and Al's best friend, returned to Brooklyn where he became a novelist, penning dramas based on his war experiences. While he met with a modicum of success, he found he couldn't compete with the likes of Herman Wouk (*The Caine Mutiny*), James Joyce (*From Here to Eternity*), Leon Uris (*Battle Cry*), and Nicholas Monsarrat (*The Cruel Sea*).

He discussed with Al whether to do a tell-all about *Oregon Grinder* and Ploesti, but they both decided, even with the war a quarter century in the rearview mirror, that the story of the raid and their tales surrounding it—a female pilot in combat, a *Luft-waffe* officer who had spared American lives—remained a bit too controversial to put in front of the general public, let alone a military audience.

George instead turned to writing noir mysteries and found his true calling. Two of his novels made it to the silver screen, one starring Humphrey Bogart and the other Jimmy Stewart, who, ironically, had flown B-24s in the war.

Sorey, *Oregon Grinder's* copilot, except on the Ploesti mission, hooked up with Western Airlines and did quite well, remaining with the airline as it grew from a large regional operation into a major carrier. Last Al heard, Sorey, now a captain, flew a regular route between Anchorage, Alaska, and Seattle. And true to their vow made during the war, Al and Sorey and their families attended the Pendleton Roundup as often as they could.

Kenny Brightman, the bombardier from Georgia Tech, became an engineering professor at North Carolina State University (formerly North Carolina State College) in Raleigh. He sent Al a Christmas card every year, highlighting the events of the previous twelve months.

Billy Cummings, the tail gunner from South Carolina, recovered from his head wound—though he suffered a mild case of what later became known as PTSD, Post-Traumatic Stress Disorder—then took advantage of the GI Bill by returning to college. He earned a degree in psychology, went into the real estate business, and hooked up with some guys trying to develop an island in the Low Country of the state into a high-end resort. Al had never heard of the place, Hilton Head Island, and hoped Billy knew what he was doing. *Real estate development . . easy way to lose your shirt,* Al thought.

Blaine Witkowski, Stumpy, the bottom turret gunner, returned to New Jersey where he founded a chain of successful steak houses. One thing he told Al, he always made sure he had good stash of Mosel Valley wines in his restaurants, in deference to the German who had spared their lives.

Master Sergeant Maurice, "Moe," Gallagher, the top turret gunner/engineer who'd declined to fly the Ploesti raid because of Vivian's presence, had found himself shunned by his fellow crew mates in the wake of the mission. They'd been unable to forgive his absence, especially since the guy who'd stepped in to replace him, Tech Sergeant Bryce McGregor, had been killed in action. True, Al had offered Moe the option not to fly, but the crew viewed his choice more as abandonment than anything else.

Moe had been reassigned to an Eighth Air Force B-17 Bomb Group flying out of England. In a twist of fate, he lost his life over Schweinfurt, Germany, in an October 1943 raid that became labeled a total failure. Sixty of almost three hundred Flying Fortresses that flew the mission were blasted from the sky.

Sergeant Ned Reeser, the waist gunner who'd brought down Egon Richter's Messerschmitt over the Ionian Sea, remained in the service after the war. He made it to Master Sergeant, then lost his life in a B-29 crash during the Korean War. Al attended his memorial service in Burkburnett, Texas.

Though Al kept the tale about Vivian Wright and Ploesti under wraps, he did relate the story to his wife. In fact, she and Vivian became friends of sorts, trading letters frequently and even a few phone calls.

After the war, Vivian tried time after time to land a job as a commercial airline pilot, but no carrier would offer her a chance. It was pointed out to her ad nauseam that she was a woman and women didn't fly airplanes for a living. Period. End of discussion.

In a letter to Sarah, she related one interview she'd had.

"I'm sorry, honey," the interviewer had said, "but even if you were qualified, veterans are given priority for pilot jobs." He paused. "I would think, however, with your smile and great looks, you'd be a perfect fit in our service operations."

"You mean as a stewardess?"

"I'd certainly love to have you serving me."

She reached into her purse, fished out the Purple Heart Al had sent her, and slammed it onto the desk in front of the interviewer.

"I didn't earn that, buster, because of my smile or cuteness, or by offering 'coffee, tea, or me,' to troops on a C-47. Screw your service operations."

She snatched the medal from the desk and flounced out of the office, leaving the interviewer sitting with his mouth agape.

After numerous rejections, she opened her own flying school near Omaha, Nebraska, teaching both men and women —women, preferably—how to fly multi-engine aircraft.

"Someday women *will* be flying commercial airliners," she wrote Sarah, "and I want the ladies I teach to be first in line for that."

Her prediction turned out to be prescient. In 1973, several commercial carriers in the US hired female pilots for the first time.

Al never came to grips understanding Vivian's personal life. He learned that after the war she'd married and divorced twice, but whether that stemmed from her independent and assertive nature or because she didn't find men sexually attractive, he didn't know. And didn't care. He admired the woman and would always hold her in exceptionally high regard.

He knew the surviving crew members of *Oregon Grinder* felt the same way. In fact, they began planning a special reunion for the fortieth anniversary of the Ploesti raid in 1983, a reunion that would include and honor Vivian.

Al, in the meantime, began to think about a different kind of coming-together event.

"I want to go to Germany," he told Sarah. "The kids are

grown, we're still in good health, and we've got a little money and some free time. Let's travel."

"To Germany?" She sat down next to him on a well-worn couch in the living room of their 1920s brick home in southeast Portland.

He nodded.

"Ulterior motive?" She knew him too well.

He nodded again.

"Let me guess. It has something to do with that German fighter pilot?"

"I've thought about it a lot," he said. "If he has any surviving family, I'd like them to know what really happened over the Ionian Sea thirty years ago. That Egon Richter spared the lives of seven Americans. That he is a man whose memory is worthy of honor and respect."

"How would you find out about the family, if there is one?"

"I looked on a map. The place he mentioned where he lived, Zell, on the Mosel River, is just a few miles from an American air base, Hahn. I could write the base commander there, tell him who I am, why I'm interested in coming, and see if there might be somebody who could poke around in Zell and find out if there are any Richters living there. Especially ones named Inge or Christa. Those are the two names Egon whispered before he died."

Al paused, feeling emotion constrict his throat. Even after three decades, the German's unnecessary death still distressed him.

He continued. "I don't know if those names belonged to his wife, a daughter, a sister, or maybe even a mother. It really doesn't matter. I just need a connection to start from."

Al followed through with his plan to write to the base commander, and things actually went well. The Public Affairs Officer at Hahn Air Base contacted the *Bürgermeister's* office in

Zell and discovered that, yes, an Inge Richter, age sixty, lived in Zell. Further probing determined that Inge had indeed been Egon's wife.

Friendly explanations and negotiations followed and resulted in a meeting being set up between Al, his wife, and Inge Richter. The translator for the gathering—since Inge spoke no English, and Al's guidebook-German wouldn't get him far—would be Egon's daughter, Christa, now in her early forties and married.

Al and Sarah undertook their long journey in May 1973, flying from Portland to New York City on a United Airlines DC-8, then New York to Frankfurt on one of Lufthansa's new wide-body 747s.

West Germany
May 1973

The trip on the autobahn from the Frankfurt *Flughafen* to Zell proved harrowing for someone not used to routinely driving at over one hundred miles per hour. Al quickly learned not to let the anchor drag in his rented Opel Ascona saloon, especially in the passing lane. The Mercedes and BMWs and Porsches running up his tail pipe at one hundred fifty miles per hour let him know with flashing headlights or their left-hand blinker winking to get the hell out of the way.

"Not like driving in Oregon," he said, his heart beating like an up-tempo metronome. "Lord, I think I felt safer in my Liberator dropping bombs on these guys."

The German countryside, green and lush with spring growth, reminded him of western Oregon. Sunshine, sharing the sky with popcorn cumulus, burned through a gauzy haze of diesel exhaust and factory emissions.

"A testament to West Germany's industrial might, I guess," Al noted.

"Frankfurt looked like an ultramodern metropolis," Sarah added.

"Yeah, I suppose when you're forced to rebuild from nothing, with a little help from your newfound friends, that's what you get."

Sarah stared out the window as the landscape raced by. "It's so hard to believe the destruction and death and misery that must have prevailed here."

"The Third Reich will never be remembered for its glory."

They reached the Mosel Valley in mid-afternoon and checked in at the Hotel Schloss Zell, a castle-like structure that had stood in the town since the fourteenth century. They hurried to their room and, without bothering to unpack, collapsed into their bed for a long and overdue sleep.

Shortly after noon the following day, they arrived, feeling refreshed, at the home of Inge Richter for a meeting with Inge and her daughter. The meeting had been arranged through the Public Affairs Office at Hahn Air Base. Hahn sat on the *Hunsrück,* the high ground south of the Mosel Valley, about five miles from Zell.

Inge's home, one of several that shared a three-story stone structure, sat near the intersection of two main roads, one paralleling the Mosel River, the other crossing the river on what appeared to be a fairly new bridge. The traffic—cars, trucks, motorcycles—while not heavy, appeared to be steady.

Al rang the doorbell. The door opened and an attractive blonde with an ingratiating smile greeted them. She wore a tan blouse and dark skirt and carried herself with what seemed an almost regal bearing.

"Welcome," she said, and gestured for Al and Sarah to enter. "I'm Christa, Inge Richter's daughter. I'm so happy to meet you."

To Al, the sentiment seemed genuine, but he had to wonder if she really felt that way. He assumed she probably had been told by German authorities she would be meeting the pilot of the American bomber that had shot down her father during the war. She, of course, would have no knowledge about what had really happened.

Al introduced his wife and himself, and added, "We're so pleased you agreed to see us. We're honored by your hospitality."

"And we by your visit," Christa said. "Please, follow me."

Trailing Christa, they mounted the stone stairs of the house up to the living room, dining area, and kitchen on the second floor. The windows of the home sat open, ushering in the warmth of the spring afternoon. A soft breeze bearing an amalgam of vehicle exhaust and lilacs rippled their lace curtains in lazy undulations. Occasionally, the muted growl of the traffic outside rode the zephyrs into the house.

"My mother has lived here since before the war," Christa explained. She ushered Al and Sarah into the living room.

A woman arose from an armchair in the corner of the room.

"This is my mother, Inge," Christa said. *"Mutter, das sind Al und Sarah Lycoming aus Amerika."*

Keeping things formal but friendly, they shook hands.

Al could see that Inge had likely been beautiful once, but time and war had taken an obvious toll. More furrows and creases than might be expected for someone near sixty lined her face, and she stooped slightly when she stood.

"Thank you for inviting us into your home," Al said.

Christa translated for her mother, who nodded her acknowledgement.

Only then did Al notice a fifth person in the room, a man sitting in a dimly lit corner. He stood and walked to Al and Sarah. He appeared to be in his fifties and carried himself with the bearing of a military man. His piercing dark eyes suggested an alert and curious nature, and immediately reminded Al of many of the senior officers he had known in the Army Air Force. The man smiled warmly and extended his hand.

"Gustav Rödel," he said in German-accented English. "I know you weren't expecting to meet with anyone other than Inge and Christa, but they were kind enough to invite me when they learned who you were."

Though puzzled by his presence, Al gripped the man's hand. "You mean the American who"—he struggled to find the right words— "was with Egon at the end?"

"I was *Hauptmann* Richter's wing commander when he flew his final mission out of Kalamaki Air Base in Greece."

Al stared. *Shit.* He'd wanted this meeting to be private, to tell Egon's wife and daughter how Egon had really died, how he'd spared American lives. Now he didn't feel comfortable doing that. Even with the war now relegated to history books, he didn't know if this man, Gustav, still harbored Nazi sympathies or not. If he did, it could still prove dangerous for Inge and Christa.

"I see," Al said, hesitant to say more.

Gustav studied him, apparently trying to figure out the reason for Al's reluctance to be more open.

Christa seemed to sense it, too, but took a stab at what might have triggered it. "You're concerned, aren't you, that Herr Rödel might still hold certain, how shall I say it, political views?"

"I'm a bit apprehensive, yes."

"Then I should tell you that *Herr* Rödel could also be addressed as *Brigadegeneral* Rödel. He worked with NATO and recently retired from the West German Air Force."

Brigadier General? West German Air Force? Al relaxed a bit. If the man had held a position like that, it would mean the Allies had vetted him thoroughly.

"Honored to meet you, sir. I'm sorry if my concern seemed a

bit transparent." *Still, you never know . . .* Al's disdain for Nazis ran deep. Death camps and the loss of tens of millions of lives could do that.

"I understand," Gustav said. "If I were in your shoes, I would harbor the same concerns." He paced to one of the windows, hands locked behind his back, and stared out through the jiggling curtains into the spring afternoon and the traffic in the intersection below. He seemed lost in thought, or perhaps remembrances.

Without turning, he said, "You probably wonder if I was one of those, what Americans call Nazis, a member of the National Socialist German Workers' Party. We referred to it merely as 'the Party,' by the way." He turned to face Al. "Well, allow me to tell you a story." He returned to his seat.

Christa gestured for Al and Sarah to sit, also.

"Please," she said, pointing at a low table in front of the couch, "help yourself." Cups, a steaming porcelain coffee pot painted in Edelweiss, and a delicious-looking assortment of pastries and cookies rested on the table.

Gustav waited to begin telling his story until everyone had poured a cup of coffee and retrieved something to nibble on.

"It's not something that's talked about much," he began, his voice soft, "but in early 1945, within the *Luftwaffe*, there was something that became known as 'the Fighter Pilots Mutiny.'"

Al set his coffee down and sat up straight, listening carefully.

"A group of senior fighter pilots, myself included, confronted *Reichsmarschall* Göring over his conduct of the war."

Al interrupted and turned to Sarah. "Hermann Göring was commander-in-chief of the *Luftwaffe* and second in command to Adolf Hitler."

Gustav nodded his agreement, then continued. "By 1944, we knew the air war over Europe was lost. Göring blamed us, the fighter pilots, for that. The truth was, we'd not been given any new aircraft or updated weapons for quite some time. For instance, the new Messerschmitt Me 262s, the jets, were being sent to bomber forces, of all things.

"A group of us under the direction of General Adolf Galland, the chief of fighter pilots, decided to challenge Göring directly, face-to-face, and call him out." Gustav paused and cleared his throat. "In truth, there were some of us who thought stronger measures were required, but we also realized that if Göring were to be, well, eliminated, there would likely be someone else in the Party hierarchy just as militant and inept who would replace him."

Gustav paused, took a swallow of coffee, then continued.

"The encounter did not go well. Göring had been fore-warned. We offered him a typed list of 'Points of Discussion,' hoping we could have a civil back-and-forth with him. We should have known better.

"Göring flew into an irrational rage, red-faced, cursing, spittle flying from his mouth, and accused us of treason. He swept our 'Points of Discussion' onto the floor and shouted, 'Galland will be shot first to set the example.' At that point, we assumed we all were condemned men.

"In the end, we obviously weren't executed, but most of us were banished to relatively minor jobs. The worst thing was, as we departed the confrontation with Göring, we knew with certainty that Germany was doomed."

Gustav fell silent and seemed to stare into blankness. Al realized why he had told the story. Gustav Rödel clearly held no love for the Nazi Party.

"Thank you for your candor, sir," he said. "I guess it's my turn now. I want to tell you what really happened thirty years ago over the Ionian Sea, and why I love Egon Richter like a brother. He's the only reason I am able to be here today."

The three Germans in the room traded glances with one

another, probably wondering what they were about to hear.

Al told his story, leaving out no details, even the one about carrying a female copilot into battle. His small audience remained in rapt attention, the only sounds interrupting him floating in from outside—the occasional beep of a horn or throaty roar of an accelerating motorcycle.

As he neared the end of his account, spelling out how Egon had spared *Oregon Grinder* and her crew, a glint of what seemed admiration flickered in Gustav's eyes. Wonderment shone on the faces of Inge and Christa.

But tears flowed down their cheeks, too, and Inge broke into soft sobs as Al explained the circumstances of Egon's death. Gustav appeared stunned and could only shake his head in what seemed sorrow and incredulity.

"Thank you, *Herr* Lycoming," Christa said, dabbing at her tears with a tissue. "Thank you for coming all this way to tell me about my father. It gives me new appreciation for what he did and who he was. He'll forever remain larger than life for me."

Al responded. "He was an honorable man, and I consider it my privilege to have met him, though it was only for a brief moment, and only at the end of his life. I'm so sorry."

"*Danke, danke, danke,*" Inge said as her sobbing subsided. Christa went to her mother and embraced her. Then Inge stood and said, "*Wir feiern das Leben meines Mannes.*" She disappeared into the kitchen.

"She wants to celebrate Egon's life," Christa translated.

As they waited, Gustav spoke. "You know, one thing I always emphasized to the pilots under my command is that you never, under any circumstances, shoot a man in a parachute. Once a battle is over, it's over. I think Egon stretched that edict to its maximum. He decided that for your bomber, the battle was over. He knew it was for him, too. Why shed more blood on either side? In the end, it wouldn't have won or lost the war."

"Thank you, General," Al said, "for teaching your men compassion and integrity. Perhaps if there had been more like you in the *Wehrmacht*, there wouldn't have been a war."

"There were many who harbored similar thoughts. But the key was we should have asserted ourselves much earlier."

"Yes, but I suppose you couldn't see the future."

"Sometimes you don't have to see it, but only know the character of the men leading you there."

Inge reentered the room with wine and glasses on a silver tray.

Al and Sarah and the Germans spent the remainder of the afternoon polishing off two bottles of *Zeller Schwarze Katz* and too many pastries. They offered numerous toasts to the memory of Egon. They chatted about their lives and families as if they were lifelong friends, which Al guessed they probably had become.

Al spoke of Al Junior and his two other children, a girl and a boy. Christa said she had married and given Inge four grandchildren, three girls and a boy. Inge had never remarried, she explained, since most men close to her age had been killed in the war.

Gustav offered few details about his family, but talked mostly about his career in the West German Air Force. After a series of training courses in the US, he'd stepped into his new military role in 1957 and retired in 1971.

When the get-together ended after several hours, Al and Sarah traded hugs with Inge and Christa, and handshakes with Gustav. Then Gustav accompanied them down the stone stairs to the street.

"Again, I can't thank you enough for coming from America to tell us about Egon," he said. "Although what he did would have been viewed as treasonous thirty years ago, we can now see it as honorable and ethical. In the end, that's more a measure of warrior than how many targets he destroyed or how many enemies he killed. An enemy never remains an enemy, but a man's integrity is eternal." He spoke the last words in a quiet but clear voice.

The late afternoon had slipped into early evening, and the sky had morphed into a panorama tinted in tones of soft purple, gold, and pink. Bats, presumably pursuing evening meals, darted in and out of a cone of brightness cast by a nearby street light as it flickered to life. High overhead, still illuminated by the bright rays of the setting sun, a flight of four F-4 fighter jets, American Phantoms, roared northward.

"From Hahn Air Base," Gustav said, looking up.

"The new warriors," Al added.

Gustav returned his gaze to Al. "With the old ones relegated to the ground and their memories."

His sentence seemed wrapped in melancholy and Al sensed he had something more to say, so remained silent.

"Memories," Gustav repeated softly. "When heroes flew." He quit speaking and stared past Al, as though gazing into the past. His eyes seemed to reveal a deep sadness.

He lifted his right hand and placed it on Al's shoulder. "I'm so glad you survived the war, my friend, that you got to return home and meet your son, raise him, love him, watch him mature. I didn't wish to say anything in front of Inge and Christa—this was their gathering—but I lost an infant son in an RAF bombing raid. Let us hope the generations that follow us will never again have to go through what we endured."

He removed his hand from Al's shoulder, stepped back, and saluted. "I honor your service."

Al, his heart aching over what Gustav had just revealed, returned the salute. "And I, yours, sir."

The Phantoms disappeared over the horizon, leaving only thin, smoky trails of exhaust hanging in their wakes.

ALSO BY H.W. "BUZZ" BERNARD

Eyewall

Plague

Supercell

Blizzard

Cascadia

When Heroes Flew

Never miss a new release! Sign up to receive exclusive updates from author Buzz Bernard.

SevernRiverPublishing.com/Buzz

AUTHOR'S NOTE

When Heroes Flew began life as a short story, "Oregon Grinder," almost fifteen years ago, well before I knew anything about crafting a novel. Then, after writing five thrillers, a couple of which did well on Amazon's Kindle bestseller lists, I went back to "Oregon Grinder," took it apart, and rebuilt it into a novel. Much of the rebuilding process centered around developing the character of Egon Richter, the German fighter pilot, and wrapping my wife's experiences of growing up in prewar and wartime Germany into Egon's family story.

Besides employing many of the tales my wife, Christina, told me about being a child in Nazi Germany, I used a memoir, *Christmas Trees Lit the Sky—Growing up in World War II Germany* by Anneliese Heider Tisdale, to gain additional insights.

The small town on the Mosel River, Zell, described in the novel really exists. I've walked its streets many times. It's where my wife grew up.

Except for the engagement between Oregon Grinder and the German Messerschmitts over the Ionian Sea, the major events depicted in *When Heroes Flew* actually occurred. The details of the raid on Ploesti, Operation Tidal Wave, were gleaned from numerous sources, the most valuable of which was the book *Ploesti—The Great Ground-Air Battle of 1 August 1943* by James Dugan and Carroll Stewart.

A large number of sources describing the raid can be found on the Internet. One of the best is a video on YouTube, "The Ploesti Raid." The video features the late Robert Sternfels, a decorated pilot who flew the mission.

I tried hard to get the details of the two aircraft, the American B-24 and the German Messerschmitt Bf-109, featured in the novel correct. To that end, I used a number of references, including *American Warplanes of World War II* and *Warplanes of the Luftwaffe*, both edited by David Donald; *B-24 Combat Missions—First-Hand Accounts of Liberator Operations over Nazi Europe* by Martin W. Bowman; and *The Wild Blue* by Steven Ambrose.

To make sure I got the descriptions of flying the Liberator correct, I had a B-24 pilot, Allen Benzing, review what I'd written.

Allen is a pilot of one of the two B-24s still flying, Diamond Lil. Diamond Lil belongs to the Commemorative Air Force of Dallas, Texas. The other airworthy Liberator is Witchcraft owned by the Collings Foundation of Stow, Massachusetts. I flew in Witchcraft as part of my preparation for the novel.

Albert Lycoming and his wife, Egon Richter and his family, the crew of Oregon Grinder, and Vivian Wright are all fictional characters, figments of my imagination. But most of the other military officers, both US and German, portrayed in the novel really existed.

Much of the material I used to paint a picture of the Luftwaffe came from the book, *A Higher Call* by Adam Makos with Larry Alexander.

In addition to my wife, Christina, and Diamond Lil's pilot, Allen Benzing, a lot of other people contributed to making the

ovel as authentic as possible. A B-24 bombardier, Irving
harles Rowe, who served in the Pacific Theater during WWII,
ffered some insights on what flying in a Liberator was like for
he short story version of what became the book.

A long-time friend and former Air Force weather officer, Bill
ulver, offered helpful insights on Libyan weather and
pography.

A group of sharp-eyed beta (or initial) readers of the novel-
ength manuscript helped make *When Heroes Flew* a better
ook. They included my brother, Rick Bernard; Barbara Brauer;
d Davis; Tom Howley; Skip Karas; and a superb critic who's
een on "my team" since Day One, Gary Schwartz.

Ed Davis and Skip Karas are both former Air Force fighter
ilots and Southeast Asia veterans. They helped me craft the
epictions of the fighter tactics described in the book.

When Heroes Flew couldn't have been brought to life, of
ourse, without the trust placed in me by Andrew Watts and his
ard-working team at Severn River Publishing.

So you see, it took an entire squadron of people to get *When
eroes Flew* airborne. Again, my profound thanks to them all.

In closing, I believe it's worth relating a bit more about the
eroism of Lieutenant Lloyd "Pete" Hughes who was posthu-
ously awarded the Medal of Honor for his actions with the
ky Scorpions. The citation that came with his medal read in
art:

*"The target area was blazing with burning oil tanks and damaged
refinery installations from which flames leaped high above the
bombing level of the formation. With full knowledge of the
consequences of entering the blazing inferno when his airplane was
profusely leaking gasoline in two separate locations, Second
Lieutenant Hughes, motivated only by his high conception of duty
which called for the destruction of the assigned target at any cost, did*

not elect to make a forced landing or turn back from the attack. Instead, rather than jeopardize the formation and the success of the attack, he unhesitatingly entered the blazing area and dropped his bomb load with great precision."

We should never forget what men like Pete Hughes and the hundreds of others who flew Operation Tidal Wave did or, in many cases, sacrificed. The courage and heroism displayed on that mission remain among the most remarkable of WWII.

Indeed it was a time when heroes flew.

ABOUT THE AUTHOR

H. W. "Buzz" Bernard is a bestselling, award-winning novelist. A retired Air Force Colonel and Legion of Merit recipient, he also served as a senior meteorologist at The Weather Channel for thirteen years. He is a past president of the Southeastern Writers Association and member of International Thriller Writers, the Atlanta Writers Club, Military Writers Society of America, and Willamette Writers. Buzz and his special needs adult grandson live in Georgia with their fuzzy, strangely docile Shih-Tzu, Stormy... probably misnamed.

www.SevernRiverPublishing.com/Buzz

Made in the USA
Coppell, TX
05 August 2020

32446008R00166